IN THE SAME BOAT

IN THE SAME BOAT

HOLLY GREEN

Scholastic Press

New York

for Woody
for Dad

Copyright © 2021 by Holly Green

All rights reserved. Published by Scholastic Press, an imprint of Scholastic Inc., *Publishers since 1920.* SCHOLASTIC, SCHOLASTIC PRESS, and associated logos are trademarks and/or registered trademarks of Scholastic Inc.

The publisher does not have any control over and does not assume any responsibility for author or third-party websites or their content.

This book is a work of fiction. Names, characters, places, and incidents are either the product of the author's imagination or are used fictitiously, and any resemblance to actual persons, living or dead, business establishments, events, or locales is entirely coincidental.

Library of Congress Cataloging-in-Publication Data available

ISBN 978-1-338-72663-3

1 2021

Printed in the U.S.A.   23

First edition, July 2021

Book design by Keirsten Geise

"I was praying a snake would bite me
so I could get out of this thing honorably."
Unknown competitor, 1963 Texas Water Safari
Life magazine, June 7, 1963

1

The green glow on the watch taped to the front of my canoe cuts through the darkness. It's a smack in the face. How has it only been six minutes since I last checked? I'd swear an hour has passed.

"Constant forward motion, Sadie," Dad says.

His words echo in my head, drowning out the cicadas and the frogs and the rush of the river. I dig my paddle into the water for a hard stroke. My shoulders, my lower back, even my legs all scream with pain.

The race started yesterday morning, which means we've been on the water for . . . twenty-four and then . . . I can't hold the numbers in my head. I can't hear them over the scream of my shoulder. The last mile marker I saw was 187. That's whatever 265 minus 187 is.

Eighty-three?

No.

Too many.

It's too many freaking miles.

My eyes go blurry with tears. Which makes it harder to spot obstacles in the river. Especially on this dark, dark night lit only by a pair of Maglites strapped to the nose of the canoe. I try to blink the tears back in, but it doesn't do any good.

And I can't wipe them away. Because I can't stop paddling.

Because Dad would know I'm crying. Again.

"You're sagging," Dad says. "Get a snack if you need one. We're making good time, and I don't want to lose this pace."

"I'm okay," I lie. I'm not hungry, but I lay my paddle across my lap and rip a GU packet off the inside of the canoe. The boat rocks a bit with the effort. I bring the packet up to my lips. A burst of orange-flavored energy gel hits my tongue.

After a few minutes, the fog in my mind clears.

My body still hurts.

Three days ago, Dad and I used epoxy to glue the tops of the GU packets into the side of the boat, so that when we ripped them off, we would be ripping them open. I'd thought we were geniuses. That we'd be masters of this race. That we'd have a sub-fifty-hour finish. Maybe we'd even cross the

San Antonio Bay at sunrise when it's supposed to be the calmest.

I want to punch myself in the face for being so stupid. So overly confident. Because it's not just the pain and the fatigue, or the mayflies that somehow got inside my shirt and down my sports bra. We're in a boat, paddling downriver in the middle of nowhere. Threatened by snakes and submerged trees and rapids and low branches and dams and logjams. Fishing line caught between branches that could knock us out of the boat. The woods could be crawling with murderers.

We spent so much time preparing. Scouting the river. Obsessing over water levels. I've followed this race for as long as I can remember. I thought I knew what to expect. But for the last few hours . . . Even longer than that, really . . . For the last day, maybe, with the finish line still an eternity away, the words *I want to quit* have been perched on the tip of my tongue.

And about thirty minutes ago, they actually came out. I wish I could suck the words back in my mouth, because I know he heard me, and he didn't say a thing. Maybe he thinks I didn't mean it.

I tuck the empty packet into my trash bag, rub the tears out of my eyes, and start paddling again. Everything hurts. I've never been so tired in my life. But I keep going.

Because we are Scofields.

Scofields don't quit.

Scofields don't even stop to rest.

Every Scofield for the past three generations has finished the Texas River Odyssey, 265 miles of sweat and pain and paddling. My brother, Tanner, finished the race with Dad last year and is somewhere behind us in a solo right now. He's probably never even thought of quitting. My mom has finished. Even my grandmother has.

We race because it's hard. Because it's pushing yourself further than what a lot of people think is even possible. It's finding out what you're made of.

And doing the race, finishing it, is what makes you a real Scofield.

"That's good, Sade. Now let's pick up the pace a little."

As I dig in harder and faster with my paddle, the tears well in my eyes again.

≈

Inside the cone of light from our flashlights, there's a bend in the river ahead.

"Let's ride the eddy line here," Dad calls.

He steers us into the place where the fast-rippled water meets the slower flat water, but it's hard for him to see from the back of the boat, so I make a tiny draw to the right, putting us on the line. It'll keep us moving with the fast water, but we can jump into the slow water to avoid an obstacle if we need to.

The nose of the canoe starts to veer off into the eddy, the slow water. I jab my paddle into the water on the left and pull. I pull too hard, and as we round the bend, we're sucked into the current.

But it's okay. No sweeper ahead—a fallen tree waiting to sweep us out of the boat. No strainer, either—a submerged tree with branches sticking up, straining the water. Some rocks and a log to our left, but smooth water ahead. I keep paddling.

And then we're almost on it. The water is breaking around something black. A branch or a piece of wood or something. My heart thuds as I dig my paddle into the water to draw us off it. The bow clears it by a hair and my body softens with relief.

Then the current grabs the stern and pushes the boat sideways.

I backsweep, but it's too late. I should have done it sooner. I should have called to Dad that I was drawing us off something. My stomach drops as Dad yells, "Backpaddle!"

And I do. I reach as far back as I can, put in my paddle, and push it forward, willing the boat to back up. The boat rocks as Dad draws us to the left. Too late. The current's got us. The boat *whams* into the branch. And it must be more than just a branch under the surface. There's a sickening crack and I'm lurched to the side.

I crash into cold water. It seeps into my clothes and my

shoes and covers my face as the current pushes me forward. I hold what's left of my breath. My body scrapes against something hard. I kick and pull with my arms and claw my way to the surface. My head breaks through. Water streams into my mouth as I gasp for breath.

I scramble to get into position—feet first, but the water's pushing me too hard, turning me. My right side slams into a rock. There's a sharp pain and something inside me cracks and all the air is knocked out of my lungs. I can't let the river take me any farther. I grab, tear, kick at the rock, scrambling to the top, and finally, I kneel hands and knees on it, out of the water.

I gulp down a few hard breaths. And then the pain hits. Something sharp in my side. My rib cage. I try to suck in more air—but can't get enough. My chest heaves as I gasp for more.

"Dad."

My voice is barely above a whisper. My heart beats in my throat. I scan the river. Where is he? The only light comes from the other side of the river. From the flashlights attached to the bow. The boat must have floated into an eddy. The light moves across the water and the trees onshore, but Dad's not in it.

His voice comes from upriver. "Sadie! Sadie, where are you? Are you okay?"

I take the deepest breath I can. "Dad!" It comes out louder this time. Hopefully loud enough.

"Where are you?"

"Downstream. On a rock. River left."

"You safe there?"

"I'm okay," I say, but my voice is tight. I take the biggest breaths I can manage, trying not to cry. "You?"

"I'm okay."

The flashlights turn, illuminating Dad for a moment. He's standing in the shallow eddy. The light moves again and blinds me, then shifts downstream.

"I'm on my way."

And I'm able to take a deeper breath.

My dad is coming to get me.

"It took a serious hit." Dad crouches next to the boat on a sandbar and examines the hull in the light of his headlamp.

"I'm on it," I say between shallow breaths. I hold my side as I crouch down and dig one-handed in the front of the boat.

We do some duct tape repair work before we get back in. I swallow a couple of Advil. The pain gets worse when I move my right arm. I don't tell Dad. What good would it do? Gingerly, I put my right hand on the top of the paddle and my left on the shaft, brace myself with my right foot, and take a stroke.

Constant forward motion.

Paddle through the pain.

Don't cry.

"Probably another fifteen minutes to Victoria," Dad says. "We'll have a good story for your mom."

Victoria is the next checkpoint, where our bank crew, Mom, will give us food and fresh water and sign us in with the race officials so we can keep going. I think Dad expects me to chuckle or agree or something, but I don't. I'm grasping for anything to focus on—the river, the trees, the breeze on my face—because it's like a knife is jabbing into my side.

"Can I get a hut?" I ask, desperate to paddle on the other side.

"Hut," Dad answers as I begin my next stroke.

I finish the stroke and switch sides, paddling on my right. But even keeping my right arm close to my side while I paddle doesn't help. The knife is still there, twisting its way into my body.

"You hurting?" Dad asks.

"My side."

"I'll take a look when we pull in. We'll see what we can do to make you more comfortable."

We must have missed a crack, because water is seeping into the bottom of the boat by my feet. Not so much that the pumps can't handle it, but we don't want to burn them out. I'm starting to think we might need to pull over and fix it when I spot lights up ahead. One of them must be Mom's headlamp.

In another minute, the beam of our flashlights hits her, standing waist-deep in the river, waiting to give us water and food.

I pull off my hat. I'm dripping sweat and shaking.

"Why did it take so long? Did you stop for something?" Mom asks as we pull in. The light on her headlamp hits me. "Oh god, Sadie!" She grabs the side of the canoe and pulls it up the boat ramp as Dad tells her about the crash.

"We've got a pretty good crack in the hull," he says. The boat rocks as he climbs out. "Grab the repair supplies, Sadie."

"Forget the boat," Mom says. "Look at your daughter. She's covered in blood."

"Sadie's fine."

"God, Will. Have you even looked at her?"

I reach up to touch my face with my left hand, because it hurts too much to move my right. It comes away dark and sticky.

Between fixing the boat and the pain in my side, neither of us noticed my face.

Mom takes a dry part of her shirt and wipes my hairline with it, then studies my head in the beam from her head-lamp. "It might need a stitch or two," she says. "Where else do you hurt?"

"My side," I say, pointing to the right side of my rib cage. "Pretty sure I cracked something." I've known this since the rock, but I didn't see any point in saying it out loud. Plenty of people have finished the Odyssey with broken bones.

I take Mom's offered hand and climb into the shallows. Dad slides an arm around my waist and they both help me to shore. I sit on the boat ramp, dripping water, and take breath after breath, finding just the right depth so I get oxygen without the stab of pain getting worse.

"I think we've got a butterfly bandage in the first aid kit. That should take care of the cut," Dad says. "And maybe a bandage tight around the ribs."

Dad has paddled with more than one hernia. *Stuff it back in and wrap it up,* he says. *Paddle through the pain.*

"Will, she needs the hospital." Mom's voice is cold. Hard.

Her headlamp illuminates Dad's face. His jaw is set. "Fine. Take her to the hospital. I'll fix the boat and put a couple of big rocks in her seat to balance the weight. Call Ginny. She can meet me at the next checkpoint and take over as bank crew."

"Forget the race." Mom's voice is granite. "This is your daughter. You're coming to the hospital with us."

"It's a cracked rib and a few stitches. They don't do anything for cracked ribs. Just make you rest." His voice has gone cold, too. They're not usually like this with each other. "This is twenty finishes in a row for me, Nic. I can't give that up."

My insides churn. I've failed my dad. I can barely breathe

because of the pain. And now my parents are fighting. I hate when they fight.

"The ribs and the cut are all we know about. She got ejected from the boat. She could have internal injuries."

"Sadie, do you have internal injuries?" Dad asks, like it isn't really possible. How am I supposed to know what's happening in my gut? Anyway, Scofields probably paddle through internal injuries.

Mom bends down next to me. "Which side again?"

I nod toward my right. She lifts the bottom of my shirt and shines her headlamp on me.

"What do you think now, Will?"

I look down at the jagged, dark purple bruise that's erupted on my abdomen, stretching from my bra line to my shorts.

And I vomit.

One mega bruise on my side.

Two cracked ribs.

Four stitches in my head.

Three hours in the hospital.

One nineteen-year Texas River Odyssey streak dead, thanks to me.

Painkiller-induced sleep in my own bed with my dog at my feet. A midday drive to Seadrift on Monday to watch Tanner finish the race.

I spend hours snoozing on and off in a reclining lawn chair, the hand from my good side resting on Mazer, my shaggy old golden retriever. He doesn't leave my side. It's what I always expected to do when I arrived here on Monday, the third day of the race. Except I expected to be in my wet river clothes dripping with exhaustion and satisfaction and pride at completing the race I waited my whole life to paddle.

A few people, old family friends, stop by to say things like, "You'll make it next year" and "Sorry you got hurt" and "I finished with a torn hamstring back in the eighties." How is that supposed to help?

I make some small talk, but mostly I sleep. Or pretend to sleep.

Mom comes to get me when they spot Tanner in the binoculars.

I sit on the seawall and let my legs dangle down the side. He just canoed 265 miles, from central Texas to the coast. By himself. In fifty-eight hours. It's not just a respectable time, it's a good time. He'll be happy. My heart practically bursts for what he accomplished. When he's close, I bring my hands together to clap and try not to think about how Dad and I might have been paddling up to the finish alongside him. That sharp ice-pick pain hits me again, but I keep going. He deserves clapping at the finish. Everyone does.

When Tanner reaches the finish line, I stand, gingerly, trying to make it hurt as little as possible. He puts a hand on the railing and climbs the stairs out of the water, so unsure on his legs you'd think he was drunk. That's what fifty-eight hours in a canoe will do to you.

Dad hops into the water and carries Tanner's boat up

behind him, leaving it on the grass beneath the arch that is the finish line. Mom hugs Tanner, and Dad claps him on the shoulder before pulling him into a hug. I'd go in for a hug, but they're already taking pictures of Tanner with his paddle and his boat. And then Dad, with his arm around Tanner, his face exploding with pride.

There's a hitch in my throat. I might as well be back at the starting line, 265 miles away.

I return to my chair.

They line Tanner's boat up with all the other finishers in order of arrival. As they walk back, Dad pauses to look at Johnny Hink's six-man boat at the front of the line. Even from here I can read the white vinyl letters on the black hull. NEVER SAY DIE. It must kill Dad to know that his biggest rival took first when we didn't even finish. But he follows Tanner to the pavilion. My brother settles into a folding chair at a table, with a burger and fries and my dad by his side.

Later, when Tanner has showered and settled into a lawn chair for a nap, Mom and Dad exchange words I can't make out. Both of their faces are tight. Mom walks away, and Dad shoves his hands deep into his pockets. His face is all hard lines. He walks over and sits in the chair next to me. We're silent for a few minutes, which isn't unusual, except that all I can think about is how I let him down.

"Dad, I'm . . ." I say, ready to apologize, but he holds a hand up in the air, like he doesn't want to hear my apology. Like he can't even stand to hear it.

He watches the horizon as a speck on the water turns into a canoe, paddling in to the finish. Then he turns his head toward the finish line and the row of finished boats behind it, where ours should have been.

"We had a good run. Shame we couldn't make it to the finish together," he finally says, before he rises from the chair and walks away.

Shame we couldn't finish together.

Shame.

Maybe that was supposed to make me feel better. But how could it, when I know how wrecked he is about not finishing? When I know that Mom just made him come say this to me?

His words are salt in both our wounds.

And I know it now, that next year it won't be enough to just finish. I have to nail it.

3

ONE YEAR LATER

The sun glistens off Spring Lake. It's the headwaters for the
San Marcos River, surrounded by an honor guard of giant
cypress trees with feathery leaves that shake in the breeze.
This is where the race will begin tomorrow.

The grassy lawn around the lake buzzes with people dropping off their canoes and getting their boats checked by race
officials who mark things like GPS trackers and life pre-
servers and snakebite kits off their boat inventory lists.
There are tents and folding tables set up for information and
registration, and boxes of T-shirts for racers and bank crews,
and for spectators to buy.

Doug Hammond, one of the race officials who paddled all
through the nineties, clears our boat and wishes us luck.

Racers, all in jeans and T-shirts, begin pouring into a big open tent filled with a sea of folding chairs. Tomorrow we'll all be in leggings and river shoes.

"Orientation?" I ask. It's not like we're going to learn anything new. None of the rules have changed from last year. But there's free barbecue afterward. Hard to say no to that.

"I heard someone scouted the cut yesterday," Tanner says. "We should find out if it's open."

"That would be a gift," I say. He and I are planning a sub-fifty-hour finish, and taking a shortcut on the water instead of hauling our boat on foot past a two-mile logjam—a mess of branches and debris in the river so thick that you can't paddle through—will go a long way toward making our goal.

For a couple of months, I hoped that I'd be doing all this with Dad again. That it would be the end of Dad getting that just-socked-in-the-gut look on his face every time he saw me. That his eyes would stop lingering on the scar just below my hairline.

But when I asked him if we could give it another try, his eyes drifted away from my face so he wouldn't have to look at me. "I think my racing days are over."

My heart crumpled.

At seventeen, I'm a year short of being able to race on my own. But Tanner didn't much care for solo racing, so we rebuilt the cracked tandem and trained for half a year.

There's a shrine to the Texas River Odyssey in my living

room. The pages of the 1963 *Life* magazine article about the Odyssey hang framed on the wall. It's the story that inspired my grandpa to race in 1964, back when you had to paddle past Seadrift, along the coastline all the way to Corpus Christi to finish. My grandpa swamped in the ocean and had to get rescued by the coast guard. But when Dad was old enough, they paddled it together and finished in Seadrift. Then Dad paddled with my grandma, and later with Mom. Below the framed article, finisher patches for everyone in the family are mounted on the wall. Every day I envision mine right there with them.

They're the real Scofields, and I'm still on the outside, doing everything I can to get in.

We file into the tent with the other racers, and it's a relief to be out of the hot sun. We're surrounded by at least two hundred people. Maybe more. Over a hundred boats registered this year, and most will have at least two people. Some will even have six. We sit in white folding chairs set up on the grass, facing a small stage.

Doug Hammond stands at the microphone. The sound system makes one of those awful high-pitched feedback squeals, and then Doug's gravelly voice welcomes us all. I listen to the first few minutes, and then I start reviewing the river in my head, because everything is the same as last year. Except that this year I won't miss a beat. I won't make a bad call. I won't cause a wreck. I'm not going to choke.

I'm not going to choke.

In my head I paddle and draw and backsweep and we dodge other boats, and I've got us just about to Scull's Crossing when Doug says, "I went myself to scout the cut yesterday. It's a no-go. Not enough water to get through."

I join the collective groan.

Tanner is already at a table with the Bynums by the time I've made it through the line with a brisket sandwich, coleslaw, and iced tea.

Awesome.

I glance longingly to where Ginny sits with No Sleep till Seadrift, a team made up of Molly and Mia Hernandez, Erin Davies, and Juliette Welsh, but their table is full. Anyway, I should probably sit with my partner, so I brace myself and head for my brother's table.

Tanner sits across from Hank and Coop, next to Randy. Hank and Coop have taken up one side, which means I get stuck on the other side of Randy, and it's a squeeze. He isn't fat, but he's massive. I put my tea next to his Coke, pull the last empty chair a few inches to the left, and sit with my butt hanging a little off the seat to avoid Randy's elbows. It's like they're epoxied to the table.

"Yeah, but what makes you think you can beat a six?" Tanner asks.

"What's going on?" I lean past Randy to get a look at my brother.

Tanner shoots a skeptical look at his friends. "These three think they're taking first place this year."

"The last time a three-person boat won, none of us were even born," I say.

"But we only missed first by ninety minutes last year," Coop says.

"You gotta look at who's racing this year to see it." Hank leans half his body on the table. "We beat Conner's boat last year, and he still can't pace for shit. Half the Wranglers decided to solo this year, and the guys taking their seats are all novices. Your dad's not racing. It just leaves Johnny's boat."

Johnny Hink's six-man boat took first last year, and no matter what Hank says, I'm sure Johnny expects to win again. I glance again at the women of No Sleep till Seadrift. They're good. So good that Hank shouldn't count them out. If a six doesn't take the top spot this year, I would love for it to be them.

"But Johnny only pulled together a three this year," Hank continues. "Kraft just had knee surgery, so he's out. Ryan's wife said she'd divorce him if he missed seeing his baby born, so he's not racing. And Greg just got sick of dealing with Johnny."

Can't blame him. The Hinks' property borders ours, and I've known them for as long as I can remember. Even though it's a truth universally acknowledged that Johnny Hink is a humongous asshole, he and my dad were actually friends once. They raced in the Odyssey together six years ago. I don't understand exactly what happened between them on the water, only that by the finish, they hated each other and have ever since.

The Scofields and the Hinks are the ugliest rivalry in the Odyssey community. If we're Hatfields, they're McCoys. Most everyone who's been racing for a long time comes down on one side of it or the other, and the Bynums are firmly in the Scofield camp. My dad used to race with both of the Bynum dads. They set some records together.

"Anyway, they've gotta take piss breaks every five minutes because their prostates are the size of grapefruits," Randy says.

Randy is cousin to Hank and Coop and pulls like a monster truck with a paddle in his hands. Kind of acts like a monster truck, too.

Hank and Coop are brothers. Hank sits in the back and drives the boat, using pedals to control the rudder. He's twenty-three, and the brains of the whole operation. Coop started racing when he was sixteen. He graduated from my high school with Tanner a year ago. He sits in the bow, setting the stroke, and is supposedly so tuned in to the boat that he knows who stopped to pee just by feeling how the boat changes.

"What kind of time are you shooting for?" Coop asks.

"Sub-fifty," Tanner says.

"So you guys are really in it." Hank's eyes land on me. "Not planning to stop and rest?"

"Nah, man," Tanner says.

Everyone knows Scofields don't stop to rest.

"Yeah, but . . ." Coop starts, but he doesn't finish.

"Sadie's got this," Tanner says.

But the hush that falls on the table says that no one is convinced. It says that all they see when they look at me is how I made a mistake last year and got hurt. How I dropped out.

Then Randy picks a piece of meat off his plate and holds it up to my side. "Look, Sadie—ribs!" He cracks up.

I chew and swallow and force myself to act like I didn't just get that stab-of-a-knife feeling.

"Dude," my brother says. "Not cool."

I echo that *not cool* in my head, because in the beginning, Tanner didn't want to race with me this year. It took a lot of training to convince him I could make it to the finish, and I don't need any of these guys putting doubts back in his mind.

Coop and Hank both shake their heads. All this protectiveness just makes everything worse.

Randy stares at his plate. "Sorry, Sade."

"I know you're sorry," I say. "I've seen you paddle."

Hank's face splits into a smile. "She burned you." Now the whole table is laughing. Even Randy.

Taking a joke at your own expense is the only way to belong with these guys. But I need more than that. I need them to take me seriously.

I know we can't take first, but what if we still did really well? Like plaque-on-the-wall well. "We're going to make the top five," I say before I can talk myself out of it. Top five will erase last year from everyone's mind. Maybe even Dad's.

Tanner chokes on his water.

Coop's eyeballs almost fall out onto his brisket. "Top five?" he says. "You know there are some really fast boats this year, right?"

"You've got to look at who's racing this year to see it," I say, echoing Hank.

Coop's cheeks go pink, and he's decent enough to look away.

But the whole exchange flies right over Randy's head. "Plus, you should rest, so you don't wreck again," he says, like a big sack of stupid.

Hank looks like he's going to garrote Randy. Then he turns to me. "I'm glad you're in it one hundred percent." He says it like I'm his middle-school sister. "Just sucks you guys didn't get your number."

Tanner pounces on the subject change. "We should have

registered early. I can't believe a couple of novices got our number."

Scofields always race under the number 1964. It's the year Dad's dad first raced. We were wrecked when we didn't get it. It feels like a bad omen.

"What number are you using?" Hank asks.

"Three-twenty-four. It's our street number," I say. It took forever to come up with another number that meant something to both of us, and it's still no good.

Just as Randy puts his jumbo cup to his mouth, someone bumps him from behind and Coke sloshes everywhere. It's so crowded here.

Randy groans and pulls at his wet shirt.

Brent Hink stands behind him, his weasel face cracked in a smile and his stupid shoulders shaking with quiet laughter.

Tanner spits the words out. "Eat me, Hink."

"You eat me."

Randy turns around, sees who hit him, and pushes his chair back into Brent, who stumbles. This could get really ugly really fast, because Randy is as hotheaded as he is massive.

"You better leave now," Tanner says. He presses a hand flat on the table and rises out of his seat.

"Tanner!" I shake my head at him. The Hinks have it coming, and Tanner wants to be the one to give it to them.

But getting in a fight today could mean an injury. It could ruin our chances tomorrow.

He looks at me and back to Brent. But he doesn't sit down.

"Move along, Brent." It's Johnny Hink's voice.

I turn around just in time to see him clapping a hand on his nephew's shoulder. His eyes sweep the table and land on me. "This is no time to stir up the riffraff."

We all watch Johnny and Brent leave. The entire table is like a stretched-out rubber band waiting to snap.

"Johnny was talking trash about you guys in the bathroom before orientation," Tanner says when they're well out of earshot.

Hank's face is puzzled. "He was talking trash about the way we use the bathroom?"

I almost take back what I thought about Hank being the brains, until one side of his mouth twitches up and all that rubber-band tension is gone.

"Courtesy flush, dude," Randy says. "Use the courtesy flush."

It's a terrible joke. But Coop's lips press together, and his trying-not-to-laugh face is all dimples. And then Hank's laughing, and Tanner's laughing, and I can't help but laugh, too.

When the laughter dies down, Hank looks from Tanner to me. "You guys should watch out for Brent and John Cullen, too."

John Cullen Hink is Johnny's son. He's paddling for the first time this year with his cousin Brent, even though he never had any interest in racing back when we were kids. Back when we used to call him Cully.

"They were talking like they were going to bust out some old-school shit on your asses."

"Old school like ramming our canoe?" I ask. That could do some damage.

Hank shrugs. "Just don't be surprised if you show up tomorrow morning and one of them has taken a dump in your boat."

The sky is wide open and blue as Tanner and I walk back to the other tent, where we left our boat. It's an absolutely perfect summer day, and yet all I can think about is Brent or John Cullen fouling my canoe. It's not too late to plastic-wrap it. Racers do that sometimes with their canoes if they're worried about people messing with their stuff.

Unlike when we arrived, the tent is now full of canoes and kayaks. Full of people and talk and laughter, too.

"I'm going to go look around," Tanner says. "Wanna come?" My brother likes to see how everyone else kits out their boat. How they arrange their water bottles and bags for food and trash. He likes to talk to them about their lighting systems and all the gray foam we glue into our boats to hold everything in place.

"I'm just going to check a couple of things," I say, not wanting to leave our boat alone.

"You can't prepare away being nervous, Sade," my brother says, but I ignore him and walk around the other boats to ours. It's not just nervousness. John Cullen broke Tanner's nose last fall. He's wrecked other things, too.

I crouch low, inspecting the mesh snack bag attached to the inside of the canoe by my seat. I've already counted and recounted energy blocks and checked the flashlights and batteries a million times, but I check everything again. It's all here. Everything is fine.

"What the hell, Hink? That's our number."

It's my brother's voice booming from across the tent. Crap.

I whip my head around. At the edge of the tent, Tanner is charging toward Brent, who turns around, shoulders back. John Cullen is right behind him, the sun shining through his orange hair, making it look like it's on fire. My stomach churns, and it's not because of the way he finally grew into his long arms or how his jaw has squared off or how he carries himself with this quiet sort of confidence. Every time I see him, it's like being in the ocean, caught in the waves, getting hit over and over again with anger, sadness, confusion. Mostly anger.

"I didn't know that was your number," Brent says loud enough for the whole tent to hear. So loud that nobody would believe it's actually true. Everyone knows that's our number. It's obvious that the Hinks took it to eff with us.

"Bullshit." Tanner's all puffed up, like someone hooked him up to an air compressor full of anger.

"Well, it's our number, too. It's—"

"It's Brent's IQ," John Cullen says from over Brent's shoulder.

Which is ridiculous, and not just because IQs don't go that high. It could be the number of jelly beans in Brent's head. But all I hear is that it was John Cullen's idea to take our number. Brent's not capable of coming at us with anything other than rude hand gestures and insults to our mom. But John Cullen is.

I hate John Cullen.

So much.

"It's not our fault you didn't register it sooner," Brent says.

"Doesn't matter. The skills don't come with the number," Tanner says, still sticking his chest out like he's inviting something.

He is inviting something.

He's been waiting for this since last fall.

I zigzag around boats, trying to get to my brother. And I'm not the only one heading his way. Randy takes huge strides in the same direction, his shirt still wet with Coke.

"Low blow, little Hinks," Randy says, still a few feet out from the argument.

"Did you just call me a little Hink?" Brent yells.

"Damn straight I—"

"We can't do this. It's just a number." I step in front of Tanner and push back into his chest to keep him out of this.

"This is about a lot more than a number," Tanner says.

I know he's right.

I dig my heels in and throw my arms out to keep my brother behind me as I stare into Brent's pointy face. Tanner's feet stay planted, and after a long second, his body relaxes. "We'll settle it on the water."

"Nah," Brent says, his eyes trained on Randy. "I need an apology right now for that little Hink shit."

"Here's your apology." Randy holds out his meaty fist in a single-finger salute. He takes a step closer to Brent. "Now where's mine?"

"I've got it right here!" Brent shoves his hands into Randy's chest.

Randy shoves him back.

John Cullen tugs on Brent's shoulders, trying to pull him away. Tanner and I do the same to Randy.

"Leave it, dude. You've got to race tomorrow," Tanner tells Randy.

But Brent breaks free and shoves Randy backward into Tanner. Randy doesn't fall, but Tanner lands on the grass.

Then Randy is chest-to-chest with Brent. "Screw you, Hink."

"Stop it!" I yell, grabbing Randy's arm, but he shakes me off, and I grab both arms from behind, trying to pull him back. He lunges, yanking me onto his back and pushing Brent, who falls into John Cullen, who tips like a domino. A big green canoe stops his feet, but the rest of his body keeps going. Brent comes down with him.

The crack is deafening.

There is one collective gasp, then everything is silent.

Everything is still.

We *broke* a *boat*.

And then people in Day-Glo-green race official shirts are pulling Brent and John Cullen off the boat and running their hands over the crack in the hull. They haul the five of us into the building where, on normal days, they sell tickets for the glass-bottom boat tours on the lake.

God, I wish this had been a normal day.

Inside, the race officials are all tight mouths and wrinkled foreheads while they line up a row of four chairs.

"Boys, take a seat," Donny Billingsly says, like I'm not even there, and I don't know whether to be offended or relieved that I'm not being included.

Randy and Tanner scoot their chairs a few feet away from the Hinks before they sit down.

"Disqualified," Becky Lamont says. Her bright race

official shirt is tucked neatly into a belted pair of khaki shorts.

"No!" Brent shouts.

"No," Tanner, Randy, and I echo.

John Cullen is the only one who stays silent.

"Yes," Becky says. "This behavior is completely unacceptable. We pride ourselves on being a supportive community."

"And throwing punches at the starting line isn't supportive," Donny says, pulling his sun hat off his poofy gray hair and letting it hang around his neck by its cord. "You boys put a hole in a two-thousand-dollar boat."

And that's it. My chance at proving I can do this, at fixing things with Dad, it's gone. Again.

"Hold up. What can we do to fix this?" John Cullen says, because he's a rich, entitled little creep. "I need to race."

Which I don't get. Three months ago, I'd never seen him out on the river, and then suddenly, he and Brent were a near-constant presence.

"You should have thought about that before starting a fight," Donny says. "Think about those people whose race you just ruined. Think about all the work they put into getting here. There is absolutely no question that you boys are out."

Boys. I'm standing against a wall, and the boys are sitting. They're not even including me.

"So I'm still in?" I ask.

"Well, yes. Of course you're not in trouble," Donny says, tilting his head to the side. "But I know you wouldn't want to race without your brother. You don't want to be out there at night on your own."

I was literally on Randy's back when he knocked Brent over, and I'm not being disqualified.

Because I'm a girl.

"She can't race by herself. She's only seventeen," Becky says, like Donny is just a regular idiot instead of a patronizing, sexist idiot.

"But I'm still not disqualified because I didn't fight? Right?" I ask.

"Of course, dear," Donny says.

Becky stares at me like she's trying to peer inside my brain. "Yes—"

"Tanner didn't fight, either." I cut her off before she can put any conditions on it. "Tanner tried to *stop* Randy, same as me. So you can't DQ him, either. There are witnesses."

Becky glares at me, like I just caught her in a bear trap. Which I basically did.

My brother is on the edge of his seat while Donny and Becky conference together in the corner. John Cullen is on the edge of his seat, too. The red second hand ticks its way around the clock on the wall twice.

"Fine, Tanner can race," Becky finally says.

Tanner lets out a breath the size of Houston. So do I.

Then John Cullen is on his feet. "I didn't fight, either. I tried to stop it, too."

Donny and Becky exchange a look.

"Ask anyone," he says.

Becky turns to me and asks with her eyebrows instead of her mouth.

I could knock him out of the race right now if I wanted to. It would be perfect payback for taking our number. For being a dick to us out on the river while we trained this spring and for the ways he's treated us for years. For the tree house.

He's staring at me, hope perched on the tip of his nose. I know that look, back from the days when his face was round and soft, before it was ever touched by a razor or acne. Back before his nose lost that cute-as-a-button look. Back when he was my best friend.

I yank my eyes away from him and back to Becky. The words are like tar in my mouth. "He's telling the truth."

Bouncing. That's the only way to describe how I get to Tanner's truck. I'm bouncing because we're still in the race. I'm bouncing because as soon as we walked out of that office, my brother looked at me like I'd suddenly grown a foot and said, "Well played, Sadie."

I roll down the window and let the wind whip my hair as we drive back to the house. In three days we'll be at the finish line and I'll have earned my patch. Everything will be better. I've been dreaming about this for so long. It's like finishing the race is this hole in my chest because my heart is already there at the finish waiting for the rest of me to arrive.

"Sucks for Randy, though," Tanner says, picking up the conversation again after we've driven a few miles toward home.

"It does suck," I agree, because I was almost in the same situation. But truthfully, I'm not too broken up for Randy. He's already finished a handful of times and has a first place under his belt. He doesn't need this. And he's the one who dove into a fight that had nothing to do with him. Who it sucks for is the rest of the Bynums. They've got a three-person boat and only two paddlers.

"Do you think they'll run with his seat empty? Or do they have a tandem they can paddle?" I ask.

"Dunno," Tanner says.

"Do you think John Cullen will paddle alone?"

Tanner's laugh lasts from County Road 234 all the way to that old broken windmill somebody made look like a *T. rex.*

"I don't think so, either," I say, although racing seems pretty important to him. Maybe he'll make it happen. I don't know what kind of stake he could have in this race, though.

"He won't make it to the finish." Tanner switches on the radio and drums along on his steering wheel.

I force a laugh so he won't know how much that stings. "He won't make it past the first afternoon. I doubt he'll get to Leisure Camp."

The truck kicks up a cloud of dust on the long gravel drive on our property. As we pass the fork where the road splits off and goes down the hill to the river, we decide that I'll wipe down the ice chest and Tanner will start organizing the water jugs and checking the tubing.

Tanner's phone rings and he grabs it from the cup holder as we park next to Dad's truck in front of the house. He answers with a "Yeah."

By now, Dad should be in the kitchen, making spaghetti for the traditional prerace feast. On the front porch, Mazer does a lazy stretch, getting up from his nap. His whole body wags as soon as he sees me step out of the truck. He breathes his warm roadkill breath all over me when I crouch down in front of him on the porch.

"I'm going to miss you, buddy," I tell him.

He leans against my leg and puts his head under my hand. I sit down on the porch and give him the all-over scratch he deserves.

Tanner steps down from the truck, phone to his ear. "Hey . . . Wait, seriously? You mean it?" My brother's eyes hit me for a second before he takes a sharp turn toward the garage.

"I'll stink like the river when I see you at the finish Monday," I tell my dog. "You'll love it."

Mazer rolls over and offers me his belly. I indulge the furry old man for a few minutes, even though I need to get started on the cooler. But it's hard to say no to this dog. Even if most of my heart is already at the finish line, a piece of it will be with him.

Probably five minutes pass before I hear the creak of the garage door opening and Tanner coming back out, his face tight. His feet thud past me on the porch, and he walks inside the house. Something makes me uneasy. He didn't say anything. He didn't even look at me, and I don't hear any noises from the house.

Mazer paws at my hand, reminding me that I stopped petting him. I give him a couple more pats. It's just race nerves. I'd better get to work.

"Come on, boy," I tell Mazer.

He rolls back onto his feet and follows me into the barn.

By the time I've finished washing the cooler, Tanner still isn't back to work on the water jugs. Slacker. I grab the milk crates and wash the jugs and tubing we'll need, and then I organize the electrolyte tabs. My stomach growls and I glance at my watch. It's time for dinner. My brother is so freaking lucky I'm more responsible than he is. But I don't want to grumble too much. He's got two finishes under his belt, and one of them is a solo. If I can't race with Dad, I'm glad I'll be on the water with my big brother.

When I get to the porch, I can just make out the low tones of Dad's and Tanner's voices in the kitchen.

"What's going on?" I call as I walk into the house.

Their voices stop. The only sound is Mazer's happy tail thwacking against the end table. A little stone forms in my stomach.

"Anyone there?" I ask. The smell of spaghetti and garlic greets me in the kitchen.

Dad and Tanner stand at opposite ends of the island, a loaf of garlic bread between them. Tomato sauce bubbles and pops in a saucepan on the stove behind them, next to a big bowl of noodles.

Tanner's eyes move from me to Dad and back to me before he gets interested in the garlic bread. The silence in this room makes the stone in my stomach grow spikes.

Dad slaps a hand against the counter. "Let's take this to the living room," he says, leading the way. He chooses a spot right beside this hideous deer lamp with a plaid shade that he inherited from my grandma.

When I was little and just experimenting with swear words, I was apparently getting it all wrong, saying things like, "I'm going to punch the damn out of you." So one day Dad took Tanner and me into the living room and flipped the lamp on. "Kids, I'm going to teach you some shit. Notice I said *shit* there, not damn or hell. If you're going to cuss, I want you to do it right."

That's the day the Cussing Lamp was born. If the lamp is on, we can curse all we want.

Tanner stands beside Dad, his eyes fixed somewhere around my shoes. I'm struck for the millionth time how alike they are. Both just over six feet. Both blue eyed, straight nosed, their skin permanently gold from being on the river.

Tanner's hair is the sandy color Dad's was before it was taken over by gray. When I was little, I wished I could trade in my dark hair and dark eyes, things I got from Mom, to be more like them.

The spiky stone inside me grows a size bigger. Something bad is coming. For a moment, I'm back in the river on that dark night last year, clinging to a rock.

"Whatever it is, just get it over with," I say.

Tanner glances at Dad and then at me. "Hank Bynum offered me Randy's seat in the boat."

I know what Tanner's answer was. I do. But there's a little part of me hoping that maybe I'm wrong. Maybe I still have a partner. "And?"

"You know the Bynums don't call twice."

"No!"

I knew it was coming, but his words hit me in the gut, knocking me back a step.

"Hank's right. We could be the first three to take the race this century." His stare pushes against mine, like he's forcing me to understand. "I had to."

I grit my teeth, because he didn't *have to*. He ditched me. Betrayed me.

This is the race I've spent a year—no, I've spent my whole—life preparing for. You can't just pick up a new partner at the Buc-ee's with a tank of gas and some beef jerky.

Tanner knows this race is supposed to make things right with Dad.

The lines on Dad's face are hard and stony.

My skin vibrates. "You knew? You're letting him?"

Dad doesn't answer. He reaches for the knob on the Cussing Lamp. "Thirty seconds, kid."

The lamp clicks and the plaid shade glows.

"You asshole!" I yell at my brother. "You donkey dick! How could you fucking do this to me? I've trained for a year to do this race and you just pissed away all my hard work like a little shit weasel. I fixed that damn boat out there with my own hands and now you're dicking me over for the damn—"

The lamp clicks again and goes dark. Mom's hand is on the knob. I didn't even know she'd walked in.

"What on earth? I thought I was coming home to spaghetti and garlic bread, not a cursing war."

"Wars aren't one-sided," Tanner grumbles, rubbing a hand over his short hair.

Mom's dark hair is pulled back in a ponytail because she just came from the bakery she owns. A bag of cookies dangles from her hand. Desserts for the happy night that just vanished.

"It's not my fault. It's them." My voice shakes. "Randy Bynum got disqualified, and now Tanner's taking his seat in the Bynum boat and I can't race. And Dad's letting him do it."

Mom looks at Dad with her eyebrows up in a question.

"He's a grown man. He makes his own decisions," Dad says.

"He's nineteen and he lives in our garage and calls it an apartment!" I shout. "That's hardly a *grown man*."

"Sadie, why don't you head up to your room for a little while?" Mom says. "Maybe you could take a bath."

I look at my brother, but he just shrugs. People don't say sorry after you call them a shit weasel.

Mazer follows me to my room, panting because he's getting old and the stairs take more effort than they used to. I let him climb on the bed and I don't even care if I get in trouble for it. I snuggle up with my dog and listen. Mom's and Dad's words travel up the stairs and through the crack I left in the door. They've never figured out that I can hear them.

"How could you let him, Will?" Mom's voice is angry. "She worked her ass off for this. She even loaned him the money to register."

"This is a chance at first place in a three," Dad says.

"Only sixes take first," Mom snaps.

"You gotta look at the field. The best guys aren't in sixes this year," Dad says. "And Hank, Coop, and Tanner, they've got the experience, the strength, and they won't quit for anything."

More salt on the places that never healed.

"I'll make sure she gets her money back," Dad says, his tone a little softer.

"Do you really think the money is the problem?"

"Of course it's not. But it's better this way."

"No. It's not. He could wait. They could form a six next year."

"Nicole." Dad's voice is softer now. "Our kids don't belong in a boat together. Can't you see how much drive he has? He'll never slow down. He'll never quit."

There it is.

No matter how many times Dad's said that he doesn't care about it, he's still upset about our DNF. *Did not finish.* He doesn't want me in the boat with Tanner because he doesn't think I'm as good as my brother. He doesn't think I can finish.

I cover my face with my hands and let the tears roll down my cheeks. At least if I'm not paddling, I can't prove him right.

I turn down dinner when Mom knocks on my door half an hour later. I take a pass on her offer to talk, too. There's nothing more to talk about. It's done. On my bed, I play last year's race over and over in my head. Which is worse, wrecking the boat and ending our race, or never even starting?

A tapping noise on the window shakes me out of some kind of stupor. It's ten thirty. I must have fallen asleep. I rub my eyes and yawn. There's the tap again. Probably a tree branch. Or a really big, stupid bug. But then there's a knock.

I climb out of bed and flip off the light switch before I pull my curtain aside. I squint until I can make out the shape in the branches. He's grown over a foot and gained about a hundred pounds since the last time he was in that tree, but there's no mistaking that it's John Cullen.

"Are you spying on me?" I ask as soon as I pull the window open. Then I fold my arms across my chest to hide that I don't have a bra on under my tank top.

"If I was spying, would I knock?" he asks.

"How would I know? If you were a normal person, you'd use the phone. Or the door."

"Yeah, I can call your house. 'Hi, Mr. Scofield. This is Cully Hink. Is Sadie home?' You know it doesn't work like that. I don't have your cell. And your brother would jump me if I knocked."

"You did break his nose."

His face hardens and looks back at the tree like he might climb down. But then he meets my eyes. "Can I come in or what?" he asks. "You want to hear this. Trust me."

I don't trust John Cullen. I haven't trusted him since I was eleven and he was twelve. But it would have to be something good to send him up my tree after years of loathing. I give him enough space to climb through. "It'd better be an apology for ruining my life."

He thuds onto my floor. Shoot. That was loud. There's another thud. Mazer jumping off the bed. In an instant he's wagging his whole body and trying to climb into my enemy's arms.

John Cullen bends down, grinning, hands already scratching Mazer's ears, and the whole thing would be heartwarming if it wasn't for all the betrayal.

"Keep quiet," I whisper.

I tiptoe to my door, although stealth is useless since Mazer is making enough noise for all three of us. I poke my head through the crack. No sign of my parents. Thank goodness they're heavy sleepers.

I pull the door shut and turn on a lamp before I return to the lovefest by my window. "Keep it down."

"He remembers me," John Cullen whispers.

"He does this to everyone."

"He knows I named him." His eyes go from my dog to my chest, and quickly back to my dog.

I go to the closet and pull down the biggest sweatshirt I own, and try to press down all the memories of the nights he snuck over to my house and we stayed up playing board games and reading books. Try not to think about the stuffed racoon he gave me, stored in a shoebox on the shelf with a few other mementos I was too soft to throw away.

I leave the closet and shut the door on all that.

"Why are you here?" I ask.

"None of that was my fault, you know."

I slide the sweatshirt over my head. "Stealing our number was your idea," I say as I put my arms through the sleeves.

My traitor of a dog rolls onto his back, offering his belly for a scratch to my biggest enemy.

"Blame your brother. Or the Bynums. It's not my fault they poached him," he says.

News travels fast.

"Why are you here?"

"I still need to race tomorrow."

"Good news! You're eighteen." I do a slow clap. "You didn't get screwed over by this whole thing like I did."

"Could you be a decent person for five minutes? I'm trying to ask you something important."

I stop the golf clap. Mazer scrambles to his feet to lean against John Cullen's leg. That dog is a terrible judge of character.

"I need to race tomorrow, and I don't have a boat to solo." He stops and waits, like I'm supposed to fill in the big blank at the end of his sentence. Like . . . Like . . .

Oh.

"So are you going to race with me or what?" he asks.

I can still race tomorrow.

I can prove my dad wrong.

I can do it *if* I race with John Cullen.

I sit on the bed.

How am I supposed to decide between my family and finishing? I'm not sure Dad will ever speak to me again if I get in the boat with a Hink. Especially Johnny Hink's son. Tanner definitely won't. Not after the fight they had last fall. But Dad and Tanner are the reason I'm stuck without a partner. They don't even think I can finish.

I need to finish. It can't wait another year.

"Gonzo's on board to bank crew. We'll have to use your boat."

"Wouldn't set foot in your boat, anyway," I say automatically.

"Wouldn't want you to."

I flip him off.

"Is that a yes?"

"No . . . Do your parents know about this?"

His hand is on Mazer's head. "They'd lock me up if they knew."

Since Dad and Johnny first raced together, things have gotten ugly. They've both called foul on each other in shorter races, and both have been disqualified. I even heard Dad telling Mom that Johnny had cost him business. This is a total betrayal of my family, and it's not like I can beat Tanner and make him feel bad. He'll be in first or second place. There's no way we could beat his boat. But maybe we could make top five. I'm good enough for that. I know I am. I think I am. And if we placed, Dad could see it, too.

"Goulash." He spits out the challenge.

My fingers itch to knock the smug little smile off his face with my fist. "We're not friends. You can't freaking goulash me."

But I already know my answer.

One of John Cullen's copper-colored eyebrows ticks up, like he knows he has the upper hand, and he must see the decision in my eyes, because he says, "Let's hammer out some details."

It's completely dark in the house when I creep downstairs at five thirty in the morning, carrying my bag of clothes for after the race. Mom and Dad will be up in an hour and I want to be long gone. I flick the switch on the dim light above the sink and heat up a bowl of spaghetti and a slice of garlic bread. I sit on a barstool at the end of the island and eat. The spaghetti is lukewarm, and the cheese on the garlic bread is so hot it burns the roof of my mouth.

Last year, on this day, I'd had a good night's sleep. A lot more than four or five hours. The sun was up, and the lights were on. The entire house smelled of eggs, biscuits, and bacon. Mostly bacon. There was a bowl full of berries on the table. Mom, Dad, Tanner, and I all sat down together. That was before Tanner moved into the detached garage.

Mom and Dad told stories of their Odyssey together, back before they got engaged. They were already training for the race when Dad went to my mom's dad to ask for permission to marry Mom. "You get in the boat with her and do that race," my grandpa said. "If the two of you still want to get married when it's all over, you have my blessing." Apparently, it was touch and go around the checkpoint at Invista, 230 miles in, but by the end they were solid. Dad got down on one knee at the finish and Mom said yes. They even did the race together again a few years later, but that was the last time for Mom.

Then Dad and Tanner talked about portaging—carrying their boat around—Gonzales Dam the year they raced together. I'd heard all these stories before, but I never get tired of them. Last year, on this day, I couldn't wait until our next meal together at the finish, when Dad and I would tell our own crazy stories about the race. I would finally be a part of it.

But the next meal Mom, Dad, and I had together came from a hospital vending machine. We never tell stories from our race. And I doubt anyone in my family will ever want to hear about me racing with John Cullen, either.

I force down as much breakfast as I can, but the garlic smell makes me queasy this early in the morning. Maybe it's just the guilt. Or the anger. I head outside and put my bag in my car. Then I go to the barn and load the race food Tanner and I prepared from the freezer into the cooler. I pack up the water jugs and electrolyte tabs and make a couple of trips from the barn to my car. I double-check the race supply list on my phone and confirm that I have everything. Then I sit in my car with my hands on the steering wheel. I don't turn the key. Everything about this feels wrong.

An idea hits me as I stare at the windows of our dark living room. I've never turned the Cussing Lamp on in my life, but right now it feels like giving the middle finger to everything that happened yesterday.

I go inside, straight to the lamp, and turn the knob.

Light floods the living room, and I turn to go back to my car, but another light flips on. The one in the kitchen. Dad walks in wearing gray pajama pants and a bakery T-shirt.

"I see you're dressed for racing." His voice is scratchy from just waking up.

Damn.

White tights under shorts, quick-dry shirt, river shoes. My dark hair in pigtail braids. The orange hat he gave me. There's no way I could pass this outfit off for anything else. I'd planned for them to find the note I left on my bed after I didn't come down for breakfast. I thought I could hide in the crowd around Spring Lake and be on the water before anyone could try to stop me.

"How'd you know I was up?"

"Your dog tried to climb in bed with us. He only does that when you're not around."

"Did you read my note?"

"Didn't see it," Dad answers.

I open my mouth a few times, but there's really nothing helpful I can say right now.

"How'd you find a partner so fast?" Dad asks. Is he going to try to stop me? "Did you pull Ginny out of retirement?"

I shake my head to buy some time. "She can't race," I say. "Her shoulder."

Dad nods. "So who is it?"

I don't want him to know. If I could make it so that he never finds out, I would. But there's no use in lying. I've never been good at it, anyway. "John Cullen."

Dad's mouth drops open, and his upper lip goes back. It's like he's watching a horror movie. He walks to the couch and sinks into it. He leans back and puts a hand in his hair. Everything stays quiet for a long while. He's so mad he's actually not speaking to me. I don't want this. I hate it. But I want to race. It's best I get out of here, so I head for the door.

"Wait another year," Dad says when my hand is on the doorknob.

"I don't want to wait any longer," I say, my back to him.

"You'll be eighteen next year. You can solo if you want."

I turn my head. He's still got his hand in his hair.

"I don't want to solo. I wanted to do the race with you. Or with Tanner."

"Sadie." He takes his hand out of his hair and puts his elbows on his knees, leaning forward. "You don't have any business getting in a boat with a Hink. You need to be on the water with someone you can trust. And that's not John Cullen. He's volatile. Just like his dad. How do you think he's going to handle it when things go wrong? Look what he did to your brother last fall. I wouldn't want you on the shore with him, let alone in a boat for the next sixty hours."

"Then you get in the boat with me. You race with me. Give me another chance." I hate the pleading sound in my voice.

His hand goes to his forehead, half covering his eyes and rubbing like he's trying to get rid of a headache. "I can't do that."

"That's what I thought." I turn the knob. He can't bear the possibility of another DNF with me. "Bye, Dad."

As I drive through the morning fog, I try not to think about the worry I saw on his face.

"Good god, the sun isn't even up yet," my best friend, Erica, says, climbing into the passenger seat of my car and shoving a duffel down at her feet. "Your family is extreme."

Her dyed black hair is stuffed into a messy bun. She's wearing shorts and a T-shirt, but she still took the time to put a ring of thick black eyeliner around each eye. She intimidated the hell out of me when she first came to my school two years ago, even after we started sharing shifts at my mom's bakery.

But two Aprils ago we spent a night and half a day making a million little organza flowers together because Lacy Siddens hired Erica's grandma to copy a prom dress out of a magazine, and four days before prom, Lacy declared the flowers they'd already made "anemic." Lacy is horrible, but the dress turned out just like the picture. She didn't deserve it.

When I called last night and asked Erica to bank crew, she didn't even ask for details. She said, "Yeah. Of course." Which is good, because if I'm going to do this, I need someone on my side.

I hand Erica the bag of cookies that didn't get eaten last night. "Payment for taking care of me for the next three days."

She crams her hand in and pulls out a sugar cookie with gumdrops in it. Mom calls them Sadie Bears, which is embarrassing. "You'd think I'd be sick of these by now, but I freaking dream about them." She takes a bite and chews. "What kind of dark magic does your mom put in these things? Crystallized baby joy?"

"It comes premixed in the flour," I say. "Special blend."

I put the car in reverse and back down her driveway.

"Shoulda guessed," she says with a full mouth. "So explain why you're doing this."

"Because it's hard."

Honestly, we've had this discussion before. She knows the Odyssey is about digging down and pushing yourself further than you ever dreamed.

"Yeah, I've seen the cross-stitched pillow on your couch," she says. "I can't believe your family motto is a double entendre. It's so weird."

Ugh. No. "Don't be gross. It comes from that JFK speech

about going to the moon. He says we do things 'not because they are easy, but because they are hard.'"

"Suuuuuure," Erica says, and even though I'm staring straight at the road, I can feel her side-eye.

The clock on the dash shows seven fifteen as we drive down the road that cuts through the green grass surrounding Spring Lake. My brother won't show up until eight, which gives me some time to train my new and completely inexperienced bank crew in peace.

I take a deep breath.

This'll work. It has to work.

We park next to John Cullen's truck. It's navy and shiny. I bet he got it new. I bet he's never even washed it himself. At least he didn't pay a bunch of money to have it lifted.

He's standing by the tailgate with Ricky Gonzales, who everyone calls Gonzo. He's one of those guys who stand out, and not just for sharing a nickname with a Muppet. He's slight, shorter than me, and he wears his hair in a pompadour every day. Even right now. He's followed by a wake of *he's gay, right?* whispers every time he walks down the hall. It's strange seeing him in shorts and a quick-dry T-shirt instead of a bright-colored button-up shirt and suspenders with dark cuffed jeans. He just graduated a few weeks ago, like Erica. I suppose John Cullen did, too.

In a million years I would never guess that the two of them would be friends. John Cullen is the kind of guy who breaks people's noses. And Gonzo's a really nice guy, the kind of guy at risk for getting his nose broken. They're an odd pair for sure, but I guess ever since his parents started sending him to a private school a few towns away, I lost track of what John Cullen gets up to, aside from fighting and talking shit about my family and not washing his own car.

We climb out of my car, and Gonzo picks Erica up in a big hug. They took art together last year.

"Sooby-sooby-roo," John Cullen says, walking around the back of my Subaru and running a finger across my VISUALIZE WHIRLED PEAS bumper sticker. "Can't believe this thing hasn't peeled off yet."

My insides prickle at the familiarity. I don't like that we have so many shared memories. That we nicknamed the car together and spent so many hours riding in the back when it was my mom's. That we spent all those afternoons watching Shaggy and Scooby.

Our eyes lock. God, it's annoying that he turned out nice-looking. I'd forgotten how his eyes are that shade of light brown, and I'd forgotten how he got that little scar beside his left one working on the tree house.

I haven't forgotten what he did to my tree house.

A years-old fire ignites inside me. My foot itches to kick him in the shin.

Am I really stepping into a boat with him for the next 265 miles?

Dad's word echoes in my ears.

Volatile.

"Is this a staring contest?" Erica asks.

I snap my eyes away from John Cullen's.

"Does not bode well," Gonzo mutters.

"Not at all," agrees Erica.

I cut both of them down with a glare, and then I pop open the back of my car. "Gather 'round, kids. This is Bank Crew 101."

I hand Erica a green binder that has driving directions and a printout of an Excel spreadsheet with every place they meet us and whether it's a checkpoint where they have to sign us in, or just a place where they need to restock us with water and food.

She and Gonzo stand under my open hatchback and flip through the laminated pages. Something inside me twitches, because I've just handed the Scofield family bible to outsiders.

"Ice socks," I say.

Both their heads pop up and the binder closes. They stand next to me looking at the supplies loaded into my trunk. My thighs bump against the bumper.

I've never been this close to Gonzo before. He's got a sweet, kind of powdery smell to him. I think it's coming from his hair.

My so-called partner sits on his open tailgate, legs dangling, staring into the distance.

I tear open a bag of tube socks and teach them how to use a Solo cup with the bottom cut off to stuff ice into a sock. I show them the milk crates with pool noodles zip-tied around the edges so they float, even with full water jugs inside. We go over how many electrolyte tabs to put in the jugs and how to attach the tubing we'll drink from and bite valves that keep the dirty water out. They see the vacuum-sealed food in the cooler and we talk about trash collection. I show them how to check our location on the tracker app so they'll have an idea of when we might show up at checkpoints and water stops.

"If you run into trouble, don't be afraid to ask questions. There's a wealth of knowledge out there among the other bank crews, and Odyssey people are some of the nicest. They'll help you."

I look to John Cullen to fill in the gaps.

He shrugs.

Moocher.

By the time we head over to the boat, more cars have arrived. But not my brother's truck. And I haven't seen any of the Bynums yet, either. Or Johnny Hink.

But they'll be here. They all will be.

Erica and Gonzo leave us to pick up their team captain shirts and driving guides, and to wander around a bit. They don't really have a job until our first water stop in a few hours.

My canoe is twenty-one feet long, narrow and black with low gunnels and a rudder controlled by pedals in the stern. It weighs about fifty pounds. That's light compared with the aluminums. John Cullen should already be pretty comfortable with it. It's probably just like the one he and Brent were planning to race. But still, everyone makes their canoe theirs.

We take out Tanner's extra shirt and the rest of his stuff and put it on the grass. Part of me wants to throw it in the trash. John Cullen puts his things in. We push his seat forward a bit, since Tanner has a couple of inches on him. He needs to be able to press his feet against something to get a more powerful stroke. Hopefully shifting the seat won't affect our trim, the way the weight distribution in the boat affects how it sits in the water. I give him the rundown on everything up front. Where to find the life preserver and how the lighting system works. Our food and trash systems. The bilge pump that keeps our boat from swamping if we take on water.

He examines the pump like he's never seen one before.

"You know how to use it, right?" I ask.

"Yeah. Of course," he says, and after a long pause, "Ours was just different."

I can't think of anything else to do with the boat, but he's still crouched close to me. So close I can feel the warmth of his body. So close I can smell him, and it's not the same dirt and sweat and river scent from when we were kids. It's shaving cream and deodorant. And greasy diaper cream and sunscreen. Wait. No. The diaper cream and sunscreen are me.

I stand up. "You don't smell right."

"I didn't know Axe Body Spray was a race requirement." He stands, too. "One whiff of your brother says different, though."

"You need to Desitin up or you'll chafe all over." Everyone knows you smear your whole body with the stuff. "And you need sunscreen. Don't you know you're a redhead?"

He cocks his head to the side and puts a hand to his chest. "Look at how much you care."

"I care about you not being a dead fish in your seat because it hurts too much to move your arms."

"I was going to put it on in the bathroom. Didn't want to stink up my car."

My car will probably smell for a week after the race. Dad's truck always did.

I push him toward the bathroom. "Get in there before everyone who did laxatives makes their final trip."

"Slow down," he says, and goes to his seat, fishes out a Desitin tube and some sunscreen, and stands back up. "You don't do laxatives, do you?"

I shake my head. "Too risky. You?"

"No."

Some people would rather not poop during the race, so they try to get it all out ahead of time. But getting the timing wrong can throw a *serious* wrench in your first day.

John Cullen walks away. I make myself small, sitting next to my canoe, using the people around me as a shield. I'm not going to hide behind a building or something, but I don't want to be noticed, either.

In the gaps between a team of racers one boat over, I spy a couple stopping him on his way into the bathroom. I move my head so I can see as they pull him back toward the picnic tables. They're smiling, and he's smiling back, and they're all talking. I've never seen these people before. They must be novices. The woman mimics wobbling and maybe falling out of a boat, and John Cullen laughs and she laughs and then he shakes hands with the man and the woman pulls him into a hug, and he takes the sunscreen from his pocket and walks into the bathroom.

I wish Erica hadn't gone off with Gonzo. Everyone is milling around and talking and laughing, and I'm sitting next to my canoe, wishing I were invisible. I pick a blade of grass and tear it into little pieces.

A hand presses into the top of my head. "Hey there, Sadie."

It's Ginny, lowering herself onto the ground next to me.

She's short and plump and old. Her long gray hair is pulled into a braid that goes over one shoulder. She mentored my dad when he started racing.

"It's weird seeing you here without your racing clothes on," I tell her, even though she didn't race last year, either. Ginny racing is a staple of my childhood. If she hadn't injured her shoulder a couple of years ago, she'd still be out there cutting a wake.

"Still strange knowing that I'm leaving here in a car instead of a canoe," she tells me.

"I know that feeling."

"I suppose you do." She gives me a small little smile. "Heard you and Cully have teamed up." Ginny mentored Johnny Hink, too. She's the flag tied to the rope in our families' game of tug-of-war.

I nod.

"It's like a duck and a moose decided to climb into a canoe together," she says.

I'm still trying to work out which of us is which, and what it means, when she says, "If you ask me, you're better off waiting a year and going solo."

"Why?" I ask. "How come you never raced with a partner?"

"I did in my first few races. Learned pretty quick that when I get on that water, I want to do it my way. I don't want to be responsible to anyone but myself."

"Ginny!"

I recognize Mark Siegfried's voice. He reaches out a hand, and Ginny's face lights up. Mine probably does, too. Mark has golden skin, bright blue eyes, and looks like he was chiseled out of stone. Ginny lets Mark pull her to her feet and he lifts her in a hug. He's someone else Ginny mentored.

"You gotta meet my girlfriend, Kimmie!" he says. "You'll love her. She's like lightning in a boat."

Mark is one of the fastest paddlers I know. If Kimmie is anywhere near as good as him, they'll take first in class.

I get up to hug Ginny goodbye, and as she whispers *good luck* in my ear, I see him.

Tanner.

Walking up from the parking lot with Hank and Coop.

Coop locks eyes on me, elbows my brother, and points. And now my brother sees me.

His face is a war hammer.

My chest, my throat, my stomach all go tight. I want to hold Ginny there like a human shield, but Mark pulls her away and I'm left completely exposed.

If we have to do this, I don't want it to be in the middle of a crowd. I weave my way through the canoes on the grass toward my brother. I wish Hank and Coop would leave, but they stick with Tanner.

"Are you really racing with John Cullen?" Tanner's voice is only about two notches below shouting.

"Only because I didn't have another choice," I say. "This is on you."

"It's not about me," Tanner says. "How could you do this to Dad?" He swings an arm out and wraps his thick hand around my wrist. "Come on. I'll find someone to drive you home."

My heels dig into the ground. "Stop it!" I twist my wrist from between his fingers and wrap my own fingers around the spot. It burns from the friction.

"Tell you what, Sadie." Coop claps a hand on Tanner's shoulder, even though Tanner is a couple of inches taller. He digs his fingers in. "We'll consider him on loan this year. Next year when Randy's back, you and Tanner can have your race. We'll give him back to you better than we got him."

Hank winces at his brother's words, but Coop keeps going. "You'll make top five for sure after he paddles with us."

He smiles, like he's just offered me first pick from a box of chocolates.

I'm so glad I turned the Cussing Lamp on, because, "Fuck you, too, Coop."

"God, Sadie. What's wrong with you?" my brother asks, like Coop didn't just completely dismiss me. Like he didn't just offer my brother back to me next year as his leftovers. Like them having a good race is so much more important than me racing at all.

I step forward, nose to chin with my brother, and pull myself tall.

"I don't need you to make top five. John Cullen is fast. Faster than you are. We'll probably make first in class."

It's the stupidest thing I could have said. Boats that train for years don't make top five. And clearly Mark and Kimmie have first in our class locked down.

"Really?" Tanner asks, his mouth curved into a smirk. "Your partner's going to have to stop crying first."

I follow Tanner's eyes to the corner of the tent, where Johnny Hink is red faced, fuming at his son. And John Cullen—I don't think he's actually crying, but I've seen that face on him so many times. Eyes trained on the ground. One cheek pulled in because he's biting it, willing himself to keep the tears in. The back of his neck is on fire.

When we were kids, things like this happened over the stupidest stuff. A missed catch in a baseball game or a half gallon of ice cream forgotten and melted on the counter. Tears always ran close to the surface for John Cullen, which just made things worse with his dad.

So much shame. I guess we have that in common these days.

A lump swells in my throat. This could be the end of our race, right here. And not because of me and my brother.

Gonzo is walking up to the two of them. They both turn their heads in his direction, and Johnny turns his back on

Gonzo, putting himself between them. He's still laying into his son, and Gonzo must be the bravest person here, because he steps around Johnny and pulls on his friend's sleeve.

I stalk back to my boat. There's nothing left to say to Tanner and the Bynums, and I don't care to watch John Cullen get raked over the coals.

A few minutes later, he walks back alone, hands shoved into his pockets and head down, the brim of his blue baseball hat covering his face. Gonzo is gone again.

A blonde girl—*why is Allie Davis here?*—puts a hand on his arm as he passes, but he pushes it away without a word.

I expect wet eyes when he gets here. They'll be pink rimmed, like when we were kids. But his eyes are dry and steely. His face is volcano red.

I wait for him to say, *I'm out. This was a bad idea.* But he brushes by me toward his seat.

The words spill out of me, like a habit. "Are you okay?"

The answer was always more tears when we were kids.

But instead, he stares at me, searching my face and biting the inside of his cheek, turning something over in his mind. I wish I could peer inside and see what he's thinking. He shakes his head.

"Fuck him," he says. "Let's do this."

Spring Lake is closed to boats, aside from the glass-bottom boat tours John Cullen and I used to go on when we were kids. We could see the springs that feed the lake bubbling up through the sand on the bottom. There's an old building that used to be a hotel back when this was an amusement park. There used to be women dressed as mermaids doing water ballet, and at one point there was a swimming pig, but that was all over before I came along. Texas State University bought the land. Now the whole place is called The Meadows Center and is dedicated to environmental education and preservation.

But on this one day a year, they let about a hundred canoes on it for the start of the Texas River Odyssey.

It feels like a lifetime has passed since Tanner and I

dropped our boat off here yesterday. Now I'm under the tent, among all the other boats, getting ready to launch my canoe with someone else. Everything about this is so wrong.

The back of John Cullen's neck is still red.

"I told my brother we'd make top five," I tell him.

His forehead wrinkles up and his head kind of tilts.

"Why the hell would you do that?" he asks.

I don't answer.

"We should put in in the shallows." I point to a narrow strip of dirt between the cypress trees that surround the water. Most of the shore is covered in bushes. This is one of the only access points aside from the stairs. "It's a good place to test the trim and make adjustments."

"Aye aye, captain." He mocks me with a stupid little salute.

"Don't pull that," I say. I know more about the river and the race and we both know it. It's only natural that I should take charge. I don't need to catch any crap for it.

I pick up the stern handle and he takes the bow handle and we carry the boat across the grass to the water. We wait behind two other boats before we get our chance to put in.

If I were with Tanner, he'd march into the shallows, but John Cullen stops at the edge of the water and feeds the boat in.

"What are you doing?" I ask when I've pulled up even with him and the whole boat is in the water.

He grabs the side and pulls it toward him. The nose of the canoe makes a slow arc around, finally coming up parallel with the shore. "Just thought I'd enjoy another ten minutes of being dry before I'm wet for three days."

I plow through the water, step a leg across the boat, and put my butt in my seat. Cold wetness floods my shoes and runs right through my tights, soaking me up to my knees. I won't be dry again until after I shower at the finish, and there's no point in putting it off. There's no room for hesitation.

John Cullen carefully stays dry.

How are we going to survive 265 miles when I already want to kill him?

"Ready?" I ask.

John Cullen pushes off with his hand and I push off with a foot. We paddle a few strokes out of the way to make room for other boats putting in.

"I've gotta move my seat," he says.

I throw a leg into the water over each side of the boat because these things are tippy as hell. We shudder as he scooches it forward.

"Good?"

"Good."

I lean back and check the rudder, and it looks like it's in the water at a good height. We need to run bow heavy for at least these first eighty miles to get through the patches of shallow suck water that slow you down, and right now it looks like we are.

We join the crowd of canoes and kayaks. One hundred and thirty-nine is the official number registered. Every single boat on this water is planning to make it to the finish line. Somewhere between a third and a half of them won't. Some of them won't make it past noon.

I can't be one of those boats again.

We wait, our boat rocking slightly in the water. We're at the very back of the pack. Your place in the Odyssey Marathon, a race that runs in the spring, determines your starting position for the Odyssey. Tanner and I were going to be toward the front. Since we didn't compete together, John Cullen and I are stuck in the back. Thanks to the roster change in their boat, so are my brother and the Bynums. They're about ten feet away in highlighter-yellow shirts, holding double-bladed paddles.

Tanner and I never double-blade. They're faster than the single-blade paddles we're using, but they wear on your shoulders. Nobody double-blades the whole time. That means carrying single blades, too. You've got to be pretty sure those double blades will pay off, because carrying two sets means more weight when you want to travel as light as possible. Ounces turn into pounds and pounds turn into pain.

With every little ripple that leaves my brother's boat and

hits ours, I can feel how angry he is. I stare at John Cullen's back and the way his gray shirt stretches across it. The way his hairline is square on his neck below the bottom of his royal-blue ball cap.

He isn't paying attention to anything ahead. He's stealing glances at the shore. A distracted partner. Just what I need. I don't care what it is distracting him, I just want him to focus on the race. Except that after about his fourth peek in two minutes, I have to look.

Hundreds of people are crowded on the side of the lake. About a dozen have squeezed into the spot between the trees where we put our boat in, which shouldn't even be possible. I don't know who among this crowd could be significant. I don't see John Cullen's sister or his mom, and his dad's in a boat somewhere up front.

But I do see Allie Davis. Her hand lifts in a stupid little finger wave. But John Cullen's got his head trained straight forward again.

High-pitched feedback cuts through all the chatter. Doug Hammond starts talking through a loudspeaker. He goes on about race stuff. Some good stuff about spotting hyponatremia, or water poisoning, and electrolyte consumption and staying safe around dams, and then he says a prayer, and someone sings the anthem, and then he says, "Get ready. This is it."

I sit taller. John Cullen raises his paddle, right hand

planted on top and blade on the left side of the canoe, pointing straight down into the water. I raise my paddle to the right. All over the lake, the same thing is happening in every single boat.

My brother and the Bynums have their double blades poised above the water.

This is probably the last time I'll see them until the finish.

If I make it to the finish.

"Three." Doug's voice echoes over the now silent water.

I can do this.

"Two."

We'll glide through this mess. We'll pick them off one by one.

Bang!

9

9:00 A.M. SATURDAY

The world erupts into splashes and grunts and shouts and
cheers as I shove my paddle into the water and pull hard.
The Bynums' double-bladed oars slice through the air. My
brother's boat surges forward. Their waves rock my canoe
and I miss the catch on a stroke. The lake is littered with
boats, like sprinkles on a sugar cookie, and we have to navigate through them. But they're all moving, too. We're pulling
past an aluminum on the left, and John Cullen's oar slaps
the oar of another racer.

"What the—" the guy in the boat shouts as we pass him.

I keep my eyes trained ahead, looking for openings, using
my rudder pedals to steer the boat, all while trying to match
John Cullen stroke for stroke. But he's constantly drawing

and pulling up short or putting in late so we don't hit another boat, and we move jerkily. I steer us to the right and we paddle through an opening between two aluminums. We follow on the tail of a guy in a C-1, a solo canoe you only paddle if you're a glutton for punishment. As he tries to pass a standard, he overdraws, and suddenly his boat goes over. His head pops out of the water next to the hull of his boat, and we're plowing straight for him.

Too many boats on the right.

"Draw left!" I shout as I press my foot on the rudder pedal.

He draws us left. The bow of our canoe grazes the tail of the C-1, but we avoid the man.

It was a good call. Up ahead on our right a four goes over. A longboat. An aluminum hits it with a bang, knocking it sideways with a splash. Shouts erupt from the guys in the boat and the other boats that start stacking up behind it. We keep pulling and glide past.

Thunk.

The whole boat rocks to the side, and I lay the blade of my paddle flat on the water to keep us from tipping.

"Sorry," comes a gruff voice. It's a big guy in the bow of the kayak that just hit us.

We paddle by the glass-bottom boats and the dock, and I keep my eyes trained on the water up ahead.

Waves from the other boats rock ours.

We're about to pass a tandem on the right when another boat slams into us from the left. I pull my paddle up to keep from stabbing it into the woman who just appeared in the boat next to me. I wedge my paddle between the boats and push them away, but it's no good. No room to paddle on the right either. We're too close to the other canoe.

"Sorry," the woman beside me says. Her paddle hovers above the top edges, the gunnels, of both our boats. The man in front of her takes timid strokes on his open side. The boat on the other side appears just as flummoxed. So is John Cullen up in the front, even though there's enough open water for him to paddle.

"Power!" I yell to the front.

It takes him a moment to realize I'm talking to him, but then he takes a massive stroke. And another one. We inch ahead. Space opens up for my paddle. I put in and pull as hard as I can. Our boat glides into a less congested area. I think we've made it out of the crush.

He keeps up his pace and we're flying to the dam at the end of Spring Lake.

The dam is the first portage of the race, only a quarter mile from the start. It's a bottleneck. The shore is already three deep with boats waiting to get out. Johnny Hink and his teammates disappear into the trees, carrying their three-man canoe. My brother probably came through a couple of minutes ago.

If John Cullen and I really get into sync, is there any chance we can keep up with them?

"Let's go to the left," he shouts above the mess, and I steer us to the side of it all, where there are fewer boats.

We nose toward the shore. I throw a leg on either side of the boat to steady it for John Cullen to get out. But he doesn't. He backsweeps to the left, sending the stern into another boat.

"What are you doing?" I shout.

The boat rocks as he turns around. "Getting you closer to shore."

Getting me closer to shore?

"Are you kidding me about this stuff?" I ask. "This isn't a date, it's a race."

His chin jerks back like he's been jabbed.

I slide out of the boat and it's so deep I can't touch. Cold water soaks into my clothes.

I saw him training with Brent this spring. I thought he knew what he was doing. I thought he took this seriously.

He puts his hands on the gunnels and climbs out. While he pulls the boat, I swim it forward until my feet find the muck at the bottom. He pulls the bow onto shore.

I bet we've been passed by ten boats.

John Cullen picks up the bow handle, and I take the stern. We carry our boat at a trot along with the other racers, forging a trail through the woods, but he's all starts and stops and

I'm jerked around at the back of the boat. Finally, we make it down the hill to the bottom of the dam.

Across the river in the calm, shallow water, people swim and spectate under the canopy of cypress trees. Sometimes as kids we'd play here together.

"You swim the bow out to the deep water, I steady the boat for you. You climb in, then I climb in."

"Don't tell me this stuff like I'm five," he shouts, but he's already wading into the water.

"You were smarter when you were five."

"You two aren't even going to make it to the first checkpoint like this," says some woman, setting down her half of an aluminum.

She's wearing flip-flops. What the hell does she know?

Calf-deep, I set my end of the boat in the water, climb into my seat, and put one foot in the muck on each side to steady the boat for John Cullen.

He's watching the bowman of another boat climb in, and then he puts a hand on each of the gunnels in front of his seat, pushes down, and throws his body across the canoe. The boat rocks back and forth while he pushes and wiggles and twists over and finally gets his butt in the seat. He wiggles a bit, we both pull our legs in, and we go.

We paddle and I call the huts, and we pass the university where later today people will be sunning out on the lawn in swimsuits. Pass City Park and the place where all the tubers will put in later with their beers in coolers, getting drunk and floating downriver in a cloud of one another's pee. Pass houses with balconies slung with hammocks.

The rushing sounds of the water and the noise of the paddlers and the crowd hit us before we actually see everyone congregated to watch at the dam at Rio Vista. It's not much of a dam. Three small drop-offs making three big rapids, and a spillway down the center of each. Almost everyone portages the first rapid on race day, but some people jump back in and run the last two in their boat.

It's another bottleneck when you're coming from the back. Boats everywhere. Spectators everywhere. At least a hundred people are scattered all over the rocks, clapping and cheering.

"Let's run it," John Cullen says.

Such a Hink thing to say. All bravado and no sense. "Don't be a dumbass."

"Brent and I ran it all the time in training. It's faster."

It's true. There's a crowd of boats waiting to get out of the water, and nothing about portaging is fun. But it's the better call here.

I hit the rudder pedal, steering the boat to the left. "Hut," I call.

We finish our strokes and switch sides. The boat points left.

"Hey!" He draws us to the right. "We don't have to wait in line this way."

"Stop it!" I dig my paddle in on the left and backsweep, trying to pull the nose to the left.

He draws right again, overcoming the rudder and pointing the nose straight at the dam. "Half the boats here are running it!"

"I'm the one driving!" I shout, backsweeping again.

But now we've missed the takeout I wanted on the left and are headed straight toward water spilling over a wall of rock. We can climb down the rocks into the pool below. We'll have to cut through the crowd, but we can still portage around the last two rapids.

"You have to climb out as soon as we get to the wall!" I shout.

"I know what I'm doing!"

What a lie.

Our nose bumps the wall. John Cullen scrambles onto the top of the rocks, water flowing around his ankles. He takes the front handle and scuttles forward while I climb out. Holding the handle for the back, I follow him down the slippery wall of rocks and get into my seat again. He jumps into his. That's when I look ahead, about twenty feet across the water to the place I want to portage the next fall. There's a couple with an aluminum blocking our path. The man is clutching his shoulder and the woman is grabbing the gunnels, trying to lift the boat all on her own. We won't have space to get out and get around them.

"We're running it," I call. We're coming from the left, which is good, because it's the best angle for approaching the V at the bottom of the rapid. The sweet spot, where you know the water is deep and moving. "Line us up."

He does a tiny draw to the side.

Here we go.

The nose tips down the spillway and I'm riding it down with a *whump* when everything goes sideways. We've tipped off balance. Damn. I lean left to stabilize us, but it's too late. I fall out of the boat, clutching my paddle in a death grip. Cold water rushes around my face before I pull my way to the top. Water drips off my hat and my eyes and into my mouth as I gulp for a breath. John Cullen and his blue hat bob in front of me. The black hull of the canoe floats on top of the river.

My stomach drops with the water as I'm sucked down the next spillway. The water throws me left, right, and under before I surface and swim for the canoe. The river sends it into an eddy, where the water swirls back upstream. By the time I get into the shallow water, John Cullen is already there. Thank god his paddle is still in his hand.

He's knee-deep in the river and his shorts cling to his body, and there's a lump. Not like a boner lump. Just a regular lump. But it's there, and now I can't unsee it. And now the fact that John Cullen has a penis is in my head, which I never want to think about again.

"This is why we don't run the rapid on race day!" I shout. "If you'd listened to me in the first place, we could have portaged all three!"

"Half the other boats here are running it," he shouts back.

"And every one of those boats has run it together in practice. This is our first time on the water together."

"So we're not going to do anything hard? Are we going to portage Cottonseed? Maybe we should just walk our boat down the river? That would be—"

"Works better if you stay in the boat, Sadie," shouts someone passing by. My stomach drops at the sound of the voice.

I whip my head to the left. It's my brother.

Our eyes meet before he passes me and paddles away with the Bynums, their double-bladed paddles moving in unison.

I was in front of my brother?

10

Works better if you stay in the boat.

My brother is the biggest jerk.

We have to catch him.

John Cullen and I flip the boat over and I shove my water jugs back in their holders. Everything else is still there. "Quick," I tell John Cullen as we join the crowd paddling downriver under the canopy of cypress trees.

We used to play here together all the time, the three of us. Summer days we piled into the back of Mom's Subaru and drove here. Weekday mornings, when there were fewer tubers clogging the river. We stormed the park a quarter mile up the road, playing until sweat stuck our clothes to our bodies, then we'd retreat to the river and jump in.

Usually, we chased one another around the water, climbed on rocks, splashed and tried to dunk one another. We'd sit together, arm to arm, on the rocks that dammed up Rio Vista, and watch the white-water kayakers in their short boats surf through the rapids of the falls, flipping upside down on purpose and popping up again without coming out of their boats.

There was this one day—I was seven. It was hot, as usual. We'd been out of waffles at breakfast. Everyone was tired and hot and grumpy with everyone else. And Mom was perched on a rock, reading another book about small businesses, because she was planning for her bakery. Tanner accused Cully of losing some of the pieces to one of his LEGO sets, even though we all knew it was Tanner who lost them.

"Leave him alone," I said, slapping Tanner's arm.

"You're such a traitor, always siding with him," Tanner said.

It was just the latest in a morning of fights, and I wanted it all to stop. For us all to get along. And then I had it. I pulled the rubber bands out of my braids and dunked my head. I rose out of the water folded in half, with my head and hair hanging down. Then I flipped my head back and stood, leaving a roll of hair right above my forehead, just like Ms. Trout, our assistant principal with her old-lady beauty-parlor style. I ducked out my lips. "Students who fight over LEGO sets will have to sit out at recess," I said, using my best Trout voice. Making students sit out at recess was her favorite pastime.

Tanner laughed.

Cully laughed.

And suddenly everything was right again between the three of us.

It wouldn't work now. Everything that's gone down between the Scofields and the Hinks, between the three of us, it's all way too much for a Ms. Trout impersonation to fix. I don't even want to fix it. I want to get this boat to Seadrift as fast as humanly possible.

I want to make my brother sorry he ever said *works better if you stay in the boat.*

He and the Bynums are already out of sight.

I want to make John Cullen sorry he tried to take over. If he'd been a decent teammate, we'd still be ahead of my brother. I paddle as hard as I can, trying to burn holes in the back of his stupid head with my laser stare.

Which would be counterproductive if it actually worked.

"Faster," I tell him.

"We should be pacing ourselves," he says. "You know this is two hundred and sixty-five miles, right?"

"Shut up and paddle."

We pass three boats on our way to Thompson's Island, which splits the river in two.

"Left!" I call.

We follow a line of boats to the left and weave past two aluminums. The light is dim from the cypress branches that make a canopy overhead, and the air is cool. But the path is narrow and the water almost stagnant. The current slows. I take us too far to the left. The rudder scrapes the bottom and someone knocks us in the stern, jerking the boat forward.

"Sorry 'bout that!" I hear, but I don't even bother to look for who it is. I still don't see my brother.

We're paddling hard to get out of the shallows, which slow you down, and we're ducking under branches, and then we come to a stop, right before the portage, and wait two back in line while a team struggles to lift their long, four-person boat out of the water. Boats stack up behind us. Finally, it's our turn. We push up to the front, parallel to the concrete barrier. The boat rocks as we climb out. Water drips off the boat as we lift it by the handles and jog across the concrete to the other side of the island. We feed the boat back into a tiny stream and follow it into the water, where we climb back in. It's a short paddle, and then the bridge comes into view. People lean over the rail, cheering and waving. I don't even bother to look.

"Current's coming fast. Draw left, then right," I shout, pressing hard into the rudder pedal, because we're about to join a much stronger current, right as we make a ninety-degree left turn under a bridge. If the current pushes us too far, we'll hit concrete. I steer us to the left, but as soon as I know we'll make the turn, I even out the pedals to make the rudder straight. "Draw right! Draw!"

John Cullen reaches out too far, and I have to correct, but we keep paddling, and then we're under the shadow of the bridge, and we make it through.

There are boats ahead of us, but they disappear behind the turn and I don't see Tanner up ahead. We weave past a few more boats. And it's not just boats. We dodge a pair of kayakers out with their fishing poles and a spectator who thinks it's a good idea to stand chest-deep in the river on race day.

This section is constant drawing and backsweeping, navigating from one near crisis to another, and I usually love it. I'm usually listening to birds and frogs, but today all I hear are dips of our paddles in the water and other racers shouting directions at one another and my brother's words echoing in my ears.

Works better if you stay in the boat, Sadie.

Jerk.

He's getting away.

We come out of a bend where a small island splits the river, and I want to go left, like usual, but somebody's upended a longboat on that side. It's floating sideways, causing a traffic jam. Better to follow the four-person boat ahead of us on the right. Fours usually know what they're doing.

We pull up beside them. John Cullen is even with the third person in the boat.

Thud.

Their boat stops. All four bodies lurch forward.

"Log," John Cullen yells with his paddle up in the air. Useless.

"Backpaddle!" I tell him as I do the same, pushing the water forward. It's not enough. *Thunk.* The whole boat shudders as our bow hits and beaches on the log just under the surface.

"That was a surprise," one of the guys next to us says, laughing.

I stick a leg in the water on either side of the boat to stabilize us.

"I'll get out," John Cullen says, hands on the gunnels. He swings his legs over the side.

"Use your paddle to check the depth." Honestly.

I use mine to do the same and it hits bottom. Water pulls fast underneath logs like that. Jump out when it's too deep and you can get sucked right under into god knows what.

The guys next to us climb out as John Cullen dips his paddle into the water and hits bottom mid-shaft. Another boat slams into the log, inches away on the other side. Right where I was about to climb out.

What did they think we were doing here, having a tea party?

"Watch it there," John Cullen says, all fake friendly to the middle-aged man and woman.

"Dave! It's Cully!" The woman's face lights up as she calls to her partner in the back.

Their entire boat rocks as Dave perks up and says, "Cully!" like they're old friends.

"Oh. Hey," John Cullen says.

"We've already gone over twice!" the woman says. She's the one he was talking to at the starting line. Only now her hair is dripping and her shirt is wet and stuck to her, making wrinkles across her back. Her partner's, too.

"Yeah, that thing's not as stable as your other boat," John Cullen says as I check the depth on the other side, the empty one, and slide into waist-deep water.

I push the boat forward, but with John Cullen in the bow, it still sits too low in the water to clear the log.

"Hurry up and get out," I say, rocking the boat and interrupting the woman's story about how they fell out going under that bridge a few minutes ago. They act like we're here for fun.

"We'll watch how you do it. Get a lesson from the pros," Dave says. As if John Cullen has been doing this more than a couple of months.

The four-man is already on the other side of the log and the guys are climbing in.

"Check your depth before you get out," I tell Dave,

because even if he's annoying, I don't want one of these newbies to get sucked under a log on my watch.

John Cullen climbs out, balances on the log, and I push the boat forward a few feet across it.

"Thanks," Dave says.

That's when I see it.

1964.

In white vinyl stickers.

On the side of their boat.

"You gave them your boat?" I spit the words out and they taste sour.

Some random novices are paddling with my number.

"Oh my goodness, it was so crazy!" the woman says as her partner slides into the water. "A fight broke out under the tent yesterday, and some guys fell on our boat and broke it."

I push the boat forward, past John Cullen, still standing on the log, water rushing past his ankles.

"We thought we were out of luck," Dave continues. "We were talking to the race officials about getting our fee refunded, and then Cully came over and told us we could use his boat."

"Such a nice boy," the woman says.

Not too bright, this one. Does she even know he's the one who landed on her boat?

"What a crazy welcome to this race, right? I mean, it's such a fluke, I love it," the man says as his wife pushes up on the gunnels to climb onto the log. She loses her balance and falls back into her seat.

"Wouldn't have it any other way," the man continues as John Cullen holds out a hand to help the woman out of her seat.

Their hands are almost touching when I shout, *"No!"*

Three pairs of eyes bore into me. Because I'm the only one who bothered to learn the rules.

"You get disqualified for helping people, unless it's life or death. Same for accepting help. You could have ended our race right there."

I'm even with the log now, and John Cullen towers over me with narrowed eyes. His jaw muscles flex, and his neck is already flushing red.

Volatile.

It makes me miss that ten feet of boat between us.

I glance at my watch as I climb back in. Four minutes wasted.

We'll never catch my brother like this.

9:45 A.M. SATURDAY

We hit the confluence of the Blanco and San Marcos, and the world opens up. We paddle into the wide, flat river with its steep banks and big sky. It feels like taking a deep breath when you didn't even realize you needed one. It's a break from hairpin turns and constant steering.

But not today. Today my body is tight and my jaw is sore.

Ugh. I've been clenching. Our boat is jerky. We don't get the smooth glide that's the whole reason for being out on the water. The sky is perfectly clear and the sun beats down on my arms. Sweat trickles down my neck. And my brother is getting farther and farther away.

I'm tired, and we have 255 miles to go.

I rip a GU pack off the inside of the boat and suck it down. Too-sweet strawberry-banana all over my tongue. I tuck the packet into my trash bag before I grab my water tube from the bottom of the boat, sit back up, and get my paddle moving again.

Constant forward motion.

I bite the valve and take a hit of water. It's cold and full of lemon-flavored electrolytes. I take three long pulls before I spit the tube back into the hull.

"Eat and drink," I tell John Cullen, because he hasn't taken care of either yet. We've got a long way to go and he needs to take care of this stuff or he'll crash.

"I'm not hungry yet."

"Doesn't matter," I tell him. "You need calories, water, and electrolytes. These are Odyssey basics."

His paddle in the river is all the answer I get.

And his paddle in the river is all wrong.

It's my job to make sure that I match him stroke for stroke, but I'm always coming up too short. And it's not me. *I* know how to do this.

He's fast. He's strong. If he got his stroke right, maybe that would be the difference between catching Tanner and not.

"You're leaving your paddle in the water too long," I say. His whole body tenses, but he needs to know this. We'll go faster. "You should pull out at your hip, but you're going way past." Water swirls around his blade and, "There! That's when you should pull out and start a new stroke—there—and there."

Nothing changes in his stroke, but the air is suddenly thicker.

Trying to match his too-long strokes is like having an itch that moves every time you try to scratch it. That's what just being around him is like.

The concrete tower of Cummings Dam peeks out from behind the trees. We're getting close to our next portage.

The tower is river left. Water rushes over the spillway, reaching between the tower and the middle of the river. At the bottom, it churns into a pit of concrete and rebar, construction debris leftover from when it was built. Terrifying when you really think about it.

From the spillway to the bank river right is a wall that stands a few feet above the water. We've got three portage options here. The safest and slowest ones involve pulling over on the bank river right. It's a narrow strip of shore between the dam and the trees, and it gets crowded. You can portage through the woods or down a ladder. But lucky me, there's only one other boat at the pipe.

The roar of the water spilling over the dam floods my ears as we pull in just right of the wall that juts out perpendicular from the dam. The pipe is on the other side of the dam, to the right of the spillway. It's giant and runs at an angle from the top of the dam down to the water. The guys ahead of us are already walking on the concrete wall. They lift their boat and hold it balanced on the dam while one of them climbs down.

"Forward," I tell John Cullen as soon as they start lowering the boat and there's enough room for us to pull closer. We're in, next to the wall that juts out, and I climb on top of it and walk to the edge of the dam, just a few feet from the second guy in the team ahead, careful not to get close enough to spook him or anything. John Cullen waits in the front for the boat to be out of his way.

The bowman from the boat in front is down on the ground now. The sternman holds the handle of his end and sits his butt on the pipe, ready to scoot down it.

"You'd be better off holding the stern rope," I tell him. *Obviously.*

"I've practiced this," he snaps as he scoots his body forward.

John Cullen is standing next to me on the dam now, holding the bow rope. "Don't mind Sadie. She likes telling people what to do. Ask her when you should eat and take a bathroom break."

"Shut up." Now I'm the one snapping.

The guy on the pipe ignores John Cullen and slides most of the way down until his partner has stopped with the boat. He bumps against the stern, wobbles, and falls off a couple of feet above the concrete. Which is why you use a rope. The words *are you okay* are forming in my mouth when he gets up, grabs the stern handle, and climbs down, into the water.

My mouth opens and instructions for John Cullen almost come out, but I clamp it shut again. We'll see how this goes.

We raise the bow of the boat and balance it across the dam before he climbs down the buttress to the platform below. I feed the boat down to him, using the pipe to support it, and then I use the stern rope to lower it farther before I climb onto the pipe and slide down it in a straddle.

We guide the boat into the water and climb in.

And I guess we managed to get something right.

But our paddling is still out of sync after the dam, when the river is wide and easy. We almost tip in a rapid my brother and I cruise through all the time. A few people clap and cheer at Westerfield Crossing. We paddle past the River Retreat and navigate some really shallow stuff and I have to kick us off a rock.

John Cullen rips an energy-gel pack off the side of the canoe. He groans. "I'm not even going to tell you what this looks like." But he eats it and washes it down with some water.

We have to lie down in the boat for a low branch. Coiled on top, six inches from the boat, is a dark snake with white on its face. Cottonmouth. Water moccasin. Poisonous. Aggressive. My throat goes tight and my heart races as I glide closer and it stretches its head over the boat.

Don't drop in the boat don't drop in the boat don't drop in the boat.

I sit up and turn back in time to see it slither off the branch into the water, but we've left it behind.

"Did you see that water moccasin?" I ask.

"Water moccasin?" John Cullen asks. "No."

"It was half a foot from your head less than a minute ago."

He shudders. "Just let me out of the boat now. I'm done."

But he's joking.

And then I remember—god, it's so funny the way my dad tells it—

"Did I ever tell you a water moccasin chased my dad down the river once? It tried to bite his boat."

John Cullen laughs, but he shakes his head. "That can't be true."

"That's what I thought until he showed me the fang marks on the hull."

"Now I really do want out." He draws to the right, but he doesn't mean it. He's laughing.

And then I laugh. And we're both laughing, and we're on the river together, and it's like when we were kids, swimming and splashing and having contests to see who could hold their breath the longest. His freckles got darker every summer.

As much as I hate to admit it, I've missed this. It's like a hollow spot in my chest.

This race . . . This partnership . . .

Maybe it's starting to work.

The cypress branches stretch across the river, making a tunnel. Blue sky peeks through the thin leaves. Dappled light filters through. Cypress roots tumble over one another into the water. But it doesn't even occur to me where we are until we round the corner to my family's property.

He straightens up as soon as he sees it. His family owns the property inland of ours. This is one of the places we swam together as kids.

This is where Mom waited every year to give Dad fresh water and a tube sock full of ice. Tanner and I were always with her until two years ago when Tanner raced with Dad. Last year it was just her, and I got fresh water and a sock of ice for the first time.

She's here, sitting on a rock on the side of the river. But this year there's no water or ice sock. And this year Dad is with her. One hand is in his shorts pocket. The other holds the end of Mazer's leash while my dog laps at water in the shallows.

And now nobody is laughing.

Mom's face is tight. Dad's eyes meet mine, and then they wash across the river to something on the other side.

It's not until we've already passed them that Mom calls, "Doing fantastic, Sadie. Making good time."

The year that Dad and Johnny raced together, I was eleven and Cully was twelve. We'd spent most of the race goofing off and splashing in the river while our dads paddled and our moms served as bank crew. By Monday, we were tired and sunburned and ready to go home.

The finish line was like any other finish line any other year. Twenty or thirty people buzzed around. A lot of race officials. Ten or eleven boats already lined up at the finish. Soaked and muddy racers napped under the pavilion. Some of the early finishers, the ones who had paddled in overnight, had retreated to their homes or hotels to shower up and get some sleep.

Dad and Johnny weren't super fast that year, but they had set a decent clip. The app predicted they'd be in by three in the afternoon. We were at the finish with hamburgers and fries for our dads a little before two thirty.

Three o'clock passed with no sign of them, but it didn't bother me. The bay took time. A rough bay could mean a lot of stops and starts. I didn't worry when four o'clock or five o'clock went by, either.

Cully, Tanner, and I passed the time playing together on the grass. My brother had brought a baseball and gloves. We played catch. And when Tanner went around, trying to engage some of the racers in conversation, Cully and I tossed a Frisbee. Cully sketched and I did a book of mazes and word searches. When we got hot, we jumped in the water and swam.

The moms sat in lawn chairs, binoculars in their laps, staring out onto the bay.

The burgers sat in paper bags beneath their chairs.

It was six when Mom finally told us our dads' tracker app had been off for the last two hours. My stomach twitched.

Around six thirty, another boat made it in, a solo, and Mom asked whether he had seen Dad and Johnny.

"Nah," he'd answered. "I haven't seen anyone since the Wooden Bridge."

My stomach grew heavier.

It was around seven thirty, after Leslie Hink had gone out to pick up dinner and another boat came in saying they hadn't seen Dad and Johnny and my gut sank to somewhere around my knees, that Cully's hand slipped into mine.

I knew that hand so well, even though it had been years since I'd held it in mine. Since Andrew Haggarman said that us holding hands made Cully my boyfriend. Gross. That was the last thing I wanted at eight. It was the last thing I wanted at eleven. But before that, holding Cully's hand had been as natural as holding my mom's or my dad's.

At that moment, though, waiting at the finish, holding his hand was like being wrapped in a soft blanket. Warm and familiar.

But there was something different about it, too. Even though my hand must have grown, too, his had grown more. His fingers were thicker between mine. He still had the same pencil callus on his middle finger, but now his whole hand was rougher—calloused all over from an entire spring spent working on the tree house.

We held tight, until Mom jumped out of her seat, binoculars up to her eyes, shouting, "It's them!" Everything inside me loosened. We ran to the seawall and sat down, legs dangling, waiting for the speck on the water to turn into our dads.

Dad's face wasn't just tired when he paddled in. It was tight. Angry. At the finish, he rocked the boat hard, tipping to the side and dumping himself and Johnny out. Tanner splashed in to carry the canoe out. The dads climbed the steps, and then Mom met Tanner on the stairs and helped him carry the boat out of the water. Mom and Tanner set the boat under the wooden awning, and then it was hugs all around. But when Mom pulled out her camera for a picture, Dad ignored her, turning to face Johnny. Cully's hand found mine again and squeezed. The hate between them hung in the air like a cloud of poison.

One look at the way they stared each other down, the way Dad's and then Johnny's eyes fixed on my hand, wrapped warm and tight in Cully's—I knew it was all over. No more sneaking over to read books together after lights-out. No more splashing in the river. No more goofing off, putting fake spells on each other in the back of the Subaru while Mom ran errands. No more tree house. The Scofields and the Hinks, me and Cully, it was all in the past.

13

10:39 A.M. SATURDAY

We're closing in on a slow-ass tandem when we turn a bend and see the old red mill high on the hill. Which means Cottonseed Rapids is close. Which means wipeouts and crowds. Everyone wants to see one of the most difficult rapids of the race where the most spectacular wrecks happen.

This boat in front of us has their form all off. It would suck to be stuck behind them if they wreck. The river is narrowing. We need to make our move now.

"Let's pick it up and pass them," I yell to the front.

John Cullen answers with a faster, stronger stroke. I pull harder to match him. The boat surges forward with every hard pull. My muscles burn. The splash of our paddles in the water fills my ears. I adjust the rudder pedals so our nose points between the other boat and some rocks on our left. The river narrows ahead, but we have enough room to squeeze past them.

Gaining.

Gaining.

He's even with their sternwoman. I adjust the rudder again, pointing the nose a bit to the right so we don't hit the rocks.

The quiet dips of paddles in the water reach me just before the boat plows into view. Double blades fly through the air as they push their way between our boat and the other tandem. Their boat glides close. Too close. A blade just misses John Cullen's head. He pulls left to keep from getting hit and *bam*. Our nose slams into a rock. Our boat stands still.

"Sorry about that," calls one of the guys from the three that just passed us. They wear highlighter-yellow shirts.

My insides boil at the sight of my brother and the Bynums. Assholes. They did that on purpose.

But when did we get ahead of them?

John Cullen pushes us off the rock with his paddle.

"Your brother's a jerk," he says.

"That's why we have to beat them." I wait for him to agree or give a hell yeah, but he doesn't.

We catch up just in time to see the tandem approach the rapid. People cheer. "Go, boat fifty-five!" someone yells.

"You've got to draw hard on the right when we pass that first rock," I say as I line us up for the rapid. Maybe we shouldn't be running this. The thing is, you're not going to win the race by running Cottonseed, but you might lose that way. But portaging will slow us down. And anyway, Dad will find out if we do. He might even be here to see Tanner. We'll look like failures if we portage.

"You heard me about drawing, right?" I ask, because honestly, he could at least say something.

"Can't you tell when I'm ignoring you?"

"You can't ignore me! We're supposed to be a team."

"You don't want to be a team. You want to be in charge." He takes a harder stroke than he needs to. The boat rocks.

We pull past the two RV chassis lodged on the right bank, left over from a flood. Water breaks over a rock in front of us, and I steer us left of it. Our bow hits the rapid. A rush of water pushes us toward a rock on the left.

"Draw! Draw!" I yell.

John Cullen draws right. I grunt with every forward stroke, pulling with everything I have, fighting to keep us away from the rock. It's not enough. Just as the back half of the boat grates against it, I do the last thing I can. I pull out my left leg and push us off it with my foot. Water bouncing off the rock sends us in the other direction, and we've lost almost all our momentum. I dig in hard with my paddle to get us moving again.

"Power!" I yell, and the current picks us up again, sending us straight toward another rock.

"Left! Left!" I push the rudder pedal left. The nose of the boat careens toward an even bigger rock. I backsweep as he draws, and we scrape past it.

"Power!" We both dig in and paddle forward as hard as we can. It wasn't pretty, but we've made it through. The current is slower now, pushing us toward a smaller rock in the middle of the river. Pressing the rudder pedal is enough to keep us off it.

On the sandbar to the right, another team kicks a huge dent out of their boat. That's the beauty of paddling an aluminum canoe. Carbon fiber is lighter, but much less forgiving.

My brother's boat is already out of sight, but they can't be far. I take a couple of relaxed strokes. That's enough of a break. I pull hard again. We need to catch my brother.

But John Cullen has gone stiff, his head locked on the shore, turning as we move forward.

"Head in the boat!" I call. He's supposed to be my eyes up front.

The boat jolts to the side, and there's the scratchy resistance of the hull scraping against something in the river as we tip. I lean left and try to stabilize with my paddle, but water is spilling over the gunnels, and we're sliding into the river.

AGAIN.

How am I ever going to look my dad in the face?

The hull floats low in the water. I bob with it under a huge fallen tree that three kids sit on, their legs dangling down.

"Dude, what were you looking at?" one of the kids asks John Cullen as we float beneath her bare feet.

"Yeah, dude, what *were* you looking at?" I ask.

Silence.

This was such a mistake.

≈

We kick toward shore until we reach a spot we can both touch.

"Ready?" I ask, curling my hands along the gunnels underwater. "One, two, three."

The water sucks at the hull as we pull the boat out of the river. It's like trying to lift a tree, but finally we clear the surface and get the boat into the air. We roll it away from us and set it back on the water. I grab my water jugs, now floating around my waist, and put them back into their foam holders.

What a waste of time and energy.

We keep going.

My shirt clings to me and water drips rhythmically from the brim of my hat. We paddle hard. With each bend in the river, I imagine seeing my brother on the other side. I think, *This is it. This is when I'll catch him.* I've already been in front of him twice. I can do it again. But after a couple of miles and another dam portage, it still hasn't happened.

There's no breeze to make being wet feel cooler. The trees don't offer any shade. Sweat and river water drip down my neck and down my back. John Cullen glances over his shoulder at me a couple of times, but the only word between us is *hut*.

We haven't even been on the water for two hours and have only gone about ten miles. It feels like two years already. Looking at the 250 miles ahead, they feel like the rest of my life.

The rest of my life trying to match John Cullen's too-long stroke. The rest of my life wondering when we're going to flip next. The rest of my life not catching my brother.

"I'm sorry about tumping the boat." His voice is flat. Unconvincing. Just the kind of *sorry* I'd expect. Not that I expected one.

Apologizing is such an un–John Cullen thing to do.

"We're lucky we're not onshore right now, fixing a crack," I say, because apparently I'm not ready to let this one go.

"Is that how you accept an apology?"

I swear I can see the way his lip curls up right through the back of his stupid head.

His paddle goes past his hip again when I've already got mine out of the water. We've got to sort this out.

And since he's quasi-apologizing, maybe he'll actually accept some coaching.

"You need to start pulling your paddle out earlier instead

of going past your hip. It's making your stroke too long and throwing our rhythm off. I can't match your stroke and it's bugging the hell out of me."

"Didn't anyone ever teach you how to make a shit sandwich?" he asks.

"A *shit sandwich?*"

A fly buzzes around my face and my shoulders ache.

"A shit sandwich. It's when you sandwich the shitty thing you're about to say between two nice things."

Oh my god, he's asking me to baby him. "Is that what they teach you in private school?"

"No, they taught me that in being-a-decent-person school. Where were you?"

"I was busy rebuilding my tree house."

"Noted."

His stroke is still too long.

"Okay, here goes," I say. "It's great that you've gone five minutes without flipping the boat. Your stroke sucks. Pull out at your hip and we'll finish faster and never have to talk to each other again. Hut." We switch sides. "How's that for a shit sandwich?"

"Shitty."

≈

There were no shit sandwiches after that awful race between Dad and Johnny. No attempts to smooth things over and give constructive feedback. Definitely no victory burgers in lawn chairs, sharing stories about the race. We didn't even stick around at the finish, and we usually stayed for hours. Dad showered. Mom, Tanner, and I packed up the chairs, cleaned out the canoe, and strapped it to the roof rack of the Subaru. We drove the two hours home. The first raindrops hit not far from our house, fat smacks on the windshield, followed by thunder. It didn't compare to the thunder Dad was making, talking about bad calls and disagreements and Johnny lying down in the boat. But it was all background noise to me in the back seat, knowing my friendship with Cully was done for.

The storms continued for days. The river swelled, full of debris. Tanner left for baseball camp. Mazer and I spent the first few days curled on the couch watching movies. I didn't even check on the tree house we'd been building. Everything about that tree house was washed in Cully, and I missed him like a limb.

But four days later, when the sky had cleared, it was time to get back to work. I carried a bag with a few tools across the property to the giant live oak that held the tree house. The platform and ladder were finished, and Cully and I had been working on the sides. It was almost finished. Almost ready to show Dad. I kept picturing him marveling over it, telling me I'd built it as well as any grown-up could. He'd see that I was ready to do all the stuff he and Tanner did.

I climbed the rope ladder to the hole in the platform and put my head through. Someone was already in there, lying on his back, reading a book—Cully.

My face cracked into a smile. "Hey," I said, forgetting for a moment about the storm between our families.

Cully laid down his book and rolled onto his side to look at me.

He didn't smile. He didn't even say hi. No sign that he was glad to see me.

Right. We were enemies now. The night we got back from the race, I'd overheard Dad telling Mom, "I'm done. We can't be friends with them anymore."

"I don't think you should be here," I said.

His face curdled.

"What do you mean I can't be here?" Cully asked, his voice as sour as his face. It was the first time I heard the shadow of Johnny Hink in him. I saw it in his scowl.

For a moment, my throat didn't work. The words were stuck somewhere in there. "This is *my* tree house," I finally forced out.

"You're always saying it's yours. But it's not. It's as much mine as it is yours."

But that was just wrong. And not just because the tree was on the Scofield side of the property line. The whole thing was my idea. There'd been this tree-house-building book in the kids' section at the library, and instead of being all, *get an adult*, it made it sound like you could do it on your own. And . . . and I'd wanted that. Dad and Tanner had been taking a blacksmithing class, learning how to make their own knives, and it was just like all the other activities they left me out of. They always thought I was too young or too slow or too *something* to join them.

And I was sick of it.

I wanted to show them what I could do. I wanted to stop being on the sidelines. And Cully knew it.

I read that book cover to cover. *I* scouted the entire property for the right tree. I scavenged wood from Dad's scrap pile. Did extra chores and helped Ginny paint her house to get money for the rest of the materials. I watched YouTube videos about tree-house building. And yeah, Cully helped, but he didn't do all that.

Cully rolled onto his belly and scooted closer to the hole, propping himself up on his elbows, staring me down, his face above mine. I couldn't bear how different he was. How had I never seen this side of him? This side that was so much like his dad.

I could only stammer, "It's a Scofield tree house."

"We built this *together*." He brought his hand to his forehead and touched the red mark above his eye. The scar he gave himself when he was carving his name in a board and the knife slipped. He'd needed a stitch.

I opened my mouth, but I couldn't think of anything

else to say. He'd helped. But that didn't make it his.

"Look, it's not my fault your dad messed up. Not my fault my dad's pissed at him," Cully said, his tone a bit more gentle.

Wait, what? What kind of crap was Johnny Hink telling him?

"My dad didn't mess up. Your dad was a bad partner. He wasn't committed."

"Your dad's not as perfect as you think he is." Cully's voice was loud. His face twisted up again. "He almost got my dad killed!"

His words knocked the wind out of me. My face grew hot and my skin tingled.

Johnny Hink was awful. My dad was the best. How could Cully think so badly of him? We'd always been united against Johnny when he was being a jerk. Cully had practically lived at my house the week before the race because of a fight with his dad. How could Cully defend him now?

"Either you're a liar or you're stupid," I finally said. "Nobody would believe your dad over mine."

My eyes swam with tears as I climbed down the ladder.

I gave it three more days before I went back, half hoping Cully was there and half hoping he wasn't. Maybe we could reach some sort of joint custody of the tree house agreement.

I took Mazer on that hot afternoon. He trotted ahead,

stopping to sniff interesting things, knowing exactly where we were going. The same place we'd been a million times before. The tall grass tickled my legs. The sun beat down on the bare skin of my arms. Up ahead, Mazer circled the tree. But something was missing. The rope ladder. My eyes followed the trunk up to the branches, but it was gone. Everything was gone. I must have walked to the wrong tree. But how could I? I knew our property like I knew my own self.

My tree house was gone.

As I got closer, I saw them—planks of wood scattered under the tree, partially hidden by the tall grass. And on the very top, the board he had carved his name into. *Cully.*

He'd taken the whole damn thing apart. Every. Single. Board.

There's a canoe up ahead. With two—no, three—people. Tanner.

"Faster," I tell John Cullen.

"Ever heard of pacing yourself?" he asks, but he still kicks it up a notch, and even with our lousy mismatched strokes, we are cruising. He may have a terrible stroke, but he's strong. In a couple of minutes we're closer. Close enough for me to realize that their shirts aren't bright yellow, they're sea green. *The Sirens.*

My insides wilt. But just for a second, because passing a boat is passing a boat. Even if it's not Tanner, it's one boat closer to top five.

In another few minutes our bow is even with their stern, about five feet to their left. The driver, Carrie Miles, glances over at John Cullen, and then back to me.

"Heard you had teamed up, but I didn't really believe it," Carrie says.

"Is that Sadie and Cully?" Lisa Fisher calls out from the bow.

"Sure enough," says Melissa Martinez. She's got the middle.

We pull up even. Lisa kicks up the pace, keeping even with us.

"You see that boat that wiped out in the low water crossing back there?" Melissa asks.

"There were about three boats putting themselves back together when we went through," I say. "Made our portage look like the right call."

"We didn't have a choice but to portage," Carrie says. "Boat was caught sideways, blocking the whole river under the bridge. Think they lost a paddle."

"Oof." I eye the spare paddle snapped into a piece of foam epoxied to the inside of the hull. If one of us loses a paddle, that spare is our lifeline.

"What was that big dustup you and your daddy had at the start, Cully?" Carrie asks. Only she would be nosy enough to bring it up.

John Cullen takes a stroke and actually pulls out at his hip instead of past it. He keeps at the short strokes and picks up the stroke rate. We glide past the Sirens, leaving them in our wake.

15

He keeps up the pace. We pass four more boats. None of them is Tanner. But we're moving so fast. Eventually, one of them will be.

The sky is deep, deep blue and the river keeps turning. The birds are singing. I see the occasional log full of turtles sunning themselves, and once, the ripples of a snake swimming up ahead.

It's way too soon to be thinking this, but we might be able to pull off top five.

My shoulders ache with every stroke, but I am so damn alive.

≈

"Snack break," I say when we hit the wide, still waters that stretch the two miles to Staples Dam.

I rip a cherry-flavored GU pack off the side of my boat and squeeze it into my mouth. It's sweet and tart and amazing. I chase it with a handful of salty cashews I vacuum sealed last week with Tanner and tuck my trash into the mesh bag I've attached to the side of the boat. In less than a minute I'm still working on the cashews, but my paddle is back in the water.

Erica and Gonzo will be at the bottom of Staples to resupply us at the first official checkpoint. Then they'll add our names to the official sign-in sheet, to prove we were there before the three p.m. cutoff. After three hours with John Cullen, I cannot wait to see them.

I manage the boat on my own as John Cullen takes a minute to eat, too, and pretty soon the cheers and clapping of the crowd rise above the noise of our paddles in the water. We pass another boat.

And there's a white sign with blue letters, attached to the low bridge a hundred feet before the dam.

TEXAS RIVER ODYSSEY

MILE 16

KEEP PADDLING!

People stand on the bridge, cheering for us. A truck

rumbles over the bridge as we paddle underneath. The left riverbank is all trees and a gray house on stilts. On the right there's the kelly-green lawn of the big house up ahead. They open their land to the Odyssey every year. Kids play in the shallow water. Adults wade in up to their thighs. A handful of boats cluster around the right shore, just before the dam, pulling out to either portage down the stairs or run their boat around the house and down the hill.

"Portage right?" John Cullen asks.

"Left." I press the rudder pedal, steering us to the faster route.

My ears are full of the roar of the water rushing over the dam and crashing into the river below. We pass under a branch that brushes the top of John Cullen's hat. The nose of the canoe inches over the concrete wall of the dam. He stores his paddle under his seat and climbs onto the barrier. He pulls the boat forward, under the low canopy of leaves. I tuck my paddle away when I'm close. The boat rocks as I walk up the middle and put my feet into the water spilling over the dam. He jumps on the lower platform. I grab the stern rope. A couple of bank crews wait river left, but most of the spectators and the bank crews are scattered across the gravel and the river on the right. Erica and Gonzo wade into the water just before a kid arcs through the air on the rope swing hanging from that huge cypress. The splash drenches them both.

I scan the crowd for Dad's tall frame or Mom's dark hair. Mom's probably at the bakery, but Dad has time. He was going to bank crew for Tanner and me. I exhale long and hard, trying to blow all the hope out of my body. He told me not to do this, so why would he want to watch us flip our canoe every couple of miles?

"Ready?" John Cullen's eyes are on me, and they linger for a moment, even after I've said yes.

I lift the stern and he carries the bow down, feeding it into the water below. I lower the stern by the rope. He takes it and is already stepping into the water. We let the middle of the boat rest on the concrete for a moment and I jump to the platform. He swims out with the nose and I feed it to him before I step into the knee-deep water. I lean over the boat, holding it steady while he puts his hands on the gunnels, throws his body across the hull, and twists his butt into his seat. He hangs his legs out while I throw a leg across the boat and sit down.

The bow of another canoe noses into the water beside us as we push off.

"You see them over on the right?" I ask.

"Got it."

We head for our bank crew and dodge an aluminum that portaged river right.

"You guys are doing great," Gonzo says as we pull up beside them.

I dig a paddle into the water to hold us still for a moment before Erica grabs a gunnel. I detach the tubing from my water jug and throw the empty into the water next to Erica as she shoves a full jug into its space in my boat.

"Need a new bag of food?"

"No."

She holds out a hand. "Trash?"

I give her my empty GU packets and the wrapper from my cashews. She gives me a disapproving look.

"You've gotta eat more than this."

"I will. It's still early."

"Now."

I rip a GU off the side of the canoe and suck it down. Grape.

"Better." She takes my trash and grabs the jug floating by her leg.

I nod, but I'm starting to regret that there's a page about nutrition in the binder. "When did my brother come through?"

She glances at Gonzo, who's deep in conversation with John Cullen.

"Don't let her get in your head," Gonzo says.

Erica's eyes turn back to me. "Maybe five minutes ago."

Oh my god. We're still in striking distance. "Let's go!"

"Hold up. I haven't changed out Cully's water," Gonzo says.

"Then what have you been doing?" I ask. "Checkpoints aren't social."

John Cullen and Gonzo switch out water jugs and Gonzo takes his trash and I can't stop jiggling my leg. It's taking forever.

"Ready?" John Cullen asks, holding his paddle with one hand and scratching the back of his neck with his middle finger.

"I see that."

"Good."

As we paddle away, I glance back one more time.

No Dad.

16

The sun is high in the sky. The air is still. Sweat drips off the soaked sweatband of my hat as I take stroke after stroke.

"I have to pee," John Cullen says, so I'll know he's about to put his paddle down.

"Good." It means he's drinking enough. Double good, considering the dark gray sweat spread like a Rorschach test on his back. It looks like a stingray in a top hat.

But he doesn't put his oar down. He keeps paddling. And paddling.

And now that I'm thinking about it, with each stroke we take, my bladder gets heavier and heavier.

"Sooooo?" he says.

"What?"

"Should we pull over so I can duck into the woods?"

"Are you kidding me? It's just pee. Do it in the canoe."

Constant forward motion.

Dad once paddled with a guy who would hang his bare butt over the back of his seat, take a dump on his paddle, and fling it into the river. I wouldn't go that far. But there's no reason to stop the boat for pee.

John Cullen still hasn't missed a stroke. And now I really need to pee, too.

"So you don't care if I pee in the boat?" he asks.

"Not *in* the boat." Gross. The image of his pee sloshing around my feet. Seriously. "Go over the side like a normal person."

"OBVIOUSLY," he says. But he doesn't stop paddling. I think—I think he has stage fright.

My bladder pulses.

A couple of minutes pass.

"If you're not taking a break, I am." I tuck my paddle beside my seat and grab the blue plastic urinal I keep tethered to the brace in front of me. I pull my shorts aside, open the slit I cut into the upper thigh of my tights, pull my underwear aside, and put my urinal in place. It's basically a small plastic pitcher. I relax all the right muscles.

The river flows all around me, but nothing flows out.

I give it a little push.

And another.

Damnit.

"You okay back there?" John Cullen asks.

Which just makes the muscles clench tighter.

His head starts to turn.

"Don't!" I drop my urinal and put my clothes back in place. Honestly, I've never had a problem peeing in a boat before. "You should just get it over with," I say. "You're making it into a bigger deal than it is."

He holds his paddle to the side with one hand as I start paddling. The boat gets heavy without his help and I have to pull harder. I call a hut just so he'll know he'll need to switch sides when he's finished. I bet it'll take forever for him to get sta—

Oh. My whole body stiffens. I train my eyes on the trees on the opposite bank, but I can't escape the rhythmic sound it makes hitting the river.

How did he do that so fast?

And then it's in my head again. It's not even like I haven't seen it before. There are pictures of us in the bathtub together. We used to pee in front of each other all the time. And when we got older, he was the first one who wanted to change separately. I didn't care. But I keep seeing him at Rio Vista, his shirt clinging to muscles I didn't know he had, and his wet shorts—somehow knowing it's exposed to the elements up there grates at me.

And it shouldn't. It really, really shouldn't.

Even from back here I can see the water splashing up around the nose of the canoe, and over the dips of our paddles in the water, I hear the unmistakable sounds of something caught on the bow. John Cullen keeps paddling, oblivious to the stick or algae or long grass or whatever it is up there, creating drag and making us work harder.

"Are you gonna knock that off the boat?" I ask.

"Knock what off?"

"Whatever's strung across the bow up there."

He does nothing.

"It's cutting a wake," I say.

"I thought that was because we're going fast."

"It's creating drag. Slowing us down." I wait for him to knock it off the boat. But he doesn't. Maybe he doesn't know how. Geez. "Slide the blade of your paddle up against the front and knock it off."

He leans forward, holding his paddle like a sword, and makes a couple of fumbling attempts before he finally gets whatever it is off the nose. The front wake is gone when he starts paddling again, and I don't care if he couldn't tell the difference. I know the boat is moving faster.

We round a bend, and there they are, maybe a hundred yards ahead. They've switched from their double blades to single-blade paddles, but their yellow shirts are unmistakable.

"This is it," I tell John Cullen. This is our chance.

Dad always says the easiest time to pass someone is when they don't know they're being chased. He always loved seeing the other boats scramble to speed up when they realized he was about to overtake them.

This is how we have to pass Tanner. And we have a beautifully straight stretch of river to do it in.

"Quiet as a mouse," I say. "Silent huts. Switch sides every seven strokes." It's obvious he wants this as much as I do because he gives a swift nod and doesn't say anything about me trying to be in charge.

He sets a quick pace and he keeps his good form. We paddle in unison. Quietly. Stealthily. The boat surges forward with each pull. We glide past trees. Past logs full of turtles. Every seven strokes we switch sides. We're like a machine.

With each stroke we inch closer to my brother.

And my brother hasn't noticed.

My chest inflates.

This. Is. Glory.

Up ahead a fallen log stretches most of the way across the river. Tanner's boat stays right. There's enough room for them to lie down under it. By the time they reach the log, we'll be in striking distance. We might even be passing them. There's enough room for both boats. And I wouldn't mind shoving them around a bit for payback.

Almost there. Our nose pulls even with their stern. We inch forward until it's even with Hank in the back.

Hank's head swivels. He catches sight of John Cullen and startles before he turns his whole body and catches sight of me. His eyebrows fly up under his hat.

"Head in the boat, Hank," Coop calls from the front.

John Cullen pulls even with my brother and then past him, but he keeps his eyes on the water. His head doesn't turn.

Tanner twists and his eyes grow wide when they catch mine.

"What the . . ." he starts as Coop and John Cullen both lie down in the boat.

"Down!" Hank shouts at my brother.

Tanner lies back just in time, and I lie back, hugging my paddle to my chest, and look at the clear blue sky. My seat is almost even with his by the time I glide under the huge trunk of a cypress tree. A few strokes and I'll be in the—

Thunk.

The boat shudders to a stop. I stare at bark as my brother slides ahead of me.

What the hell just happened?

"What the . . ." John Cullen says.

"What'd we hit?" I slide forward in my seat until I'm clear of the tree. I crouch in the footwell in front of my seat.

"Nothing." He pokes at the water around the bow with his paddle. "There's nothing there."

My brother's already ten feet ahead, turned around looking at us.

His laughter cuts through the air.

I dig my paddle into the water and pull. The boat doesn't move. It *has* to move. I can't let him get away. I bounce up and down, jostling the boat, but it's still stuck. Now he's fifty feet ahead. He can't get away. I backsweep in a wide arc, trying to pull us off whatever it is. The stern should move, even if we're caught on something up ahead, but it doesn't. At least, it barely does.

I twist and slice into the water behind me with my paddle. It hits something taut. I jab around above and below, and then I know.

"The rudder is caught up on something."

"Okay. What do we do?"

"I've got this." I slide my paddle into the water to check the depth. I'll be able to touch, and the current is slow. Should be safe enough to get out. I slide the paddle under my seat. Where'd I put my knife? Crap. No. Tanner was going to carry his pocketknife.

I'm out here without a knife. How could I be so stupid?

No. This doesn't have to be a disaster. I put a hand on each gunnel, half stand, and lower both feet into the water. The left gunnel lifts my shirt and scrapes my stomach as I slide into the river, but I don't care about the pain.

I'm chest-deep when I hit bottom and carefully step my way toward the rudder until something hair thin presses into my stomach. Fishing line. If I'm lucky, this will just be a matter of sliding the fishing line off the front of the rudder. Over in a minute. We'll have caught up to Tanner in another five.

My right hand slides over the bottom of the boat to the rudder, and there it is, a giant tangle of it. My stomach sinks. I tug it down, but the line holds tight. It doesn't move. I jerk it, and it cuts into my fingers but stays where it is. I run my hand around the joint where the rudder connects to the cables. The line is tangled in the mechanism.

My left hand bobs up and down with the top of the boat. The rudder moves in my right. John Cullen splashes into the water.

"What's going on here?" he asks.

I push on the top gunnel, enough to tilt the boat to the side, but it doesn't move. It's caught too tight.

"Where's your knife?" he asks.

"Tanner was going to bring the knife," I mumble.

"What was that?"

"I don't have one!"

"You should have told me." He goes back to his seat and returns holding a weird pair of bent scissors over the surface of the water.

"What are those?"

"Trauma shears. Gonzo swears by them."

Why does Gonzo use something called trauma shears?

I put out my hand to take them so I can start hacking

away at the fishing line, but John Cullen swims around me to the other side and reaches both hands under the water.

"I was going to do that." I reach underwater to take the shears from him, but he pushes me away with his shoulder.

"Watch it. These things could take a finger off."

Neither of us can see what he's doing under the surface. His eyes drift shut. His mouth pulls to the left. I'd forgotten about how his mouth always did that when he was drawing. I'd forgotten how I would watch him take a pencil and paper and spill the contents of his head onto the page. A *T. rex* chasing us down a riverbank. Us climbing a building to meet King Kong. Us, in a hot-air balloon, flying over kangaroos in Australia. Always the two of us together on the page.

After our dads fought, I chucked most of those drawings in the recycling bin.

He opens one eye and glares at me. "It doesn't help, having you stare at me," he says, before he squeezes it shut again.

My gut twists. I hold my hat with my free hand and plunge under the water. It's so cool on my face and in my hair. I resurface facing downstream and swim a little farther away from John Cullen. It's not like I wanted to stare at him. I just want to be out of this mess. And since I don't have any other way to be useful, I go ahead and pee. I don't like the way the warmth fills my clothes, but I fan the waistband of my shorts and tights to let in fresh water, and soon enough, it all washes away.

Tanner is so far downriver I can't even see him anymore. We blew our chance.

"Take this," John Cullen says.

I swim back to him. He holds out a wad of fishing line. His hands plunge back into the water after I take it. Another moment's work and he holds up another tangle of line. The back of his hand is golden and dotted with freckles. The edges of his squared-off fingers are wrinkled with water. Back when we were kids, his hands were softer. His fingers thinner.

For one stupid second, I imagine what it would feel like now, to have his fingers laced between mine.

"That's it," he says. I shake that ridiculous thought out of my brain as I take the line from him and add it to the rest.

With my free hand, I pull on the gunnel. The boat glides forward.

"Checking my work?" he asks.

If I was checking his work, I would feel around the mechanism to make sure there weren't any tiny pieces of line left to gunk up the works. But I can still see his drawings in my head. They were so careful. So precise. He wouldn't leave anything behind.

We climb back into the boat and John Cullen sets a quick pace, but not as quick as it was before. Our paddles splash in the water. I call our huts. Every time we turn a corner I scan ahead for my brother.

He's not there.

17

Around every turn I think we'll see the Highway 20 bridge in Fentress. And not long after that, we'll see our bank crew at Leisure Camp.

The claps and yells of spectators up ahead fill my ears. We must be close to the bridge. And we must be closing in on another boat. And then we're passing by kids wading in the river and people on the shore and a boat getting supplies from their bank crew, we're under the bridge and paddling through twists and turns, dodging tubers, and I'm holding my breath through a cloud of cigarette smoke. We turn a bend and see the crowds of people at Leisure Camp, floating in tubes and sitting with their lawn chairs planted in the water, their shade canopies set up right in the middle of the shallow parts of the river. A couple of kids splash in front of us and John Cullen backsweeps to keep from hitting them.

I can remember when we were kids, Mom waiting for Dad in the shallow water here, with me hanging on to one of her legs, letting the current push me, and Tanner doing the same on her other leg.

I steer us toward a sandbar in the middle of the river. Erica and Gonzo are belly-button-deep in the water beside it.

It's 2:04 p.m.

Dad's not here.

"When did my brother come through?" I ask.

Gonzo checks his watch. "About twenty minutes ago."

Twenty minutes? The fishing line couldn't have cost us more than seven. Maybe ten. They're flying. They must be double-blading again to be going that fast.

"Making good time. Last we checked you were in twentieth place," Gonzo says, like he hasn't just delivered a huge blow to us. He and Erica switch out our water jugs, take our trash, and give us food.

I throw my melted ice sock in the milk crate and grab a fresh one. I cringe at the cold as I drape it around my neck, but after the initial shock, it's cool bliss.

"Hey, Cully," Erica says.

John Cullen twists in his seat to look at her.

"Gonzo told me you did that *T. rex* windmill on Highway 80. That thing kills me it's so good."

John Cullen's face lights up like a flashlight, and I see an echo of that kid he used to be. "Thanks for that."

Erica examines my trash bag. A line forms between her eyebrows. "You can't live off GU, you know." She pulls something from a plastic bag she's had tucked under the strap of her tank top and hands me something. "Eat this." It's an empanada and it's still oven warm.

Gonzo holds one out to John Cullen and says, "She made your favorite."

"The beef ones? " John Cullen asks, snatching the empanada out of Gonzo's hand.

"Our stops have to be quick," I say for everyone to hear. "No time for snacks. We should be moving already." I bet Tanner and the Bynums were in and out of here in under two minutes.

But John Cullen is already saying, "So freaking good," like he's in ecstasy or something. He waves his half-eaten empanada at someone on shore. "Thank you!" It's a mumbled yell through a full mouth.

"See Mrs. Gonzales over there?" Erica points to shore at a woman who must be Gonzo's mom.

Mrs. Gonzales cups her hand around her mouth and calls, "I'm so proud of you, Cully! Good job, Sadie!"

But now John Cullen's body is rigid.

"That nice woman made you empanadas," Erica continues. "Are you going to break her heart by not eating them?"

I shove half the empanada into my mouth and start to chew. It's spicy beef with something a little bit sweet, and it really is heaven.

I wave a genuine thank-you to Mrs. Gonzales. These are the perfect Odyssey food. They're self-contained, and she even made them small enough to eat in a few big bites. She smiles and waves back.

"Just ignore her," Gonzo mumbles to John Cullen, and they both glance toward the shore.

I can't imagine that they're talking about ignoring Mrs. Gonzales. My eyes slip past her to the girl sitting in a low lawn chair in the shallow water of the gravel shore. Watching us. Allie Davis. Tan and blonde in a tiny black bikini.

I chew quickly before swallowing. "Who's she following?" I cram the rest of the empanada in my mouth.

"Huh—oh, Allie?" Erica asks.

I nod while I chew.

"I think she's following you."

I stuff my food into my cheek with my tongue. "Us?"

Erica shrugs. "She was at Cottonseed and Staples. She packed it in as soon as you left both times."

I didn't see her at Cottonseed.

But maybe someone else did.

A solo woman in a C-1 cuts right by us, rocking our boat with her wake.

I have to focus. My brother is putting distance between us and now we're going down in the ranks.

"Time to go," I announce, busting up the conference going on between Gonzo and John Cullen.

Gonzo's pompadour is wilting. He pats John Cullen on the back. "Don't let her get into your head," he says as John Cullen raises his paddle. "Think about riz-dee."

John Cullen shakes his head as he picks up his paddle and takes his first stroke.

We pick our way through the rest of the sunburns and potbellies and the smoke from the grills piled high with sausages blowing over the river. We almost hit a tent pole to avoid a dog. When the noise and the people are all well behind us, I ask.

"What's the deal with you and Allie Davis?"

"There isn't one."

"Well, *I'm* not the one she's been following all day."

"It's not me, either," he says.

"She's distracting you."

"Salad," he says, pushing away a low tree branch hanging over the water. It swings back and I duck my head to keep it from smacking me in the face. Twigs and leaves scrape across the top of my hat.

We both duck under another low branch, and then he says, "Don't worry about Allie. I'm handling it."

"Is she the reason we flipped at Cottonseed?" I ask.

The only sound is our paddles in the water for three . . . four . . . five strokes.

I stop paddling, and after a few strokes he glances back at me.

"You're relentless," he says. A long moment passes. "She was my girlfriend."

"Was?" I put my paddle back in the water at the top of his next stroke. It was stupid to slow us down just to get him to answer. "Then why's she following you?"

He shakes his head. "Doesn't matter."

Conversation over.

Which is kind of a shame, because it's a break in the monotony. Dad and I talked a lot during the race. I even told him why I broke up with Jason Bartow.

Instead, I focus on the rush of the water. The birds in the trees. The tickle of the breeze on my damp skin.

Another twenty minutes pass. My back and my shoulders hurt. My butt, too. A spot on my right hand rubs and stings, and with every stroke I can feel the top layer of skin slip.

I need something to take my mind off it.

"Why are you racing?" I ask.

"Same reason as you. Because it's hard."

"Very funny." At least he doesn't try to make it dirty like Erica did. But paddling isn't at the heart and soul of his family, so I don't really understand. "What's riz-dee? I heard Gonzo say something about riz-dee."

"You really like to pick at all the scabs, don't you?" he snaps.

We paddle in silence.

"Did you really make that *T. rex*?" I ask.

"What?" he asks. "Oh yeah. Part of my art portfolio."

I can't bring myself to say that I love it. That it makes me smile every time I drive by. That I always loved watching him draw. He made it look effortless.

Minutes pass.

"Where do you think you'll go to college?" he asks.

So now we're people who make small talk. I can't keep track.

"Not sure yet," I say, although barring some miracle, I know exactly where I'm going to school. My college fund wasn't big to begin with, and it got wiped out when our house flooded a few years ago. It's in our floors and our rugs and the piers we used to lift the house so it won't flood again. After I graduate, I'll still be living at home, commuting to Texas State University.

"I got into riz-dee." He says it like I should know what that is.

"Riz-dee?"

"Rhode Island School of Design. R-I-S-D." He waits for a reaction that doesn't come. "It's kind of a big deal, getting in."

"Oh." He's moving to Rhode Island? "Um, good for you."

"Dad wants me to go to Texas State and major in business."

Not surprising. Johnny Hink is a developer. He'd probably love for John Cullen to help him take some beautiful land and mow down a bunch of ancient live oaks and bald cypresses and turn it into one of those neighborhoods with tiny barren lots.

But it's already summer—isn't this all supposed to be decided by now?

"I thought you had to make that kind of decision in the spring," I say.

"Yeah, well, he sent a deposit to RISD under one condition—that I race. That I make top fifteen. That's why I'm here."

Must be nice, having someone who can afford to pay for it all.

"Why the race? What does that have to do with college?"

"He thinks I can't do it. He won't say it, but . . . " He trails off for a few strokes. "He says that finishing the race will make me a man."

"That's the stupidest thing I've ever heard. You're eighteen years old. Doesn't that automatically make you a man?" I say.

But didn't I just argue the opposite about my brother yesterday? Does age really have anything to do with being a man?

I remember when they separated the boys and girls after lunch one day in fifth grade. We watched this awful, outdated video about our periods and how when you got your period you became a woman. It made me squirm on so many levels. I mean, I was ten. My main goal in life was skipping a rung on the monkey bars. Crystal Stevenson already had hers, and she still wore high-tops that looked like kitty cats. And anyway, I'd learned enough about gender at that point to know it's not about your plumbing and it's not binary. We weren't women, or anywhere near the verge of becoming them. I don't even feel like one now.

I broke up with Jason because he gave me a gift-wrapped condom. It might have been funny if I'd been ready, but I wasn't. Nowhere close to ready. At least Johnny Hink isn't one of those guys who tell their sons that having sex is what makes you a man.

"*Is* that what makes someone a man? Being eighteen?" John Cullen asks after a long while.

And all I can say is "Huh," because it doesn't. Of course it doesn't. But I'm not sure what does.

4:27 P.M. SATURDAY

The rumble of the cars hits my ears before we see the bridge on Highway 90, and I still haven't caught a glimpse of my brother. My stomach twists.

We paddle around a wall of trees, and there it is:

TEXAS RIVER ODYSSEY

MILE 49

KEEP PADDLING!

Checkpoint number two.

The crowds have thinned, but they're still there, watching from their chairs on the shore, wading into the water, kids floating in yellow and orange and pink inner tubes. We dodge past a few. Honestly, you'd think they'd know better. And then we spot Erica and Gonzo hustling into the river, water splashing around their legs.

We pull up beside them and Erica grabs the left gunnel.

"It's so freaking hot," she says, taking my trash. She's not wrong. No trees. No clouds. Just blue sky and a giant fireball overhead. Now that we've stopped, I can feel just how still the air is.

"When did my brother come through?"

Erica examines my trash. "You're eating better. Good."

"I know you heard me."

She grabs a bag from under her tank top strap and hands me a thick slice of something. I don't even argue, just shove it into my mouth. Banana bread.

"Thirty-five minutes ago."

I force myself to chew and swallow, but the bread goes down my throat like a rock.

I scan the shore again.

No Dad.

Allie's here, though, in her tiny cutoffs—zipper undone, top folded over—and that same bikini top.

Wait, no. It's different. This one has rhinestones. She's making costume changes. Ugh.

I turn back to Erica. "Rank?"

"Twenty-first," Gonzo answers.

Only sixteen boats to pass. At least there's that.

And I guess John Cullen spotted Allie, because there's a new fire under him when we leave.

≈

We paddle half a mile along the highway, getting glimpses and hearing the whooshes of cars passing by, and occasionally getting a nose full of exhaust from an old beater of a truck or an eighteen-wheeler. But the river takes a right turn and then it's all woods and farmland.

We paddle. And we paddle. And we paddle.

It's automatic, like breathing. If breathing made every muscle in your body scream. I try shifting my weight to my right side, then my left, sitting straighter, gripping my paddle a little looser. But any momentary relief it offers doesn't last.

Tanner is getting farther away. John Cullen's pace has been fading.

Hate John Cullen.

If he hadn't taken our number, I would be in a boat with Tanner right now.

But I'm here. And the river is getting shallower. The current is slowing. And I know we could be moving faster.

"Let's pick it back up," I say.

Nothing.

"Hut."

He switches sides, so obviously he can hear me. But his pace doesn't change.

"Faster."

"My entire body hurts," he says. "Just let me take it easy for fifteen minutes."

Paddling slow for fifteen minutes does nothing but get us there slower.

"The race hurts," I say. "It's not going to stop. So just shut up and paddle. People are about to start passing us."

He doesn't nod or agree or even acknowledge that I just said the truest thing you can say about this race. But he does speed up a bit. We paddle on for miles, pick through a log-jam, pass an aluminum on the banks, river left. A man is on the ground, on all fours, puking. His partner, a woman, rubs his back.

I don't understand pulling over to puke. It's something you can do over the side of the boat just as easily, and you keep moving.

Constant forward motion.

The current slows to the point that it almost disappears. We're closing in on Zedler Dam. The big building on the left comes into view. It used to be a mill, but someone remodeled it a few years ago. It has a million windows.

There's a low concrete wall, river right, that I steer us toward. Erica and Gonzo are on the shore near the wall. The backs of my hands are getting pink. I need to put on more sunscreen. We stop well before the dam and climb out of the boat onto a big concrete slab. My legs are gummy worms. I wobble and stretch and straighten my back.

"Bring it over here," Gonzo tells us, pointing to the empty spot out of the way where they've got the milk crates close to a solo boat.

Another tandem and a four pull in after us. We lift the boat over the wall and onto the concrete. It's heavy. Water sloshes in the bottom. We carry it across the pad to Erica, who is waiting to switch out our water and ice socks and food. We dump the water and our trash falls out. I grab it after we put the boat down.

"When did Tanner come through?" I ask.

Erica shrugs one shoulder. "Before we got here."

"How long have you been here?"

"Take this," she says, handing me a slice of cold watermelon. Clearly, they've been here a long time.

While Erica leans over my boat, doing all the work for me, I bite into my melon. It's cold and sweet and gone in a few bites. Juice drips down my chin and I wipe it with my sleeve.

A lean, white-haired man in shiny yellow leggings and a yellow-and-black-striped shirt paces back and forth beside his tandem, alternately stretching and rubbing his lower back.

An old woman in a matching shirt stands on the other side of the canoe. "I don't care about your back. Pick up your half of the boat. Let's move." The sun glints in the spit that flies out of her mouth.

John Cullen locks eyes on me.

I bend down and clip my water tube into my new jug. "See you soon," I tell Erica, and then we're off, climbing down a bank of big rocks, our canoe bumping my thighs. We put in on the water, climb into our seats, and we move.

The couple with the boat is still up top. The way that guy was acting, I don't think they're going to make it down the river. She might, but not him.

John Cullen skips a stroke to dip his paddle into the river and fling some water back at me. It hits my face and my arms in cool drops and leaves beads of water on my sunglasses.

"How did it feel, looking fifty years into your future?" he asks, teasing me, almost like we're friends.

It takes me a moment to realize what he's talking about. So maybe there's a parallel between me and that lady, but I'm not going to apologize for it.

"Feels like I'm still going to have terrible luck with partners," I say.

His shoulders shake a little, like maybe he's laughing, but I don't hear anything.

A gust of wind sweeps in, whipping one of my braids across my face. A cracking sound comes from somewhere onshore—I'm not sure where until a small tree branch plunges into the river with a splash.

Up ahead, beyond the river and the trees, the sky is thick with dark, roiling clouds.

I was twelve and Tanner was fourteen. It was night, and the only light in the whole house came from the TV in the living room. My thumb rested on the play button on the remote, ready to press it as soon as my brother came back from the bathroom, when the first thud came from across the house. There was another one, higher pitched, with a crack to it, and then *splat, splat, splat.*

"You hear that?" Tanner's voice came from behind me as he walked back into the living room.

"What do you think it was?" My thumb slid off the remote.

"Dunno."

It wasn't the first time our parents had left us home alone at night, but it kind of creeped me out. Watching a zombie apocalypse movie probably didn't help. Still, I wasn't one to run upstairs and hide in the closet, so I walked to the door and pulled the curtain back on the window.

Some sort of liquid goo ran down the glass. And dark pieces of something, too. Shell. *Splat!* I jumped back as something exploded on the window in front of my face. More shell. More goo.

Mazer joined me at the door and barked.

"We're getting egged," I told my brother. It was something I'd heard about but never thought I'd experience.

My brother rushed to the living room window behind the couch and pulled back the curtain. An egg hit the window and splattered in front of his face.

"Why would somebody egg us?" I asked. Our house wasn't in one of those crowded neighborhoods where you might get picked at random. We lived in the country. You couldn't even see our house from the road.

Tanner cupped his hands around the sides of his face and pressed his nose to the glass. "Too dark to see anyone out there."

Two more eggs splatted against the door. Three more thuds came from the side of the house. "Must be more than one person," I said.

Mazer bounced and barked again. Maybe they would think we were about to set a Doberman loose on them. Although anyone who actually knew Mazer would know he'd just run outside and beg to have his ears scratched.

"Turn the lights on," Tanner said. "Maybe it will scare them off. Make them think Dad might come out."

I walked to the panel on the wall and put my hand under all the switches that were flipped down until something occurred to me. Instead of hitting all the lights, I flicked up the floodlights on the porch. We almost never used them because of light pollution, but this was the perfect reason.

"Oh shit," Tanner said.

"Shoot," I corrected him automatically, because the Cussing Lamp wasn't on. I rushed back to the door and peered out the window. Two figures ran for a couple of bikes lying on the driveway. One of them I didn't recognize. The other was unmistakable.

"It's Cully," Tanner said, and even though Cully had been my best friend, not his, it was still clear he felt the betrayal. Cully was egging our house.

We watched them pick up their bikes and ride off as fast as they could.

After the tree house, it was all little things. Someone asked me if it was true that my mom's cookies were made with crickets and said that Cully had told them. His dad fouled my dad in a race. My dad called him on it and Johnny got disqualified. But egging our house . . . Egging our house after so much time had passed. I don't know, it was just so much worse.

"I can't believe it's Cully," Tanner said, sinking onto the couch.

I couldn't, either. Except, that person throwing eggs at my house, he wasn't the boy who'd held my hand at the finish line. He wasn't the boy who'd hammered board after board onto that tree house with me.

"His name's not Cully," I told my brother. "It's John Cullen."

20

The sky is getting darker. Too dark for this early in the evening.

The air is heavy.

We won't see Erica and Gonzo for another ten miles or so until we get to Palmetto.

If things go well, if we keep moving at a decent clip, that'll be about two or two and a half hours from now. But I don't see any way we could have gained on Tanner. We haven't been moving fast enough.

If I were home right now, I might be lying in a hammock reading a book. I might be curled up on the couch with my dog watching *The Good Place* on Netflix. Or *The Great British Baking Show*. I might be at the bakery, icing HAPPY

6-MONTH ANNIVERSARY on a cookie cake for some guy to give his girlfriend.

Instead, my body moves in a constant rhythm. Pull. Pull. Pull. My feet press into the bar in front of me with each stroke. I'm alone in a boat with someone I hate. Someone who hates me back just as much. Someone who thinks my future includes yelling at old men about their back pain.

The river keeps bending. The silence between us is punctuated by the huts and the splashes we make in the water.

God, I could use a laugh.

I miss Mazer. I wish there were room in the boat for him to curl up at my feet. He'd probably knock the boat over in the first two minutes. Or knock me out with his killer farts.

I wish that Tanner hadn't ditched me. That I were in the boat with him.

Or Mom.

Or even Erica.

Or Dad. I wish he'd given me a do-over. That we were here together right now.

I miss him so much. I've been missing him for the last year.

Doing this race, doing well, was supposed to bring us back together. To bridge the miles between us. But being here with John Cullen makes the divide grow wider.

≈

The sun is getting low. The fading light reflects off the water. The current is slow.

The ache in my shoulders has turned sharp.

Achoo!

John Cullen's sneeze cuts through the silence. The boat shakes as his entire body contracts.

Achoo! Achoo! Achoo!

His paddle stays frozen in the air.

I paddle one . . . two . . . three strokes before he finally straightens out.

"I forgot you sneeze in fours."

"Quadruple sneeze for life," he says, taking a stroke.

I pause a second, paddle poised, then match his catch in the water.

Everything about him is different now. His body. His voice. The hue of his hair. Even the way he laughs. His temper.

Volatile.

I'm kind of glad that this one thing about the kid I knew lives on.

That, and I guess his art.

There's a scraping noise. Something pushes up from below the canoe and we slow to a stop.

A rock?

No, a log. I can see it from below.

"Power." I dig my paddle in and bounce a little in my seat,

trying to shake us off it. He's not giving me enough. "Power," I say again, harder. I rock back and forth just enough to shake us off the log.

We're sliding off it when it hits—his body seizes up and another sneeze cuts through the air, and we're flipping as the second sneeze comes and then I'm under the surface holding my paddle in a death grip.

Another sneeze echoes across the water as I surface.

My hat. The one Dad gave me. It's beyond arm's reach already, moving downriver, sinking lower and lower. I can't survive tomorrow without it.

Achoo!

Still clutching my paddle, I kick and pull with one arm, climbing over part of the fallen tree that caught us and pushing off it, moving through the water, until my hat is in reach. I grab the brim and shove it onto my head. Water pours down my face.

I kick and pull upstream, back to the boat.

John Cullen straddles the log. He's got one hand on the boat and the other on his nose. He blows a snot rocket into the river.

"Water up your nose?"

He nods.

And then it hits me. My stomach fills with lead.

"Where's your paddle?"

He holds his hands palms up, staring at them like he's

never seen them before, and then his head jerks, looking to the left. To the right. All over. The back of his neck is scarlet.

"SHIT!"

I kick my legs and push the water with my arms, scrambling away from whatever is about to happen.

He swings his arm down over the surface, scooping up the water and throwing it at the tree.

"Shit!" he yells again, slapping the side of the canoe.

7:07 P.M. SATURDAY

John Cullen takes the extra paddle. It's like an extra life.

It's my extra paddle, which means it's a little too short for him. His stroke is messed up again. It's going to wear on his muscles.

Carbon fiber paddles are hollow and light. They float. So we search the banks and check the eddies for the next half mile. But it's gone. We can't search forever.

"Palmetto by eight fifteen," I tell him. "That's our goal."

"Fine. Whatever."

It's kind of arbitrary, but it's a good goal. "That's where we'll put our lights on, okay?"

"Loud and clear." His tone is terse.

Jerk.

We pull and we pull and we pull and the boat moves, and

we pass trees and scrape past a few sandbars and it's beautiful. It's always beautiful. This is my river, and I love it. But right now I can't actually see the beauty. It's drowned out by the pain and the miles and miles to go.

And anyway, the sun is gone now, somewhere behind the dark gray clouds. And it's easier in a way. Not as hot. The sun doesn't glare in our eyes when the river bends west. But with every breath I smell the rain coming.

And dark clouds mean an even darker night. No moon. A cold night, because of the rain they bring. A night where it will be hard to see and even harder to listen to the river and hear the rush of water that means a rapid or a dam.

Seven thirty glows green on my watch. Ottine Dam, an old, busted-out rock dam, should be just around this corner.

Or this one.

Or this one.

I grit my teeth.

We're not going to make eight fifteen.

"We need to pick things up," I say.

Nothing.

"Your stroke's kind of off with the new paddle. You need to reach a little farther forward for the catch." He doesn't say anything.

"And your elbow's dropping."

He still doesn't say anything, but his stroke does change. And he's still pulling out at his hip.

Good.

But we're not going fast enough and John Cullen doesn't seem to care.

I hear what I've been hoping for—the rush of the water through the rocks. Ottine, the rapid left over from the broken dam, is up ahead.

"We're going to run this just right of center," I tell him, using the rudder pedals to help line us up.

We paddle forward, and the nose enters the rapid. My stomach dips with the boat and the current pushes us left. I press the rudder pedal and John Cullen pulls right and I backsweep and then we're past the turmoil and the strong current and we paddle on.

But my watch shows 7:53.

We should have been through there twenty minutes earlier.

"Now pick up the stroke rating. We're off target."

He does.

"And be sure to catch past your toes."

John Cullen raises his paddle over his head and slaps the water with it so hard the handle might snap. "Could you just stop?" he yells. "My day has been total crap. I don't need to keep hearing how much I suck."

I can't see his face. Obviously. But it's in my head—the same as it looked when he lost his paddle. Red. Muscles popping out on the sides of his jaw. I can feel it in the way he holds his body and the way he attacks the water with his paddle. My paddle.

I can hear Dad's question again. *How do you think he's going to handle it when things go wrong?*

Dad is worried he'll hit me like he did my brother, but I don't think so. He knows all my weak points and exactly how to use them. It would be something more like the tree house. Something like destroying the boat.

Volatile.

I wish Dad had never said it, because now it's there.

I wrap my mouth around the word and swallow it.

There's no going back now. We're in this together till the end.

Even in the dark.

Even in the rain.

Two hundred miles to go.

8:35 P.M. SATURDAY

We've just passed under the Park Road 11 bridge and I know
the sun is setting, even if we can't see it. That's when the first
raindrops hit, fat and cold on my head and shoulders, tick-
ling my scalp. We're officially in Palmetto State Park.

I've always loved Palmetto. It's the third official checkpoint in the race. Mom would drive to the back entrance
that's closed off for everyone but the bank crews. Driving in
feels like entering a tropical forest. There are palm trees and
the namesake palmettos, and it's dense and lush and always
about ten degrees cooler than the last water stop.

When John Cullen and I paddle in, it's like walking into
an air-conditioned room.

When we were kids, Tanner and I would carry the camp

chairs while Mom carried the milk crate with the water and snacks. Sometimes ice socks, if it was a high-water year and Dad came through early when the sun was still strong. I loved the old buildings of red stone that Dad told me were built by the Civilian Conservation Corps during the New Deal. Dad loves FDR.

We'd hike down the hill to the footbridge that crosses the river. On a normal year, it's high enough above the water that you can get out of your boat and float it under. If the river is really low, you might be able to stay in and lie down without scraping your face on the underside of the bridge. But on a year when the river is high, water may rush through the six-inch-high stones on either side.

Everyone stood on the bridge or sat in chairs, and when a boat came into view, we'd all scramble to make space for them. Dad was fast, so we saw a fair number of six- and four-person boats come through, the racers hopping out of their canoes with mechanical precision, climbing onto the bridge, sometimes lifting their boat and carrying it over. Or, when the water was low enough, sometimes sending the boat under and meeting it on the other side.

The year my house flooded, the river was wild. They postponed the race not once but twice, until the river was low enough to be safe. That was the year I saw a man almost get sucked under the footbridge at Palmetto, clinging to one of the stones, trying to pull himself out of the water. My heart lived somewhere in the back of my throat as hands reached out to him from everywhere and he shouted that no one should touch him.

I knew why. His race would be over if he took help.

It went on for a minute or maybe a lifetime, until a race official rushed up and told him, "It's okay. You're still in," as she pulled him onto the bridge.

"Why didn't he just swim under?" the woman next to me asked her friend.

"Because we don't know what's under there. It could be a tangle of branches, or some barbed wire that washed away and caught there," her friend answered.

"Oh. Oh my gosh," the first woman said, realizing that we could have all stood there helpless as the man drowned beneath our feet.

The image of that man, clinging to a rock, still flashes into my head sometimes.

And I've never loved Palmetto quite the same since.

We're lucky this year, though. We've had enough rain that the river's not low—low years are slow years—but not enough rain to flood.

It takes a few more minutes before we see the footbridge, and now the rain is coming down hard enough that I grab my hat and put it back on my head. Not for the sun protection, but to keep the raindrops out of my eyes.

"Let's restock on top of the bridge," John Cullen says.

"Why?" Tanner and I always thought it was kind of self-ish, taking up space on the bridge. So I guess it makes sense that John Cullen and Brent do that.

He doesn't answer. But I don't really feel like arguing. Not after he lost it back there.

"Okay. Fine."

We round the bend and the shouting starts.

8:42 p.m.

"We've got a boat!"

"A tandem."

"Looks like they're going to the right."

"What number is it?"

"Three-twenty-four! Who's here for three-twenty-four?"

There's enough light that we can see, but it's dim. John Cullen climbs directly onto the bridge. I hop out into the water river right, where it's shallow and the current is slow and there's no way I'm getting sucked under as I swim up to the bridge. I keep my legs bent, away from the muck of the bottom, and pull with my arms. I don't want any more mud in my shoes than I already have. The bridge is rough on my waterlogged hands. My arms quiver as I push up and climb on top.

John Cullen takes the bow handle and pulls the boat onto the bridge, resting it between the low sets of stone blocks on both ends.

"How are you guys doing?" Erica asks me.

"Water and food, no ice sock. And tell me what place we're in."

"Yeah, I got that. But how are you actually doing?"

"Fine," I say. "We're fine. I've gotta do the lighting."

I push past Gonzo and Erica to the front of the boat. There's another boat, two guys in a standard, in the shallows just downstream of the bridge. They're doing the exact same thing I am. In the bow, I unscrew the end cap, reach in, and pull out everything I need.

"Headlamp," I say to John Cullen, handing him one before I pull on my own.

The raindrops are coming faster now, plunking across my shoulders and back.

"Can you get that foam under your seat?" I ask John Cullen. I grab the two flashlights, point them at the bridge, and click them on, just to make sure. Light bounces off the water and the trees all around us.

"Whoa, those are bright," someone says.

After last year, I searched the internet for high-lumen flashlights.

A hand appears beside me with the foam. John Cullen's. I slide the long handles of the flashlights into the holes cut in the foam, unclip the strap on top of the nose, and perch the foam on top of the canoe.

When I stand up, Erica, Gonzo, and John Cullen surround me.

"Water, food, trash—all taken care of?" I ask.

"Got it," Gonzo says.

"Keep eating. Every hour," Erica says.

"Sure thing," I tell her.

She holds something out in her hand. It's a gumdrop cookie from the bakery. The gumdrops were my idea, which is why Mom calls them Sadie Bears. I wish she wouldn't. It's fresh. Out of the oven within the last few hours. Or maybe just kept warm in the hot summer sun.

"What's our rank?" I ask, before I shove it in my mouth.

"Twenty-third," Erica says.

"Boat!" people on the bridge start calling.

The guys in the standard are still messing with their lighting. This is our chance to be boat number twenty-two.

"Let's move," I say to John Cullen as I head for the stern.

We pick up the boat and feed it into the water, then push it back under the bridge, so John Cullen's seat is reachable. He climbs in and hangs his legs over the sides to steady the boat as I push it forward until my seat is in view.

"Sadie," Erica says as I climb in.

"Yeah," I answer, picking up my paddle. The clouds are even darker up ahead.

"Ready?" John Cullen asks.

"Promise me that if the storm gets bad, you'll get off the water," Erica says to my back.

My insides prickle because it's nice that she cares, but it

also makes me feel guilty because there's absolutely no way I'm pulling over.

"Ready," I tell John Cullen, eager to get away before she asks me again.

I match his first stroke, and we're pulling our way downstream. We've gone about twenty yards when I hear her voice shouting downriver.

"Promise me!"

I usually didn't work the late shift at the bakery, but Mom and Dad had to go to a wedding, and I was always happy for the extra cash.

Erica and I were in the back, icing cookies, when the bell hanging on the front door rang.

"I'll take it," I told her. We'd fallen into a routine of taking turns with the bell.

I pushed through the swinging door just in time to see a big group of guys pouring in. It was like being invaded by a swarm of giant termites. They wore soccer uniforms, shin guards and all. Their cleats left dirt clods on the floor. I'd have to sweep that up later.

"Yeah, but did you see their forward try to head the ball?" one guy in the front of the crowd asked his friend.

"He went down like a fat kid on a seesaw," said another guy.

They reached the counter in one big mass.

I forced myself to smile. "What can I get for you?" I asked the group in general, because there was no clear order to this thing.

A dark-haired guy, front and center, took me in. It was like he flipped a switch the way he turned on his lazy smile and leaned forward on the counter.

"Hey there . . ." he said. The rest of them quieted down. "We heard that you have the best cookies in town. So tell me, which ones are the best of the best? Those are the cookies we want."

Hair was falling out of my sweaty ponytail, and my apron was smeared with chocolate frosting. Why this guy wanted to turn ordering cookies into some kind of seduction was a mystery. It wasn't like I'd give him free cookies just because he flirted with me. And he looked like he could afford to pay for them.

"They're all good," I answered, although if he had actually bothered to look at the case, it would have been obvious. We made twenty-seven different kinds of cookies, and the most popular ones were almost sold out. Everything in the case was going in the day-old discount basket if I didn't sell them before closing. "Why don't you just take them all," I continued. "Then you can decide for yourselves."

The dark-haired guy lifted himself off the counter and

stood up straight, not amused. He glanced at the case for the first time, probably registering that there were thirty or forty cookies left.

"Hey, Cully," he called out, his chin lifted like he was talking to someone in the back, but too lazy to actually turn his head. "Which kind of cookie did you say you like?"

Everything inside me stiffened at hearing John Cullen's nickname. That's when I finally read the school name on their soccer jerseys. St. Matt's. That was the private school John Cullen's parents started sending him to when he was in eighth grade.

These guys were friends with John Cullen. Which explained the asshattery.

"Cully's not here, man," a guy from the back called to the front.

I looked out the window to see if he was out there, but it was too dark.

"Did he stay on the bus?" the leader asked. "This place was his idea."

The guy beside him shrugged. "It's the Sadie Bars. He said the Sadie Bars were his favorite."

"Sadie Bears," I corrected him automatically. I immediately wished I hadn't.

The leader's eyes fell on my name tag. "Sadie Bears . . ." he said slowly, like he was tasting each syllable. He looked over the case again. "Well, Sadie Bear . . ."

The guys around him laughed and and I was all hot lava inside at the use of my nickname. Nobody had called me Sadie Bear in years, and even then, it was reserved for family. Certainly not for these jerks. I couldn't believe John Cullen would send them in here.

Actually, I could. I totally could. He'd turned out to be the douchiest of all the douchewaffles.

"We'll take all your Sadie Bears, the chocolate chip, the orange Creamsicle, and the rest of those iced ones."

I bagged the cookies and rang them up. He handed me a hundred-dollar bill for less than thirty dollars' worth of cookies.

"Just give me one more minute," I told him, and pushed through the door into the back. I grabbed a fresh bag and put in a couple of Sadie Bears.

"What are you doing?" Erica asked as I reached into the compost bin and took out a handful of cracked eggshells.

"Tell you later." Sharp pieces of shell pressed into my hand as I crushed them and sprinkled them into the bag on top of the cookies. I covered it with a couple of paper napkins and stapled the bag shut.

I rinsed my hand and was back to the front in less than a minute.

"For your friend on the bus. The one who recommended us," I said, and handed the leader the bag. "On the house."

The guy gave me another smarmy grin as he reached in

the first bag and pulled out a gumdrop cookie. "Thanks, Sadie Bear," he said, and tipped the cookie at me before taking a bite.

I hated John Cullen for setting this jerk loose on me.

A few months later my brother came home with a broken, bloody nose, and dark bruises already starting to form in the corners of his eyes. Another gift from John Cullen.

I wonder if he's thinking about any of this, too.

23

Tonight is an almost full moon, which should be a stroke of luck. But instead of casting a soft glow on everything, it's hidden behind a thick ceiling of clouds. The flashlights on the front of our boat cast a cone of light ahead. Everything else is inky black.

We hook a left when the San Marcos ends, leaving my river behind. We'll take the Guadalupe River all the way until it empties into the San Antonio Bay. A flash in the clouds lights the trees rising from the banks and the rain pockmarking the water. It's gone in an instant.

One.

Two.

Three.

Four.

Crash.

Thunder rattles the boat. Wind blows against the wet clothes that cling to my body. Goose bumps cover my arms. Just keep going.

Constant forward motion.

There's another flash. And another. The rumble of thunder lasts longer. The drops hit harder, fatter. Like pennies. And then a flash and a crack and John Cullen misses a stroke.

"Keep moving," I call, and then I wait to match strokes with him.

That's when the bottom drops out of the clouds and rain falls on us in sheets. I click on my headlamp, but it doesn't help.

"I can't see," John Cullen says.

"Put on your hat."

He grabs for it, and in a moment it's on and he's paddling. Water pours off the brim of mine.

"I think we should pull over," he says.

"Keep moving!"

We keep going, keep pulling.

1:05 a.m.

Another flash.

One.

Two.

Crash.

"It's getting closer. We need to pull over," John Cullen yells over the rain. I don't answer. "Come on, Sadie. Don't be stupid."

I want to scream at him, but it's too much effort. Erica asking me to pull over made sense—she doesn't really understand the race. But John Cullen knows better. He knows the serious boats aren't going to stop. And if anyone ahead of us does stop, this is our chance to get an advantage on them.

The boat rocks as he turns his head. "Stop ignoring me!"

"You'll ruin your night vision looking at my headlamp," I shout.

The sky lights up again.

One.

Two.

Crash.

It rumbles me on the inside, like getting passed by a car with its bass turned up too high.

Our lights hit the warning sign suspended across the river by a cable. Which means we're about five hundred yards upriver of Gonzales Dam.

If you hit it wrong—if you miss your takeout—people have died that way. The takeout spot is about thirty yards before the dam. Last year a boat of race officials hung out on the water, making sure that no one went past the point of no return. But when I spot the red blinking light that marks the takeout spot, the river below it is empty.

"Left," I call. A jagged bolt of lightning strikes somewhere in the trees on our right.

The crack is almost instantaneous.

We pull out onto a slick grassy bank, muddy from all the boats that came before us. John Cullen clicks off our lights, but not before they catch the edge of a concrete building. The right portage is faster, but more dangerous. Way too dangerous to do in the rain. John Cullen clips a rope onto the bow. I follow behind as he pulls the boat uphill toward a lantern-lit tent. A woman and a man in reflective race official vests sit in plastic lawn chairs and a couple of paddlers sit on the ground, each eating a bag of chips.

"How you two holding up?" I can barely hear the race official's voice over the rain.

"Fine," I answer. Water drips off my nose, even though I'm still wearing my hat.

We pull up even with the other canoe, the one we're about to pass. And then John Cullen drops the rope. My shin bangs against the canoe because I'm still moving. He bends down and—

"Are you getting a snack?" I ask.

He lifts his head and shields his eyes from my headlamp. "Yeah," he says. "There's a tent we can sit under. We're waiting this out right here."

"Are you kidding me?" I ask.

He throws his hands up like I'm being unreasonable. "Sadie, we're in a boat. On a river. During a freaking lightning storm. Water conducts electricity."

"Yeah, public school kids take physics, too." I walk to him, leaving a couple of feet of space between us. He puts out a hand to cover my headlamp. I click it off and everything goes dark before my eyes adjust. I pull myself taller. "The only people who have to stop in thunderstorms are aluminums," I say, even though I'm not actually sure of it.

"They stopped!" He throws an arm back toward the team eating chips. One of them, a young Black woman, gives me a sympathetic little wave.

"Yeah, and everyone else is on the water." I point upriver. "All those boats are gaining on us. And them—" I point downriver. "They're all getting away. My brother. Your dad. The gap between us is getting bigger every damn second."

"We were never going to catch them, anyway. I'm not risking my life for this."

"Damnit." I lift my hat and wipe the rain off my forehead. "We are making amazing time for two people who've never been in a boat together. If we keep this up, we could make top fifteen. We can make top five. But you're going to throw it all away." It's just like him to take everything from me when I'm finally so close to achieving something. "It's just like the tree house!"

His eyes widen. For a second, he looks small, before he postures again. "You want to talk about the tree house now?" He steps closer to me. His eyes are only a couple of inches from mine. His chest heaves and his breath is cold on my skin.

I want to look away. Anywhere else. But I can't back down.

Behind John Cullen, there's movement in the tent.

"Back to it," Mark Siegfried says.

Our eye contact breaks. Both our heads turn.

How did I not realize that was Mark Siegfried? Mark Siegfried, walking to his boat, wiping chip crumbs on his shirt.

What was Mark doing taking a break?

He takes the stern and the woman—that must be Kimmie—takes the bow. They disappear through the woods.

We were even with Mark Siegfried. But he said Kimmie was lightning in a boat.

Another flash. Another clap of thunder.

John Cullen's eyes are back on my face. His mouth is a hard, straight line. The muscles in his jaw flex.

I don't let my eyes move from his. I push my will at him with my eyeballs. With each breath, I imagine it boring its way into his brain.

He looks away. "God, you're intense."

He bends down again, and I think he's going to pick up

the boat, but he comes back with a chip bag. My battle of wills didn't work. And then I remember.

"Goulash," I say.

His hand clenches, crunching the chips in the bag. He glances back to the tent, to the spot Mark and Kimmie just left.

"Fine." He picks up the bow handle. "Let's move."

I pick up my half of the boat. My heart is a helium balloon as we carry the canoe through the trees, squelching through the mud, to the bottom of the hill, and put in past the white water at the bottom. We trudge through the muddy shallows and climb into our seats.

The light from Mark and Kimmie's boat shines into the rain, cruising away, already twenty feet downstream.

In another few minutes, we could be even with them again.

"Ready?" John Cullen asks.

"Ready."

We dig our paddles in and pull hard.

I just won our battle of wills, and making top five feels more possible than ever.

There's another huge rumble of thunder, and even though we're moving forward, the back current of the dam pulls on the boat, trying to keep us there.

24

1:18 A.M. SUNDAY

The light from Mark and Kimmie's boat is like a firefly on the horizon. God, they're fast. We're going to lose them.

Another flash of lightning. Another clap of thunder so fierce it shakes the boat. When my night vision returns, their light is gone.

We paddle on for another sixteen minutes. Headlights zoom back and forth across a bridge up ahead. Our light hits the sign.

TEXAS RIVER ODYSSEY

MILE 86

KEEP PADDLING!

Lantern light illuminates an easel holding the sign-in sheet the bank crews use and a couple of race officials sitting under the bridge.

There's a flash. *Crash.* The thunder rumbles through my body and rings in my ears.

Erica and Gonzo aren't knee-deep in the water. They stand on the shore under the bridge. Erica's arms are crossed tight against her chest and her face is just as tight. The milk crate isn't with them.

They know stops have to be quick—why aren't they ready to resupply us? The next stretch is thirty-eight miles. It's the longest in the race. They're supposed to stock us up for the next seven hours or more. That's two jugs of water each and at least fourteen snacks. It's all in the binder I gave them.

They walk to the bank as we pull up. Erica's still hugging herself.

"Why aren't you ready?" I ask.

"Get out. Now. This is dangerous," Erica insists. "I can't believe you didn't pull over."

"Are you joking?" I ask. "We can't pull over because of some rain."

"Not rain. Lightning," Erica says.

I turn to Gonzo for support. His face isn't tight like Erica's. "Come on, tell her, Gonzo."

His head shakes. "I'm with Erica. Don't get fried in a boat."

"John Cullen?" I won our battle of wills. He'll back me up.

Flash. Lightning branches out of the sky and hits the ground somewhere in the distance.

John Cullen dips a finger in the water, and when he doesn't get electrocuted, he slides out of the boat. "They're right. It's time to pull over."

"Scofields don't stop and rest!"

"Well, I'm not a Scofield." His face is steely. "And don't you dare goulash me again."

It's all slipping away. I have to talk some sense into them. "We'll be fine. We're in a carbon fiber."

"Not a good argument," Gonzo says. "The race officials say carbon fiber isn't any safer than aluminum."

I wince. There goes my best shot. "We'll stick near the shore. Lightning will hit the trees, not us."

"Leave it, Sadie," Erica says. Her hair is covered up in a baseball cap. Her eyeliner has run into raccoon marks under her eyes. "You can't argue your way out of this one. You're sitting it out until the storm is over."

How would Dad convince them? Tell them *constant forward motion*? But no one would ever try to stop Dad.

"Everyone else is still paddling!" I yell, desperate to get back on the water.

"*They're* not." Erica points under the bridge. Three boats are on the gravel, and at least seven people are curled up on the ground.

My heart thrums in my ears. They're being unreasonable. Every second that passes is a second wasted. There's a pull in my chest as the boats ahead get farther and farther away. I have to fix this.

Cars are parked to the right of the bridge. Sooby is there. I climb out of the canoe and pull the stern handle as I press through the murky shallows and drag the boat onto shore. John Cullen is too busy stretching to help.

"I'll get the water and the food myself," I snap.

Erica grabs my arm, but my sore muscles barely register her fingers. "I don't care if you restock your boat yourself, you're not getting back on that water until the storm is over."

I yank myself out of her grip. "You can't stop me."

"Actually, we can," Gonzo says. "This is an official checkpoint. You can't keep going if we don't sign you in. And we won't sign you in until the storm passes."

I take a deep breath and wind up, ready to launch into some amazing argument that I don't have yet—

"Do you have any more of those empanadas?" John Cullen asks.

"Three flavors," Gonzo says.

"Savory or sweet? I'm sick of sweet."

"Two of them are savory," Gonzo answers, and then the three of them are walking farther under the bridge.

I let all the air out of my chest, and I feel five times smaller. Punctured and flat and defeated.

There's nothing left to do, so I follow them and eat an empanada. It feels like it's stuck in my throat.

Erica and Gonzo laugh about getting lost on Highway 80, which should really be impossible, and tell us about the guys who got their car keys stuck in a tree at Palmetto when one of them tossed the keys a bit too high to the other. The first guy had to sit on the other's shoulders and swat at them with a baseball bat to knock them out of the branch.

Lightning flashes again and the thunder is instantaneous. The rumbles of the cars on the bridge above us are nothing in comparison.

"I'm going to get some sleep," John Cullen says, commandeering Gonzo's backpack and putting his wet head on it.

"You should, too," Gonzo tells me. He pulls off his jacket, wads it into a pillow, and hands it to me.

"I can't take that from you," I say before I pull the backpack out from under John Cullen's head.

He lifts his head off the dirt and rolls onto an elbow. "What was that for?"

"They can only give us food, water, and ice. We'll get disqualified."

I grab a couple of dry bags from the boat and throw one at him. It hits him in the chest.

"Eff you," he says as he stuffs it under his head.

I lie down and use the dry bag as a pillow. Oh god that's good. The weight on my butt, the aches in my back and shoulder, they're all gone. I let myself relax into a puddle on the ground and close my eyes.

John Cullen lets out a soft little snore. When did he start doing that?

"Lights!" someone calls.

The sounds of people moving, prepping for the boat, meet my ears. My eyes pop open. Everything in me tenses as the light gets closer and closer. Ten minutes off the water and we're already being passed.

That boat gets restocked and leaves. Ten minutes later, so does another.

The cool night air on my wet clothes makes me cold. My teeth chatter. People who plan to rest on the side of the river bring Mylar blankets to keep warm. I wish I had one right now.

How is John Cullen able to sleep through this?

I bite my tongue between my molars to keep them from chattering. To keep from jumping out of my skin. And then I'm up.

"Lie back down," Erica mumbles, but I blow right past her to the sign-in sheet and click on my headlamp.

Conner Howell and his team are in first. They came through a couple of hours ago, but they won't be able to keep up the pace. They always fade on the second day. The Wranglers aren't far behind Conner. No Sleep till Seadrift is in third place, and I am so happy they're beating Tanner.

Johnny Hink's boat is in ninth. Mike Lewis in fifteenth. His boat is propelled by cussing that puts me to shame. Tanner and the Bynums are in sixteenth. They came through about an hour ago and are currently putting miles between us.

More lightning.

One.

Two.

Crack.

This storm is never going to end. We now have eighteen boats to pass to make top five, and more could show up at any minute. If I'm lucky, a couple of them might slow down or stop to rest at some point. A couple more might drop out. Especially on the second night.

The second night. That phantom knife stab hits me in the side. I wish I could fast-forward right past the second night.

I'm with someone inexperienced. Untrustworthy. If I choke again, it'll be so much worse. Everyone will know that last year wasn't just a fluke. It was something bigger. It was me, not being able to cut it. It'll mean that nothing has changed, even with an extra year of training.

There's a hand just barely touching my shoulder. I jump. Gonzo.

"You're torturing yourself," he says.

"I'm strategizing."

"Sadie, I'm all about taking risks. You don't show up at our school dressed the way I do without getting comfortable with risk. But I don't get why you're willing to give your life for a race. It's not like finishing at the top is going to win you a million dollars or solve global warming."

I shake my head. Gonzo and I don't know each other, but I know he's a good guy because Erica likes him and she hardly likes anyone. If our paths had crossed at school, we might have become friends, aside from the John Cullen thing. Still, I don't like him being nice to me right now because I'd still be on the water if it weren't for him and Erica. And he can't tell me that the race isn't worth the risk because he can't understand how that spot on the wall where my finisher patch should go haunts me.

"Did you ever see that movie *Cool Runnings*?" Gonzo asks.

Well, that turned on a dime. "You want to talk about movies?"

"No." His forehead wrinkles. "I mean, yes. It's that movie about the Jamaican bobsledders."

"Yeah, I remember."

"At one point," Gonzo continues, "that coach tells the main guy, Derice, that if he's not enough *without* a gold medal, he'll never be enough *with* it. It's the whole point of the movie. That's like you right now."

That is nothing like me.

"The whole point of the movie," I say slowly, like a

kindergarten teacher, "is that they work their asses off and when everything falls apart, they pick up their fucking sled and keep going."

"You're you on either side of that finish," Gonzo says, like I didn't just prove him wrong. "And you're good enough right now."

"That's sweet," I say. Honestly, how did he and John Cullen ever become friends? I wish I could believe him. In my head, though, I see the dinner table at home. Mom, Dad, and Tanner, with me listening to their stories. *Theirs.* I see Dad's eyes, sweeping right past me. "But you don't get it. Everything will change for me."

I grab the pen dangling from the sign-in sheet and hold it out for Gonzo. "Please?"

"Cully's like my brother. I'm not going to let you get him killed."

I clamp my teeth down on my tongue to keep from shouting that I'm not going to get anyone killed.

Gonzo waits a moment for me to answer, and when I don't, he walks back to where the others are sleeping.

There's more thunder.

I go lie back down, but I can't keep my eyes closed for more than ten seconds because my stomach feels like a sinkhole. I watch for lightning. I listen for thunder. I don't trust them to wake me when the storm passes because I'm the only one who understands how important this is.

Anyway, eyes closed or not, I can see the boats downriver getting farther and farther away. My brother, becoming unreachable.

It's just like that camping trip we took in New Mexico. I was six and Tanner was eight.

We were eating cereal in our camp chairs for breakfast, and Dad and Tanner were talking about that day's hike. Tanner was going on and on about climbing his first mountain.

"How tall did you say it was again, Dad?" Tanner asked.

"How long will it take us?" I added.

Dad's face fell. He didn't answer. I turned to Mom, thinking she might answer, but her eyes were round and soft in that way that said something was wrong.

"The two of us are doing something different today," Mom began.

My heart sank. "I want to climb the mountain with Dad!"

"We're going on a really special hike," Mom explained. "It's through a meadow full of wildflowers."

But I didn't want Mom's wildflower consolation hike. "No!" I shouted. "I want to climb my first mountain!"

Dad's eyes fell to the ground. Mom shook her head.

"I want to climb my first mountain," I said again, this time through tears.

Dad stood from his chair and rustled my hair with his

big hand. "Sorry, kiddo. I thought you understood you and your mom were going on a different hike."

Mom tried to pull me into a hug, but I pushed her away.

"Just give her a minute," Dad said. He and Mom went to the truck to refill our water bottles for the hikes.

My brother rose out of his full-sized camp chair and bent down eye-to-eye with me in my kid-sized chair.

"Face it, Sadie," he said. "You can't come because you can't keep up."

Eleven years later and nothing has changed.

25

A lifetime passes. A cold, shivering lifetime. I'm never getting out from under this bridge. Rain comes in sheets and fat drops and torrents. Cars come and go, loading and unloading, resupplying their boats. Two stop and rest. Two more pass us by. John Cullen snores. Erica snores. Everybody snores.

I can't unclench my fists. I would pummel John Cullen for getting steamrolled by Gonzo and Erica if I didn't know I'd get disqualified.

But the rain finally slows. The storm stops.

I shake Erica awake. She rubs her eyes and yawns wider than a hippo.

"It's over. Sign us in."

She rubs her eyes again and looks around, then shakes Gonzo. She stretches and slowly gets to her feet, then confers with the race officials.

"Fine. It looks like the storm's over. We'll sign you in." She says it like she's making some huge concession.

It's too much work to bend down, so I kick at John Cullen's foot until he wakes up.

"What?"

I shine my headlamp on him. His eyes squeeze tight.

"Move. It's time to go."

"Just give me a minute." He yawns and stretches and yawns and stretches, and I give up and pull the canoe into the water.

Another team that's been resting under the bridge is stirring. If we get on the water before they do, that's one boat we don't have to pass later.

John Cullen shoves another empanada into his face and hands one to me before he gets in the canoe, and then we're off, with Erica and Gonzo waving goodbye to us from shore.

An hour passes. An hour with nothing but constant paddling and that grating pain in my shoulder and now another blister on my palm and one on my right thumb. I almost want to ask something about his college, just so it won't be so freaking quiet between us. This is the longest leg of the race. Thirty-eight miles between checkpoints, just him and me. Not a single spot with public access.

At least the moon is out again, casting a glow on the thin clouds in the sky and a soft blue hue on everything below.

"You should take a snack break," I say, because neither of us has eaten since the empanadas onshore. He puts down his paddle and bends forward in his seat.

I should eat, too, but my stomach's gone sour like I might throw up.

"Why's there so much trash in here?" he asks.

"Didn't you give your trash to— Oh no." I tug the handle of my water jug and it pops out of the holder. Too light. Water sloshes around the empty space. "Damnit."

"What?"

"We didn't resupply," I say.

"Damn," he echoes. "How long until we see them again?"

"Six hours," I answer. "If we're fast."

"Damn."

I have two GUs left. I don't know how many snacks. Maybe four. But the water . . . I would have taken two full jugs and I barely have half of one.

"Logjam!" John Cullen calls. "Every turn there's another effing logjam."

"They don't call it The Hardest Miles You'll Ever Paddle for nothing," I say. It's an old phrase. One you pull out for whiners.

"I hate you," he grumbles.

"Hate you, too," I say.

There's a steep bank to the left, so I steer us to the right and we pull over onto a muddy mess of a bank. He's right. There really are a stupid number of logjams in this race.

"I'm too tired to try to figure this one out," he says. "Let's just portage."

"Fine." When I don't know if I'm going to have enough food and water to last this leg of the race, the last thing I want is to get stuck in some gross, snaky, stagnant water.

I step out first.

"Should we go back?" he asks, just as my feet sink into mud up to my ankles. Now that the rain has stopped and the air is still and we're not moving, the mosquitoes are out. I feel a bite and slap at my neck.

"What do you mean, should we go back?"

"I mean we don't have enough food and water to last till the next checkpoint. So do we paddle one hour back upriver and get resupplied, or do we paddle for six more hours and get dehydrated?"

"Don't be an idiot. We never turn back. Constant forward motion."

He steps out of the canoe, and he's close, but he's up a slope. It's like I'm standing in a hole. My eyes are barely to his shoulders. His headlamp shines above me, but when I raise my chin to look at him, mine shines in his face. He puts his hand on it and clicks it off. Everything turns black.

"Don't call me an idiot," he says. "This is on you. You're the one who couldn't wait to get back on the water. You're the one who woke everyone else up. If you'd given us enough time to think things through, we'd have remembered to resupply."

"Don't blame me!" I yell. "We would have just resupplied and left if you'd backed me up in the first place."

My eyes have adjusted to the moonlight enough to see his hands fly up in the air. "That's right. Everything's my fault. This whole fucking thing is my fault!" He steps closer. The mud squelches at his feet. "Well, I'm done, Sadie. I'm out."

"What do you mean you're out?" I yell. He can't be—he's not quitting. Is he? He can't quit. "What about your tuition?"

"Do you really think that's the only reason I'm out here?" His hands grab at his hair. "You've been an asshole all day and I'm freaking over it. I don't have to do this with you!" His head shakes and my ears ring from the yelling.

I've poked a hornet's nest, and I don't even care. He can't quit. And it's not just about quitting. It's not about the food and the water. It's egging my house and the cricket rumor. It's being eleven years old and him shouting at me that my dad almost got his dad killed. It's my brother's nose. It's him destroying my tree house. And the fact that he never tried to make it right. His chest is right there like an invitation and I shove my hands into him and push.

He lands in the mud, and I teeter forward. My feet are

stuck. I can't catch myself. My hands and knees plunge into the mud. It splatters my face, gritty in my mouth. And he's standing back up, towering over me, angry.

How do you think he's going to handle it when things go wrong?

I'm pulling my hands out of the mud, trying to get up, when he scoops up a handful of mud and flings it into the night.

And then his hand is open, covered in mud, reaching down to me.

I look up and even in the moonlight I can see there are no hard lines on his face anymore. No more muscles popping out of his neck.

I put my own muddy hand in his, and my fingers slip out, but then I hold on tighter and he pulls me to my feet. I wait for him to walk away, to get his phone and call Gonzo. But he doesn't.

Our breaths come loud and hard, but as our standoff lengthens, they slow down.

"Are you leaving?" I ask.

His mouth tightens and I think he's going to say yes, but then it relaxes, almost into a smile. "Are you gonna try to goulash me?" Something inside me loosens, like the lock breaking on a box that's been clamped tight. Like now there's enough room for some of the good memories to seep out. I shake my head.

"Call me Cully again," he says, and there's a soft plea in his voice. "Every time you say John Cullen, it's a kick to the gut."

John Cullen is what his dad calls him.

The word is already in my mouth.

Soft.

Round.

Familiar.

Waiting to come out.

"Okay, Cully."

My parents always said my first word was Cully, before Mama and Dada. That I coined the nickname because when I was learning to talk, I couldn't say John Cullen. That as soon as I learned to crawl, they would put me on the rug when we got together with the Hinks and I would crawl straight to Cully.

The whole thing is an exaggeration. I know that. But there's some deep-down truth at the bottom of it all, because Cully was my person as far back as I can remember.

I had a roller-skating party for my seventh birthday, and Mom and Dad made me wait until after, when we got home, to open my presents. I tore the paper off a present from a girl in my class, revealing an adorable plastic dollhouse that came with a family of little bunny figures who walked on two legs and wore clothes, and another family of cat figures. My heart practically exploded from the cuteness.

"Whoever picked that doesn't know Sadie very well," Dad said.

Tanner picked up the box and laughed. "When has she ever played with little bunnies?" he said, before dropping it on the table.

Their words were a dirty boot stomping down all that excitement.

Scofields don't do cute and adorable.

I took the box upstairs and tucked it into a corner of my closet.

I pulled it out the next day, when Dad and Tanner weren't at home, and I studied each velvety little animal. The girls wore fancy dresses, and the boys wore old-fashioned suits. The dad bunny even had a tiny pair of plastic glasses.

I set up the house in my closet, complete with plastic bunk beds and a dining room table, and even a little steamer trunk up in the attic. I moved the animals around, having them at the table and putting the kids on the little couch. I switched their outfits around. I put the glasses on the little girl bunny and made the little boy cat wear the dad's bow tie. But beyond that, I wasn't sure what to do with them. Only that I wanted to keep playing.

The knock on my bedroom door made me jump.

"Cully's here!" Mom's voice was muffled behind the

closed door to my bedroom. I made sure to shut the closet before I opened the door to my room.

There he was, in a striped shirt, his red hair all mussed, his big smile revealing a missing front tooth.

After Mom was gone, my stomach turned over as I opened the door to my closet to show Cully what I'd been doing. I held my breath as he bent down in front of them.

He picked up the grandpa bunny and studied his sailor coat. "They're so cute!"

In an instant, he'd devised a whole scenario where the bunnies had to save the kitties from a ghost living in the attic of the dollhouse.

Within a year, the fuzz on those dolls was worn and dingy from being played with by dirty fingers. They'd been pirates and librarians and explorers hacking through the jungle.

I never understood how Cully did that. How he saw those stories so clearly. How when he looked at me, he saw me more clearly than my own family did.

27

4:21 A.M. SUNDAY

The hoots of owls and croaks of frogs and the dips of our paddles in the water fill the dark night. Our cone of light reflects off the water and the branches of the trees lining the river. It stinks of old fish. But all I can think about is the water sloshing around in my jug in all that empty space. We're two hours into this leg. A little more than five hours till Hochheim. And that's if we keep a good pace.

John Cu—

Cully.

Cully and I took stock after we fought. About half a jug of water each and enough food for both of us to eat twice. Not a great way to paddle thirty-eight miles. Not even close. At this point in the race we should be trying to eat every hour and drinking even more. But it's enough because it has to be.

"What if it's not? What if we need to call Gonzo and Erica?" he asked. "Are you going to rip my phone out of my hand and throw it in the river?"

My eyes flicked to the back of the boat, where my phone was vacuum sealed, there only for an emergency. Use it and you're out. Any call for help and you're out. Even if you change your mind and want to keep going.

Dad had a teammate who was losing his shit on the bay one time. Dad grabbed the emergency flare from his hand and threw it in the water.

"We'll make it," I said. We both needed this finish.

Now we're on a long, straightish stretch of river, taking stroke after stroke after stroke. My stomach churns, but I don't get to have a snack for another hour. And the last sip of water I took didn't seem to make my mouth any wetter. Add that to the cheese-grater pain in my shoulder and my sore butt and my sore hands, my sore everything. Eyelids that don't want to stay open. I'd almost like another logjam just to break the monotony.

"Hut."

We finish the stroke and switch sides, keeping the same cadence. No. Not the same. I'm putting in for the catch as he's moving his paddle through the air for his catch.

"Let's pick the pace up," I say.

But he doesn't change a thing.

"You're slowing us down."

A moment passes, and he takes a big breath. The faster pace must be coming. But he exhales that huge breath, and nothing changes.

I'd rather he just say, *We're doing this my way and I'm not taking orders from you anymore.* But he decides to be passive-aggressive instead.

At this pace, we'll be lucky to make it to Hochheim by nine thirty.

Slowing our pace doesn't just mean we're giving up any chance at top five. It means it's going to be longer before we resupply. Longer before we get more water.

When my grandfather did the race back in '64, racers didn't even have support crews. They were on their own. Grandpa and his friends had to take everything with them. Dad says they filled ketchup bottles with honey for energy and brought gross nutrition bars that tasted like cardboard. And they drank river water, purified with chlorine tablets and flavored with Tang. Getting restocked with water and ice socks came later. Having your bank crew give you food is even more recent. It's because they know people will keep going even if they run out.

The water here is milky brown, full of silt and all kinds of runoff, and a good amount of pee from the racers upstream. We're downriver of gas wells and cow fields and crops sprayed with god knows what. I don't know what it was like back then, but now, even if we had chlorine tablets, I still wouldn't drink this.

How would Dad handle it? Never call for help—that's certain. If he didn't have purification tablets, he'd probably drink his own urine.

Some racers keep going no matter what.

It's the draw of the Odyssey. Digging deep down and seeing what you're made of. What you're willing to do to succeed. And what, if anything, can make you quit.

"You're here!" Cully bounced when he opened the door. It wasn't like I hadn't been to his house a million times before, but this was the first time I'd been invited to sleep over. Who knows how long Cully had been asking before his parents finally agreed.

The whole thing was oddly formal. I was only eight, but I could tell. Mom stood at the front door behind me, even though she never walked me over to Cully's. Even though I'd been running through the open garage into the back door of Cully's house for as long as I could remember.

Leslie Hink came from around the corner to greet us at the door. Her face was tight. "Sadie. We're so glad you could be here. Cully's been talking about this all week."

Mom patted me on the back to get me through the door.

"Thanks so much for having her over," she said.

"Come on!" Cully said, waving me farther into the house, and I followed him, with my backpack and my sleeping bag, into his room. "It's going to be so fun!" he said. "Mom said we could watch a movie, and I got some new LEGOs."

And it was fun, really. We worked on a new LEGO kit he had, and then built with some other LEGOs and acted out a whole thing where the Star Wars characters had a hotel for aliens. The movie was good. Everything was going really well, until Johnny Hink got home for dinner.

I'd been slow coming around to the idea of foods mixing. If the green bean juice got in the mashed potatoes, the potatoes were contaminated. It's not that unusual. But it was a big freaking problem when Leslie Hink set a steaming dish of goulash in the middle of the table.

I leaned forward and studied the bowl. It was a messy mix of ground beef, peas, carrots, corn, smothered in juicy stewed tomatoes. And the name—it was like the sound of the slop falling into the pig trough when my class visited that farm in kindergarten.

There was only one way out of this. "I'm a vegetarian," I announced.

"Oh," Leslie Hink said. Her serving spoon hovered over my plate for a moment before she returned it to the bowl. "I guess I can make a sandwich for you."

"I'll make it." I pushed my chair out from the table,

because I didn't want to cause any more trouble for Cully's mom.

"No." Johnny Hink's hand slammed down beside his plate, rattling the empty glass in front of him. "I watched that girl put away three hot dogs last weekend. She can eat what we eat."

You couldn't be best friends with Cully and not know that his dad had a bad temper. Tanner knew, too. But as long as I could remember, the grown-ups had looked around it, like it was a tree that grew out of the center of the dining room table and there was just nothing to be done.

I sat quietly through dinner, sipping my glass of milk while Cully wolfed down his food. At the end, when Cully asked to be excused, Johnny Hink's eyes met mine. "You're going to eat it for breakfast."

Cully's face fell. His eyes grew shiny with tears. "We were supposed to have waffles."

We stayed up later than we were supposed to. Well after the grown-ups had gone to bed. And Cully was still heartbroken over the waffles.

"Truth or dare," he said.

"Dare," I answered, but as soon as the word was out of my mouth, I knew what was coming.

"Eat the goulash."

Just the thought of eating something called goulash made me want to gag. But I nodded. Cully grabbed his mom's phone and filmed me as I forced down every bite. We needed proof for his dad that we hadn't put it down the garbage disposal.

That's when the word *goulash* became a way to throw down the gauntlet. To say, *Are you tough enough for this?*

"I knew it. I knew you wouldn't back down from a dare," Cully said when I chased the last bite with half a cup of chocolate milk.

But he was wrong. I didn't eat the goulash because he dared me.

I ate the goulash because I wanted Cully to have those damn waffles.

4:49 A.M. SUNDAY

There's a light in the distance. A boat up ahead. I sit straighter in my seat and correct my form. Cully's pace has me slacking. Not cool.

"Can we pick it up? Let's catch them." I cannot believe I'm asking Cully's permission to go faster.

He does it, and in a few minutes our light is shining on a four up ahead. Only two of the four are paddling. The stern-woman holds her water tube in one hand and something else, maybe a sandwich, in the other.

I swear my mouth gets two degrees hotter, and my tongue starts to stick to the back of my throat.

After we say a quick *hey* and pass by them, I hit the button on my watch. 4:58. My next scheduled sip is in two minutes. Close enough. I reach for my water tube. I'm so thirsty it's almost dirty.

A shot of cold lime-flavored water hits my tongue. And then air bubbles.

When I reach for my bottle it almost flies out of its holder.

Too light.

I shake it.

Empty.

No.

This is bad.

I didn't pace this right at all.

At least four more hours to Hochheim. If Cully realizes I'm out of water he'll freak. He'll call for help, no question.

"You okay back there?"

"Yeah," I say. "Fine."

5:28 A.M. SUNDAY

"Hey, Sadie." Cully's voice drifts through the darkness.

"Mmmhmmm." I don't even let my lips part.

"I'm falling asleep up here. I need you to talk to me."

Crap.

My leg brushes against something in the boat. And that's when I remember. I have a bottled energy shot left. I stop paddling for a moment and try to open the bottle. My hands are permanently wet. Permanently wrinkled. They don't work right. It's like I'm wearing oven mitts. I fumble with the lid forever, but it finally twists, and I pour this strawberry watermelon whatever down my throat and swallow. The sweetness lingers in my mouth, artificial and wrong. I need something to wash it down, but obviously that's not an option. Still, at least my mouth is kind of wet.

"Start anytime," Cully says.

"What?" I ask.

"The talking . . ."

"Right . . ." What are we supposed to talk about? "How are you doing?"

"You've gotta give me better than *how are you doing?*"

I'm about to snap that he can start the conversation himself if he wants to talk, but my mouth is too dry for fighting. I need to get him to do the talking.

God, I can't wait for the next water stop. For Erica and Gonzo.

And there's the thing I've been wondering since yesterday morning.

"How did you and Gonzo end up being friends? I don't remember you being friends before . . ." I trail off. We don't need to talk about the fight.

"Do you remember Steve Ellwood?" Cully asks. "Does he still go to school with you?"

"I don't like that guy." The words fly out of my mouth before I can check them. Not that I have a good reason for not liking Steve Ellwood. I just don't, but it probably sounds too harsh. "But yeah, I remember. He just graduated," I say, going for a softer approach.

Up ahead a low branch stretches halfway across the river. Across the current. I steer us toward an empty spot below it so we can go under instead of going around it in the slow water.

"Yeah, well, the summer between sixth and seventh, after . . . you know."

After the fight.

"Well," he continues. "Steve invited Gonzo and me to this pizza dinner at his church. He said there'd be girls there. That he'd held Rachel Tillman's hand at one the week before."

"Uh-huh," I say, lips closed, to keep him talking. Rachel stole my piñata candy at a birthday party in second grade. She and Steve deserve each other.

"Anyway, everything kind of sucked that day and my mom dropped me off late and I missed the beginning, but I got there right in time for the—"

We're almost to the branch. Cully should be preparing.

"Lie back!"

"Oh, right."

He lies back in the boat, I do the same, and we glide under the branch.

"When we got there, the pizza was cold, and then they called us all into the chapel. I didn't know there was going to be a sermon. The preacher started talking about witches and the devil and kids killing their parents and how his mom was possessed by demons and the police called him because she was naked at the airport." He goes quiet for a couple of strokes. "Scared the bejesus out of me. You know my mom's pretty religious, but not that kind of religious. I didn't have anyone to talk to about it because . . ."

Because his parents suck. Because he wasn't friends with me anymore.

"Anyway, Gonzo was weirded out, too. He told his mom about it, and she took us out for ice cream the next day and talked us down. I needed a new best friend, so . . ."

Gonzo, with his suspenders and wingtip shoes. The opposite of everything Johnny wanted Cully to be. "Your dad must have loved that."

"Thrilled," Cully says flatly. "Almost as happy as he was about me having a girl for a best friend."

"I never knew it bothered him that we wer—"

"How did you miss it?" he asks.

How *did* I?

"What about you and Erica?" Cully asks.

"We work together at the bakery," I say, like it's that simple.

But getting to know Erica wasn't simple. Coming from Houston, she was skeptical of anything small town, especially the people. Which made it weird that she wanted to work at the bakery. We hardly talked for the first month, which didn't bother me much. But one day she came in with red eyes and raw fingertips, and fell asleep with her head on one of the prep tables.

At the end of the shift, I woke her up.

"Hey, are you okay?"

She lifted her head and wiped drool off the side of her mouth. "Effing Lacy Siddens."

"Did she Instagram you?"

Lacy Siddens was a senior with my brother, famous at school for posting bad candids of people she didn't like on social media. Like she'd catch someone mid-yawn with their face all messed up and make some horror-show caption about it.

"Worse. She hired my grandma to make her prom dress."

Erica pulled out her phone and showed me a picture of this ridiculous dress covered in tiny flowers. Like the whole dress was flowers. Not an inch of plain fabric. Even the straps.

"We've been making those stupid flowers for weeks, and two days ago she told us none of them were good enough. Said they needed more petals. Threatened to smear us on social media. Prom is in two days, and we're still not done."

My mom didn't mind when I told her I was going to sleep at Erica's.

I've always been good with my hands. Making daisy chains. Decorating cookies. Working on boats. So Erica taught me how to make the flowers, her grandmother fed us chicken stew, and we worked until Erica couldn't see straight. I sent her to bed, but I kept going.

"You're fucking invincible," she said the next morning

when I was cutting fabric and my laundry basket was full of flowers. "We have school today. Why didn't you sleep?"

"Because it's hard," I answered. Which was part of it. I liked the challenge. But also, being Erica's friend felt like something I had to earn. And I liked that about her. I wanted to earn it. I liked her better than all the girls I was friends with from the cross-country team.

But I'm not about to tell Cully that. He doesn't need to know how long it took to fill the hole he left in my life.

The conversation is dead now, which is too bad. It makes the boat move faster. Makes the time pass and distracts me from how the dry spot in my throat has grown. And also, his voice makes me feel warm inside.

We paddle through straightaways and turns. Cully pees, so I pee, too, and I don't drink it. It's a pathetic little trickle I pour into the river. We paddle. We dodge stumps and an owl swoops down low in our flashlight beam and we paddle. Everything hurts and we keep paddling.

"I think I need a break." Cully's words come out soft and scratchy.

"Have a snack," I say reflexively, just holding back the *constant forward motion* that Dad would tack on if he were here. Keeping your blood sugar up is his number one fatigue solution.

He puts down his paddle, and I guess he eats something, because it's quiet up there for a minute before he starts paddling again. "If I'm not going to lie down, we've gotta keep talking."

"That's fine," I say. "I just can't think of anything."

What if I just gargled the river water and spat it out? Just to wet my throat. Would that make me sick? Would I get some sort of brain-eating parasite?

There's a long pause, and then Cully speaks. "Last movie you saw in the theater."

It's been so long I barely remember. *"Hell or High Water,"* I finally answer.

"That came out years ago," Cully says.

"Drive-in," I say. But for some reason I don't tell him it was a date. It was a lousy date, but the movie was awesome.

For a while it's kind of fun, talking to Cully about movies, what books we like—school and non-school—and how he's totally come around on cilantro, even though when we were kids he swore it tasted like soap. It's familiar. Comforting. Easy.

"Who was your first kiss?" Cully asks.

"What?" The thought of talking to Cully about kissing makes me squirm. Maybe because when we were friends, kissing wasn't even on my radar. His face flashes in my mind. Not his kid face. His face now.

"Who's the first person you kissed?" he asks again.

I guess we're doing this, because there's no way in hell I'm letting him know it bothers me.

"Do you mean like a peck? Or are we talking tongue?"

"Both, I guess."

"Wes Dearington in the seventh grade. Just a peck. And then with tongue . . . I think that was Casey Ledbetter. Either him or Jake Summers."

"You can't even remember?" he asks. "Wow."

"What?" There was a lot of spin the bottle the second half of middle school. It was fun. Then I remember. "No, first tongue kiss was Luke Blackmon. Eighth grade. Final answer."

"Luke? That guy used to spit his gum on the lunchroom bench. I spent a whole afternoon with a sticky butt because of him."

"I didn't know that." Luke was in Cully's grade, not mine. He was older and I thought he was cute.

"Well, it might have been a selling point for you."

"Hut."

We switch sides and I steer us around a tree branch hanging down into the water.

I really didn't know about the gum. But Cully's right, it probably wouldn't have bothered me. Not then, anyway.

"Why? Who was your first kiss?" I ask.

"Let's talk about something else." There's something more subdued in his voice.

"Was it Allie?"

"No. You wouldn't know her. Sarah Simms in ninth

grade. And then this girl Madison when I was visiting my cousins. After that it's just Allie. And a girl named Krista, one night at a party. It was awkward after that. I don't drink at parties anymore."

"Oh," I say, because it turns out I don't like the mental image of Cully kissing all these girls. I wish I hadn't asked. Also, we went to the same school for seventh grade, and that's when all the kissing started. At least in my grade it was. And Cully—well, even back then, he wasn't bad to look at.

As if he's reading my mind, he says, "It's hard to get any play when everyone knows you cry at Disney movies."

Something inside me sinks, remembering all the times I saw him secretly dab at his eyes. During *The Lion King*. During *Finding Nemo*. It's not like it was something we ever talked about. It was just this thing I knew about him. Something that was only mine to know.

Then, in sixth grade, when I was still raw and angry from the tree house, Caitlin Sisal asked if my mom's cookies were really made with crickets.

"Of course they're not. Where'd you hear that?" I'd asked.

Caitlin shrugged. "That's what Cully is telling people."

"I wouldn't listen to someone who cries during Disney movies," I snapped.

It was something I'd loved about him, and then I turned it into a weapon. Just like I used his full name like a weapon. It's like there's something heavy in my chest.

"How long did you date Allie?" I ask, grasping at things to say.

"Still picking at the scabs," he says, but it's more resigned than annoyed. I didn't realize it was a scab. I just needed something else, anything else to say. But then he answers. "Two years."

"Did you see her at Palmetto?" I ask. "I wasn't really watching."

"I've been doing my best not to see her since Cottonseed."

Right. She's the reason we flipped. "Do you think she's finished trying to mess with your head?"

"No. I think your brother got far enough ahead that she had to choose between seeing him and seeing us."

"WHAT?" I ask. "Why would she want to see Tanner?"

"Is this a joke?" He sounds confused.

"I'm missing something."

"Don't you know they're together?" Cully asks.

Tanner and Allie? How did I not know this? I've seen a few girls leave the garage early in the morning when I set out for a run or a paddle. I guess that hasn't happened for a while. A long while. But I've never even seen him talk to Allie.

"Didn't he tell you why we fought?" Cully asks.

"He said you were talking trash about Dad."

"What do I care about the garbage between our dads?" Which doesn't even make sense. He tore the tree house down over the garbage between our dads.

"It was in the afternoon on Allie's birthday," Cully says. "She was supposed to be out with friends, so I brought flowers to put in her room. It was supposed to be a surprise. I walked in on them together."

"Together?"

"Yeah."

I shudder.

"So that's why you fought?" I ask, trying not to think about my brother sneaking through Allie's window. Or Cully doing the same.

"Yep."

"Like you fought in her bedroom?"

"No. I didn't hang around to watch. Seeing your brother's bare ass still haunts me. But I stood on the sidewalk for a minute thinking Allie might come out and, I don't know, have some sort of legit explanation." He shakes his head a little. "I wasn't thinking straight. Anyway, Tanner came out instead, and his shirt was inside out, and I don't know, I just kind of lost it."

Holy hell. Tanner had made it sound like he was just walking down the street and Cully ambushed him.

"Did you swing first?" I ask, because I know now that Dad was wrong about Cully. He's *not* volatile.

His arms droop a little. "Yeah. It was right after Scout died. I was a mess."

My heart plummets. "Scout died?" God, the way she and

Mazer would roll around together when they were both little, it was just one big ball of fluffy puppy.

Mazer. He's not allowed to die.

"Cancer," Cully says. "It happened so fast."

"She cheated on you right after your dog died? That's cold."

"To be fair, she was cheating on me before my dog died," he says. And I can see it now, that he's drenched in sadness, trying to pretend he's not. I want to get a towel and dry it off him. "I still shouldn't have done it."

"So that's why you took our number? Because of Tanner?" There's no fire left in me around that number.

"I couldn't pass it up once I thought of it."

"Are you . . ." I don't know how to ask this. "Is it going to mess with you if she's there tomorrow?" I hope to god he says no. As hard as this has been, the best parts of the race are behind us. The rest is a bunch of suck. I don't need my partner simmering over the deep noirness of his soul at every water stop. "I bet Erica would keep her away. She's intimidating as hell when she wants to be."

"Yeah. I get that about her," Cully says. "But the thing at Cottonseed won't happen again. It was an anomaly. I don't want to be with anyone who could do that to me."

Which doesn't mean that he's not still hurting. It sounds more like a mantra. One of those things you say over and over again, hoping that one day you'll finally convince yourself. Like *I welcome the pain* and *I'm not scared of paddling through the second night* and *I'm not worried about making it through the next few hours without water.*

Also, who says *anomaly*?

We round a bend to a long straightaway, and we must be facing east, because there's a glow on the horizon.

Almost through the night.

The light on the horizon gets bigger. Brighter. We take a turn to the west, and although the sun isn't all the way up, it's bright enough that we can turn the flashlights off. When the river bends back to the east half an hour later, the sun is in the sky.

It's officially the second day.

To be followed by the second night.

We paddle on, and neither of us has the energy to talk anymore.

Minutes tick by slowly. Each time I swallow, my tongue has to unstick from the back of my throat. Each stroke takes so much effort, and for once, Cully has the cadence spot on.

"You doing okay back there?" he asks. "Something feels off."

"Just tired," I say.

"Have a snack and grab a sip of water."

It's what I would have told him.

"Yeah. Thanks." I put down my paddle and rumple my snack bag so he'll think I'm eating. There's not enough moisture in my mouth for food. I wouldn't be able to get it down.

The sun shines red through my eyelids. Inhale. Exhale.

My head swims when I sit back up.

Maybe there's something left in my water bottle.

It takes forever to unscrew the lid, like my hands aren't connected to my body, but then I tip it back. Half a mouthful of wet. I'm so sick of lime, but I don't even care. I swish it around and my mouth must absorb it like a sponge, because I swear none of it actually makes it down my throat.

"You okay?" Cully asks again.

"Yeah. Fine." My head is swimming again. It aches. I take a couple of breaths to steady myself. "Fine."

Every stroke is a stroke closer to Hochheim. To my bank crew. To water.

It becomes a chant in my head. The word starts at the catch and ends when I pull out.

Closer. Closer. Closer.

Seven o'clock comes.

Then eight.

Then nine.

I slip on my sunglasses and hat because the sun makes my head worse. My eyes can't focus on the water. They linger around my toes. My stomach is beyond empty. It's nausea and pain at the same time.

There it is. In the distance. I can't keep my eyes off the shore below, trying to make out Erica and Gonzo and the boat ramp. But it's too far. Too blurry with my tired, dry eyes.

Until we're close enough that it's not.

"Here. Take it." Erica offers me the water tube before we've even stopped the boat. I take it and bite the rubbery tip and drink, trying to wet that spot at the back of my tongue. Trying to wet my whole mouth. I take pull after pull and swish it around. The dry spot isn't satisfied. It'll take more than just water. It'll take time.

I throw a leg on either side of the boat for stability. My head still pounds, and now that I have something to swallow it with, I pull out a couple of vacuum-sealed Advil and swallow them, too.

Only now, with my belly full of water and medicine, do I actually look at Erica. She's wiped off the eyeliner and her limp hair sticks to her head.

"You're an idiot for running off without food," she says. "We took turns on our phones all night making sure your dot was still moving. We were going to bushwhack our way to you on the side of the river with water and food if you stopped."

"It's okay," I say. "We made it."

"You look terrible." She hands me something wrapped in foil. "Eat this."

I unwrap the foil to find the holy grail. A warm breakfast taco full of eggs, potatoes, bacon, and cheese.

"Oh, thank god." I exhale the words before taking a bite. It is warm and soft and juicy, and having it in my mouth, chewing it, is everything. My eyes drift shut as I chew each bite until it's gone.

When I finally finish my religious experience, Erica has changed out my water and food bag. She's peering through the mesh to the wrappers and food inside.

I doubt she slept at all. "Thank you so much for this."

"How come you didn't eat all your food? You couldn't have had much to begin with."

"I ran out of water a few hours ago. Didn't think I'd be able to get food down without water." I take another long drink. My stomach cramps.

She nods toward Cully. "Did he have any left?"

"I couldn't let Cully know I was out," I whisper.

Her eyebrows shoot up to her hairline. "So he's Cully now?"

"Shut up. We had to talk to each other."

"We should put the lights away, right?" Cully twists around to face me.

"Yeah, let me do it," I say, because the whole system is finicky. It was always my job with Tanner, too.

I put my hands on the gunnels and push up. Everything starts to go black. My head wobbles. I let myself back down. I close my eyes and breathe. There's not quite enough oxygen, not enough of anything, inside me.

"Whoa, Sadie. Are you okay?" It's Cully's voice.

Someone pushes through the water toward me. A cool hand on my forehead, and then a pair of fingers on my wrist.

"How are you feeling?" Gonzo asks. I open my eyes. It's his hand. His fingers.

"Woozy," I answer.

"I bet," he says. "You're dehydrated."

"I could have told you that," I say.

"Well, I'm telling you that you need to lie down and get some more fluids and some food in your body before you go," he says. "Small sips. Small bites. I don't want it coming back up."

I am *not* lying down. "Do you think you're a doctor or something?"

"One day, maybe," Gonzo answers. "Right now, I'm an EMT-Basic and I know what dehydration can do to you."

"You're an EMT?" God, I don't know anything about Gonzo.

"I'm also your bank crew, so you don't have a choice."

He slides an arm around me and half pulls me out of the boat. My head swims again. The boat rocks when Cully climbs out. My eyelids sink shut. Cully's arm goes around my rib cage, thick and warm. He steadies me as I push myself out of the boat. We both wobble as we walk to shore. I crawl until I find enough space to sit.

Cully lies down a few feet away.

I don't fight the rest this time. Not because I think I need it. I know I could go on. Dad would push through and he'd be fine. I don't fight it because it's my fault we rushed off without food and water. I did this to myself. I own it. I'm just sorry I'm bringing Cully down with me.

I don't even ask Gonzo and Erica what place we're in.

Top five is over. Out of reach.

30

Dad always says to look strong at checkpoints. That other people are watching. That they're reporting back to their boats.

Which means I'm stewing that much more about Allie showing up under the bridge right before we leave. I don't know if I'm more offended that she's here, or that she's late. She's totally underestimating our pace. Cully sees her, too, in her sundress, with perfectly placed curls on her shoulders. I'm in muddy tights and shorts and my body is smeared with diaper cream.

But I get it now. She's not just trying to mess with Cully. She's reporting back to my brother. She's a freaking spy.

And she caught me lying on a boat ramp.

It's not just that my brother will find out. It's that my dad will. It's enough to eat me from the inside out.

But everything is worse because when we finally get on the water, Cully is stiff as a rock up there in his seat. Perfect form. Spot-on pace. But he's silent. Impenetrable.

It's like last night never happened.

And this is another beast of a leg. Twenty-five miles between Hochheim and the checkpoint at Cheapside. Probably five hours before we see our bank crew. By that time the sun will be high. The sky is already perfectly clear. It's going to be a blazing-hot day.

"Steer left. There's a branch up here," Cully says. It's the first thing he's said to me since we left.

I press the rudder pedal and the boat veers left. I peer into the water as we paddle past. It's not just a branch, but a whole fallen tree in the water.

"Good call," I tell Cully, just to soften things up. To get his mind off Allie. But he doesn't talk to me.

"So, how did Gonzo become an EMT?" I ask after a couple of silent minutes.

"He took classes."

"Yeah," I say, because that was pretty obvious. "What I mean is, *why* did he become an EMT?"

"Because he's interested in medicine." Cully's voice sounds impatient.

"You could be a little nicer," I say. "I'm just trying to make conversation."

"You could have told me you were out of water last night."

"What?"

"You could have told me you were out of water. You *should* have. I'm your partner, Sadie. I need to know these things. I would have shared mine," he says.

"You would have called Gonzo. We'd be out of the race if I'd told you."

"God, Sadie. It's like you don't take this seriously."

"How can you say I don't take this seriously? I'm ready to keep going no matter how much I want to quit. I'm in this to prove something. And you were willing to give up last night because you thought I pushed you too hard." I'm almost yelling. My throat is raw. "This race is my life."

"No. It's not. It's just a canoe race. You're worth more than that."

There's a stab of pain in my side. An echo of my ribs last year. My eyes go blurry.

"You're being dramatic," I say. "I knew I could do it."

He's silent for a long while. "Do you want to know why Gonzo became an EMT? Why he wants to be a doctor?"

"Yeah," I answer, although I'm a little afraid to find out, based on Cully's tone.

"It's because his Dad keeled over from a heart attack in the middle of dinner last summer. Gonzo's mom wasn't home. It was just the two of us there with him. Neither of us knew what to do besides call nine-one-one."

"Oh my god." I didn't know this.

"The dispatcher walked us through CPR until the paramedics got there and took over. They brought him back," he says. "It killed Gonzo, it killed both of us, not knowing what to do."

"Is Mr. Gonzales okay now?"

"He spent a few nights in the hospital, but he's better now. Fully recovered," Cully says. "As soon as he was back home, Gonzo and I took a CPR class, and Gonzo wanted to know more, so he became an EMT. He's going to be premed at UT."

I turn that over in my head, how cool, how admirable it is that Gonzo took that helpless feeling and turned it into something good. That he did it to be able to take care of his dad. That he wants to take it even further.

"Sadie," Cully says. "I've already visited you in the hospital once. I don't want to do it again."

For a moment, I'm ten again, on the couch made up like a bed with a pillow and blanket, nursing a stomachache and fever. "Must be a little stomach bug," Mom had said as she brought me a glass of Gatorade and some saltines. The vomiting came a few hours later, and after a dash to the bathroom and a lot of tears, I went back to the couch, this time armed with a small trash can, and turned my movie back on. Mazer curled up on the couch next to me, even though officially he wasn't allowed on the furniture.

The stomach cramps hit like a knife in my abdomen. I screamed.

Dad didn't consult Mom. He scooped me up in his arms, blanket and all, and laid me across the back seat of his truck. We sped down our long driveway before Mom even made it out the door.

I miss that. I miss Dad picking me up and taking care of me. I want to prove I'm just as tough as anyone else who does this race. One of the strongest, because I'm not going to be one of the people sleeping on the side of the river tonight. But how come if I'm the strong girl, I can't be the girl whose dad scoops her up and takes care of her, too?

31

It's 1:48 when we see a few spectators in camp chairs on the bluff at Cheapside, our next checkpoint. The sun is right on top of us, beating down. I would give anything for some clouds to block the sun. Instead my hands, my neck, my face, and my ears are all greasy with sunscreen and slick with sweat. Everything about the second day is worse. More time between water stops. More hours without seeing another boat. Fewer people cheering you on. Fewer people in general. Cully and I have only been exchanging huts and river logistics, so I have a lot of time alone with my thoughts.

And my thoughts are mostly about food and water and my bed. I can't imagine anything better than a long shower and then putting on dry clothes. A tank top and a loose pair of shorts. And then sliding into a freshly made bed. I wouldn't even draw the curtains to make it dark. I might open the windows and turn the fan on. I would close my eyes and be still. No paddle in my hands. And my hands would be dry, not wet and wrinkled. My feet, too. Dry feet. Maybe a pair of fluffy socks.

"Sadie!"

"What?"

Cully draws the boat right. "It's time to pull over."

"Looking good, three-twenty-four," someone calls from the bank.

"Oh, right," I say, pressing the rudder pedal. How many times did he have to say my name?

We pull up alongside Erica and Gonzo in the water. A few other people linger onshore.

"How are you feeling?" Erica asks immediately.

I shake my head, but the back and forth makes it hurt worse. "It's totally normal to feel lousy at this point," I reassure her. But then there's a woman dressed as a bee on the shore. "Am I hallucinating that?" The hallucinations usually start on the second night. Not in the afternoon.

"No, that's real," Gonzo says. He's next to me, too, his beautiful hair now under a baseball hat. Up front, Cully slides into the water.

What's he doing getting out of the boat at a checkpoint? People will think we're falling apart. And I can't even say anything, because I'm not supposed to bark orders at him anymore.

"Have you been keeping food and water down?" Gonzo takes my wrist and presses two fingers on it.

"Yes food. Yes water. And I've been peeing. I'm fine."

"I see your snark is still in working order." He walks to the other end of the boat, where Cully is floating in the water.

I grab my mesh bag and hand Erica my trash and extra food. She gives me a fresh food bag and examines my old one. "You're not eating enough."

"Do antacids count? I've been popping those like candy."

"That doesn't make me feel better," she says.

"My stomach's just a little off. It's normal."

She nods and we change out my water bottle.

"Oh, I almost forgot!" Erica grabs the plastic bag tucked under her tank top strap and hands me a beautiful peach with a rosy red spot on it.

"Yum," I say, and even though the thought of eating makes my stomach churn, I bite into it and the warm juice rolls down my chin. It is sweet and a little tart and everything a peach should be, but I have to force myself to swallow each bite.

"Ready?" I ask Cully between bites. He's still in the water, stretching.

"Another minute. Muscle cramps." He glances at me before going back to his conversation with Gonzo.

"What place are we in?" I whisper to Erica because I can't not know. And I don't want another *you're already enough* talk from Gonzo.

Erica shrugs. "Dunno." Which is total bull. She sees our place on the sign-in sheet at each checkpoint, and she sees it on the tracking app.

"It's part of your job to tell me this stuff," I say.

"Sadie, I didn't take three days off from work to help you torture yourself. I've read through the rule sheet. My job is to make sure you're safe and healthy enough to keep going. That's what I'm doing."

This is what happens when your bank crew look down their noses at the race. It's like they're conspiring against me, and there's nothing I can do.

When I finish my peach, I hand her the slimy pit.

We finally get back on the water at 1:57.

Nine minutes. Who takes a nine-minute break at a checkpoint?

At least Allie wasn't there watching.

We don't look any stronger at our next water stop, either, because Cully gets out and stretches again.

"Still cramping," he explains.

"Pickle juice might help," I tell Gonzo, since our electrolytes aren't doing the job.

The bumblebee woman is there again in a red wig and a mermaid costume, seashell bra and all.

A few hours later at Cuero, she's dressed as a nun.

Cully actually gets out at Cuero and sits onshore and eats an oatmeal cream pie. It's our surprise snack at that checkpoint. I want to die of shame. This will get back to Dad whether Allie is watching or not. Stopping makes us look tired. And weak. If we have to take rest breaks during the day, how can anyone expect us to make it through the night? And I can't say anything because Cully's words will never stop ringing in my ears.

I don't have to do this with you!

I am completely dependent on him. And this is how he wants to run the race.

It sucks.

Sitting in the boat, waiting like this, might be the most un-Scofield thing I have ever done.

32

The current has slowed down. The sweepers and log jams are becoming more frequent. Sometimes we paddle around them. Sometimes find a hole to paddle through, like threading a needle. Once we get out and portage, but only as a last resort.

The sun hangs lower now, but it's still so damn hot. My palms and fingers sting with blisters. I'm eating and drinking, but my stomach still hasn't settled. I'm afraid everything is going to come back up. We pass empty railroad tracks and a few small houses along the river, and a parking lot half full of RVs. A couple of kids are swimming in the shallow water of the river. Their parents sit in camp chairs on the shore. It's hard to believe that people are still doing these things. Hard to believe anything exists outside of this race.

I'm weaker than I was at this point last year. I'm with an inexperienced partner. And with every stroke we're getting closer to my DNF with Dad. If the second night took Dad and me out last year, what will it do to Cully and me? What if it's worse? I would give anything to fast-forward past it.

If I'm right, we're about a third of the way between Cuero and Thomaston Bridge. My body is heavy. Each arm is like a dead branch. My feet are river rocks. I think that's why, when we're dragging our boat across a sandbar, I don't protest when Cully says he wants to have a pee standing up.

I sit my butt down on the soft sand and close my eyes, counting my breaths and listening to the splatter of Cully's pee hitting the sand ten feet away.

After thirty hours on the river together, I am so over caring about Cully's penis.

When we're on the water, I know everything going on with his body. I can see from his stroke that his left shoulder hurts more than his right. When he puts his paddle down, I know from his back and his arms whether he's reaching for water or a snack or getting ready to pee. I know from the way his hips sit when his mind is drifting and when he's focused on the river.

And I know from the slowing of his stream that he's

just about done over there. As I stand, ready to carry the boat to the water, something pokes me in the butt. More pokes—no, they're stings. The stinging is everywhere. I swipe wildly at myself, shaking my butt, my feet dancing, my heart pounding, the name almost ready to erupt from my mouth.

"Fire ants!"

I jump over the boat and splash into the water, yanking at the waistband of my shorts and tights, kicking up silt and mud. I crouch in the shallows and pull everything down. My bare butt and lower back are bumpy with ant bodies. I sweep my hands all over, brushing them off. The water gives almost no relief, but after a minute, at least the ants are gone. I close my eyes and take a couple of deep breaths to slow my heart down.

Muffled laughter brings me back. Cully stands ankle-deep in the water, biting his cheek to keep from falling into a full-blown laughing fit.

"You okay?" He barely gets the words out before he has to bite his cheek again.

I reach down, sink my fingers into the oozy mud, and fling it at him. It splatters across his shirt and neck. He turns away, and the next mud ball gets him on the back. It's a nice distraction, until he flings water at me with his paddle.

I close my eyes for a second. Everything stings.

"Put the boat in the water," I tell him, because the last thing I want is our boat covered in fire ants.

Cully drags the boat away from the ant bed and pulls something out of the front.

"Stand up. Dry off," he says, and I'm half-sure he wants to throw mud at me, but he seems sincere.

I hitch my wet clothes up over my butt as best I can in the water and stand. I lift the back of my shirt and shake it up and down for some airflow. It doesn't stop the burn but it's a distraction. Cully squeezes a tube. I catch a whiff of something medicinal, and then his warm hand is on my lower back, rubbing cream all over my bites. "Hydrocortisone," he explains.

"Give me that." I grab the tube from his hand and pull my tights and shorts down in the back.

His eyes drop before they go wide and shoot back up to my face. "Whoa!" he says as he whips his body around, but I am so beyond caring if he sees my butt. Getting the cream on my bites is all that matters.

"Here," I say when I'm done with the cream. He puts a hand out behind him and takes it. Gingerly, I pull my shorts and my tights back up, trying not to disturb the medicine. It's not instant relief. Not by any means. But it's an improvement. "You can look at me again."

He pivots back around.

But it turns out, he can't quite look at me after all.

His cheeks are red, and I don't think it's from the heat. His hair is wild, with a faint glow from the sun. It's a darker shade than when we were kids, but I still like it. His hands open and close, like they don't know what to do with themselves.

There's a tug in my chest, like we're connected by a string.

33

The afternoon after my appendix ruptured, I lay in my hospital bed, bored to tears. Dad and Tanner had left an hour before, Mom wasn't there yet, and hospital TV sucked. Soap operas. Gross. I had nothing to do. I couldn't even sleep because I'd been in bed all day, and the nurses said I would have to spend a whole extra night there.

Dad and Tanner had brought the game Operation as a kind of joke, and we'd had a good time playing, but after about fifteen minutes of operating on my own, it lost its shine.

Everything was worse because I was supposed to go with Cully earlier that day to pick out his new puppy. His aunt had neglected to fix her golden retrievers soon enough and had seven puppies on her hands. As much as I disliked

Johnny Hink, at least he didn't deny his son a dog. Cully's mom had shown me pictures of the litter on her phone. It was just a pile of tan fluff with eyes and ears and tails. You couldn't see where one began and the next ended. I wanted to get down on the floor, right at the bottom of that fluff pile, and take a bath in it.

Instead I was here, propped up in this bed, by myself. Why hadn't Dad and Tanner at least brought me a book?

A voice drifted in from the hall. Mom. "It's okay. Don't be afraid."

She walked through the door. Cully peeked around her shoulder. I sat taller in the bed, excited to see my friend. Excited to hear about his puppy. Cully's wide brown eyes went from me in the bed to the IV still attached to my arm, up the tubes to the saline bag hanging off a stand, and all the machines behind me. His throat bobbed up and down.

Mom stepped aside, revealing the rest of him. He cradled a black duffel bag with mesh sides. Mom put a hand on his shoulder, urging him forward. "It's okay. She's going to be just fine."

I didn't like how he looked scared of me. How he stared at me like I was fragile. With my family, I was the littlest. The baby. But with Cully, even though I was a year younger, I was brave and strong.

Mom closed the door to the room behind her. Cully took a big breath before he stepped toward the bed. The bag in his arms moved on its own. He scrambled to keep from dropping it.

What on earth?

"I brought you something." He pulled the zipper back a few inches and a furry golden head squeezed through the hole. Its little black nose sniffed as it turned its head from side to side, taking in the room. The bag squirmed more. Cully held on tighter. It was the cutest thing I'd ever seen.

"You brought your puppy! Can I hold it?" I exclaimed.

"Shhhh," Cully said. "We snuck him in." He pulled the zipper open and placed the puppy on my bed.

The rest of the puppy's body was just as fluffy as his head. He sniffed the blanket in excitement. His whole body wagged with his tail.

"Careful with your IV," Mom said, joining us at the bed as the puppy moved up to sniff my hands.

I picked him up and brought him to my face. We touched noses, then I pulled him to my chest and hugged him, rubbing my cheek across his soft fur.

"What did you name him?"

"I named my puppy Scout. She's a girl," Cully said. "I've been calling that one Mazer."

I liked the name Mazer. It made me think of the corn maze we'd done at a farm one time, and the dog trotting ahead, leading the way. It made me think of adventures we would all have together.

"You got two puppies?" I asked. I'd been asking for a puppy since our old dog died two years earlier. Now Cully had two. Maybe he'd let me borrow one sometimes.

Cully looked at Mom.

"This one is yours, Sadie," Mom said.

I froze in the middle of rubbing my cheek on his fur. Mom and Dad said a puppy was a big responsibility. That I wasn't ready. I studied Mom's face for some sign this was a joke, but there was no sign of joking in her smile. Or Cully's.

"Really?" Even I could hear the wonder in my voice.

"Cully picked him out for you," she said. And after another moment, "The whole thing was his idea, really."

I held Mazer up to my face again and looked into his dark eyes. He held his mouth open and his pink-bubble-gum tongue hung out. He tilted his head and everything went blurry with tears.

34

"What kind of costume do you think that lady will have at Thomaston?" Cully asks when we're back on the water.

My bites itch and I've stuffed my ice sock down my pants, but at least it broke the tension between us. At least we're talking again.

"I don't know. Butterfly?"

"Too predictable."

"Yeah. I thought she was going to have a sexy theme going on until I saw the nun costume—maybe Supreme Court justice?"

"Who says Supreme Court justices can't be sexy?" Cully asks. "Did you know RBG was still planking in her eighties?" My stomach takes a hit at the loss of Ruth Bader

Ginsburg. I have a *Notorious RBG* sticker on my laptop. I wouldn't have guessed that Cully was a fan, too.

"Goals."

"We haven't eaten in a while," he says. "You take your break first."

I don't actually want to eat, but I put my paddle down anyway, because I like that we're talking again. And because I know I should eat. Erica will check. My snack bag has a pop-top thing of canned chili, nuts, a protein rice ball Tanner and I made, an oatmeal cream pie, beef jerky, a Slim Jim, and Shot Bloks. The thought of eating any of it nauseates me. Where's a banana when you need one? There's a burning in my chest—heartburn, I guess. I pop a couple of antacids, take a few sips of water, and force down the cherry Shot Bloks. They're the closest to Jell-O. That's what my mom always made when I had a stomach bug.

Cully asks me to talk to him while he takes his break, and I tell him about the time Mazer found a skunk den a couple of years ago. Dad said that a beer bath would get rid of the smell, but Mazer got loose and ran through the house. The entire downstairs smelled like skunk and beer for weeks.

It's the wrong story to tell, because I can still smell it. My stomach churns, and it doesn't stop. Not when we duck under a sweeper. Not when we drag the canoe across another sandbar. Not when we steer right of the huge pile of graying logs that's formed in front of one of the pylons that holds up

Thomaston Bridge. The same woman stands at the top of the cliff-like banks with the rest of the spectators, wearing a dinosaur costume.

A dinosaur. With giant purple glasses.

Erica and Gonzo are in the water.

"You didn't tell me we'd have to climb down a rope to get to some of these water stops," Erica says as soon as we pull up next to them.

"Surprise," I say weakly.

Erica pulls the bag out from under her strap. "Pepperoni roll. Still warm," she says.

I have to eat it. It's part of the unwritten contract we have during this race. And really, I don't want to seem ungrateful. But a pepperoni roll sounds terrible right now.

I bite into it and warm oil spills out the side onto my leggings. Gross. But I chew, and it's cheesy and terrible and I force it down my throat. On the second bite, Cully opens a bottle of pickle juice. That vinegary smell hits me and my mouth fills with saliva. I clap a hand over it. I gag once, like a warm-up, before my whole body convulses. I lean over the side of the boat. Sour water and pepperoni roll pour out of my mouth.

"Get her out of the boat." It's Cully's voice.

"Damn," Erica says, backing away from me.

"Banks are too steep here. There's nowhere to put her," Gonzo says.

I retch again, and all I can think is that it's nice my hair is already tied back in braids. My teeth chatter. I tremble. Tears fill my eyes. It's like there's a rock in my throat. Someone puts a hand on my back. Erica.

I gag again. Throw up again. And again. Again, until my stomach is empty and I'm dry heaving and it hurts. Then I put myself back together. Sit up straight. Lift my head. Wipe my eyes, wipe my mouth, and shoot a snot rocket into the water. I've always been a snotty puker. My stomach aches, but the nausea has passed. For now.

Erica's hand is still on my back. Gonzo is right there, downstream of where I just puked, his eyes squeezed tight. His hands hover over the water.

"It's so warm," he says. There's barely a current between the boat and the shore to wash it away.

"Here." Erica pushes water toward him with her hands.

"I'm so sorry, Gonzo." I wipe my mouth again and dip my hand in the river to rinse it.

He shakes his head. "It's okay . . . Just use the other side of the boat if you need to do it again."

I nod, even though there's nothing left. And anyway, we need to get moving.

Gonzo puts his hands back in and splashes water on his torso.

"Do you feel good enough to keep going?" he finally asks. The little bit of humor in him has washed away with the vomit.

They want to take me out of the race.

I try to catch Erica's eyes, but they're on Gonzo. "I'm fine. It's normal," I say, looking back and forth between the two of them, but they're looking at each other. "My stomach's better now. I can keep going."

What kind of silent conversation are they having? What have they been saying between water stops? That I'm weak? That I'm falling apart?

That's what Erica's thinking. I see it in the way her forehead wrinkles and her jaw tightens when she looks at me. I'm far from invincible now.

"It was just the smell of the pickle juice," I say, like that can negate the vomit.

"You're pushing yourself too hard," Erica says.

I turn my head to Cully, still watching me from the front of the boat. "Cully, please." I'm tearing up again. And my voice . . . I hate the pleading in it, but it's all I have. I can't get pulled out of the race.

His eyes go from me to Erica to Gonzo and then up high on the bank. But I don't take my eyes off him. We're past goulash. We're past me trying to force my will on him with my stare.

"Please."

His eyes come back down. "We'll take it easy. I'll keep an eye on her."

I let out a huge breath. Cully's eyes move back to the bank

and I follow, past the guy climbing down the rope with his milk crate.

There he is, towering over me, high up on the bank. Dad. In his jeans and his plaid button-down and his orange hat like mine. His hands are in his pockets. His mouth opens, like maybe he's going to say something; sprinkle Odyssey wisdom on us like fairy dust. But then it closes.

Nothing.

My dad is finally here.

And he couldn't have caught me looking weaker.

35

"We should pull over and put the lights on," Cully says.

"Yeah," I agree. My voice is scratchy. It's like my throat is full of gravel.

We don't need lights yet, but we will. It's sunset. We're on a pretty straight stretch of river headed southeast, but even in this direction, some of the clouds glow an orangey pink. I'd meant for us to put the lights on at Thomaston, but with the vomit and with Dad watching me, and Gonzo telling me about small sips and small bites, lighting slipped my mind.

There aren't any sandbars around, so we pull over, river right, and I hold on to a low branch while I talk Cully through the lights. I take one of the small sips Gonzo prescribed. Grapefruit. I'm sick of all these flavors, but

I take another. So far so good with my stomach.

There's a *plop* in the water from the front of the boat, and Cully's hands go up to his head. "Damnit. Damnit!"

"What?" I ask, because Cully is pulling his hat off and climbing out of the boat on the shore side. The boat shakes. My grip tightens on the branch.

"I dropped the end cap to one of the flashlights," Cully says, before he plunges down under the surface.

My stomach sinks. The end cap completes the circuit. We can't just duct tape the batteries in. I hold my breath until Cully surfaces empty-handed, wiping the water off his eyes. He sucks in a big breath before he goes back down. Again. And again. And again.

"Let me try," I say.

"You're supposed to be taking it easy." His shoulders lift and his chest swells with another breath.

While he's under, I take off my hat and fumble with pulling my shoes off. My hands still aren't working quite right. The rest of my body isn't either.

He resurfaces.

"Hold on to the boat," I say, and he doesn't argue.

I slide my feet into the water and lower myself until they reach the rocks and slippery mud. I'm so wobbly. It takes a minute for me to get my balance back, then I inch across to Cully's seat, shore side of the boat, hoping I don't step on any broken glass down there. Or a snake. The only thing I want to feel is the end cap. Cully moves toward the nose.

I drop down under the surface and grope blindly with my hands. It's all a jumble of roots and rocks and mud. When my lungs burn for oxygen I surface, gulp down a big breath, and go under again. With every failed attempt the sun sinks lower. The sky grows a little darker. The stone in my stomach grows a little heavier.

We take turns, but finally I'm shivering cold. The voices of another boat travel down the river. Two boats. We're about to move back two places.

"It's gone," I say. "Let's just go."

Cully studies his fingers on the rim of the boat. "It's like trying to use someone else's hands."

"I know," I say.

I let out a heavy breath as we climb back into the boat. My feet are ghostly white and wrinkled and don't want to go back in my shoes. I dig out my headlamp.

A minute later we're paddling away with one flashlight angled off to the side, because the whole system was made for two lights and Cully can't manage to get the remaining one centered.

"I'm sorry," he says.

My mouth fills with a million mean things I could say, each one more biting than the last, and I swallow them all. "It'll be fine. One light is all we need."

Before the crash last year, I never gave much thought to

lighting. But after it, I worked so hard to get this lighting system right, researching flashlights and lumens. So many test runs on the water at night to get the angle of each light perfect.

Now it's the second night, we're coming up on the place Dad and I wrecked, and the left side of our boat is going to be a dark void.

All I can do is repeat my stupid mantra in my head over and over again.

I'm not afraid of paddling in the dark.

I'm not afraid of paddling in the dark.

It's dusk now.

"Want to go ahead and click the lights—light—on?" Cully asks.

"Let's wait a little bit longer," I say. Just to save on batteries.

"What's—ugh—what the . . ."

And then I see it. A buzzy cloud and we're heading right for it.

Cully swats at his face.

"Mayflies."

I should have already put my bug net on, but they don't come out every dusk. It's a crapshoot every year whether you're going to run into a hatching or not. We cruise right into it.

They buzz in my face and tickle my ears and my neck. They're on my shirt. If I opened my mouth, I'd end up with half a dozen perched on my tongue. I've already got my hat back on. I dig one-handed in the space behind me for my bug net and slide it over my head. My hat brim keeps it from sticking to my face. Mayflies bounce around on the inside of the net now. I squish a few of them between my fingers and shoo the rest out before I tuck the ends of it into the neck of my shirt. The bag comes with a drawstring, but I'm never comfortable having something tied around my neck on the river. If I fall out of the boat, it could snag on something.

"Do you have a mosquito net?" I ask.

"Nobody ever mentioned a mosquito net."

Which sucks for him. But if he'd asked around enough, someone would have told him.

"Not everyone uses one," I say. "My dad doesn't."

I think Dad likes that part of the Odyssey. I think he kind of likes anything that makes it harder. When I was a kid and he would race, bank crews weren't allowed to give anything but water and ice socks. They couldn't even put electrolytes in the water. Racers had to do that themselves. Racers had to take all their food the whole way down the river. Run out and you were stuck making some tough choices. It rubbed Dad wrong when they started allowing bank crews to resupply food. Like they were making it too easy on the paddlers. But I get it. What if you lose your food? What if you were trying to save some weight in the boat and packed too little? Drinking water and not replacing electrolytes can lead to hyponatremia, water poisoning. And there are plenty of people who do this race who wouldn't even think of backing down if they lost their food.

Cully puts his paddle down and sprays himself, and a second later I'm gliding through a cloud of woodsy-smelling bug spray. I hold my breath but still get that bitter bug spray taste in my mouth. He reaches for something else, and a moment later he wraps a bandana around his face and ties it behind his head.

He picks up his paddle again, but then flaps his arm like a chicken wing.

"They're in my armpit." The bandana muffles his words.

"They'll chill out in about half an hour," I tell him.

"Where were they last night?" he asks.

"Rain probably kept 'em away. But sometimes they don't come out at all. Sometimes they come in the morning."

We keep moving, trying to outrun the mayflies, and the sky grows darker and darker until Cully says, "Let's turn the light on, okay?"

I steer us to the right and we pull over. The button on the light is so far up, Cully has to balance on the bow to reach it.

Light explodes onto the right bank ahead. The left stays dim with the dusk. Not completely, because I set up the lighting with some overlap. But not enough.

Okay. This is it. For the second night, this is it. While we hallucinate. While we pass the place I wrecked with Dad. While all we want to do is stop and sleep. This is it.

9:47 P.M. SUNDAY

The sky goes from dusky to dark. The mayflies move on, and I take off my bug net and hat. Cully takes off his bandana. The sky is fully dark when we see the headlights zooming by on the bridge up ahead, and I know we're coming up on the Nursery stop.

I remember Nursery that year. It was the first time I realized something was wrong between Dad and Johnny. They got there around dusk. Tanner, Cully, and I were killing time playing cards. My grandparents were coming to pick us up later and take us back to their place in Victoria to spend the night so Mom and Leslie could meet our dads at all the overnight water stops.

They brought a dark cloud with them. Figuratively. Dad was all business at water stops. I was used to that. But before he left, I'd always blow him a kiss. I'd done it as long as I could remember. He never blew kisses back. That's not Dad. But he'd catch it and tuck it in his pocket. It made me feel like he was thinking about me, even though he was so inaccessible. That when this was all over, everything would go back to normal.

But this time Dad and Johnny were hard faced. He didn't

even throw a glance at me when I called, "Dad! Dad!" My kiss went uncaught.

This year we're pulling into Nursery just after dark. Someone's put a lantern onshore, lighting up the bank crews and a couple of spectators. And a unicorn.

"I thought the hallucinations started a bit later," Cully jokes when we pull up next to the costume lady. Her horn glimmers in the lantern light. I would have loved one of those horns when I was a kid.

"You feeling any better?" Erica asks.

"I'm eating again," I say. "No more puking."

She's still got that wrinkled-face look about her.

"Here," she says, handing me a cup of something with a foil lid. Jell-O. I rip the lid off and tilt my head back, shaking the cup until it falls into my mouth.

"Thanks," I say, once I've managed to swallow it.

Erica and I change out water and food. I'm not sure why she gives me two bottles, but I take them, and then I'm ready to move. I'd leave right now, if Gonzo and Cully weren't still talking.

"Ready?" I ask.

Erica puts a hand on my arm, like she's trying to stop me.

"Give me a couple of minutes," Cully says. He doesn't get in the water, but he stretches up in the front.

"What do they spend all this time talking about?" I ask, trying to avoid whatever Erica's building up to.

"Gonzo asks how Cully's doing. Cully asks how Gonzo's doing. Some of Cully's friends are texting messages for him to Gonzo and Gonzo passes them along. I get the feeling Cully's pretty starved for conversation up there."

"Oh." This is such a foreign way to do water stops. And also, we've been talking. "So, um, how are you two holding up?"

"I think it's time for you to pull over and rest. Sleep for the night."

"What? No." I am not one of those people who pull over to sleep on the side of the river. I'm a competitor.

"Sadie, you look like hell, you puked your guts up at the last water stop, it's freaking dark outside, and you're in the boat with a novice. I don't think it's safe for you to keep going."

My insides crumble. What happened to that night we made the flowers when she said I was invincible?

"Looking good, Leo!!!" the unicorn shouts.

Erica looks over her shoulder at the boat coming in.

We have to go now, before she tries to pull us out of the race.

I put my paddle in the water and pull. "Let's go, Cully."

"What?"

He scrambles to get in position as I paddle our boat away from shore.

36

We're a little way past Nursery and it's fully dark now. The stars come out, one by one, and I guess that's the beautiful thing about being out here at night. The moon and the stars. The frogs croaking. The crickets. Those are the things I might appreciate if I were putting in right now, planning to take out again in an hour or two. If I were here for a pleasure cruise.

Last year when my English teacher found out I was training for the River Odyssey, she told me, "I'd love to do the nights. To be alone in a boat with the moon and the stars. It sounds like heaven. Like meeting God."

She conjured up this romantic picture, and even though I've heard my parents and their friends talk about the race my whole life, she kind of sold me on that image. I went into it last year thinking about that.

Now I know what we have ahead of us. Pain and fear, confusion. The ghost of last year's race. My best friend losing faith in me.

She's probably right.

It's a miracle we've made it this far.

Last year Mom pulled us out of the race at Victoria, our next checkpoint. There's this sick feeling in my stomach that I won't make it any farther this year, either.

Over on the right, a little gnome stands on the water ahead, waving at me, and it's not until we come up even with him that I realize he's just a tree root, a cypress knee, sticking out of the water, and I pull the name out from somewhere in the back of my brain. Stump people. Dad says they're always the first thing you see when you start hallucinating.

Light creeps into the space on the left. Real light. Leo, the guy the costume lady is cheering for, pulls up even with us for a while and hangs out on the left so we can see better. It's his girlfriend dressed up at all the stops. She wants to keep his spirits up because it's his first time soloing. His brother is his bank crew. It's nice, cruising along next to Leo, because it's not so dark. Because I don't have to think about what's coming. Because he's company. But when he stops paddling for a snack, we keep moving.

Time passes slowly. A light bobs ahead of us sometimes

on the straight sections of river, and I don't know if it's another boat or my imagination.

Last year I did my best to ignore my hallucinations. But now we're rounding a bend, and I swear to god there is a giant cat sitting at a table having a tea party with a little girl. They stare at me as we pass by and I stare right back.

"You hallucinating yet?" I ask Cully.

"It's normal down here for the trees to be full of panda bears, right?"

I pop my paddle across the water and splash him as we round a bend to the right. Teasing Cully is better than thinking about how freaking scared I am.

"Hey, I'm going to get cold th . . . Wait, I don't know where the river went," Cully says. I wince. "Left," he says. "I think. Maybe."

I know that sinking feeling at night where the river just seems to disappear. I squint ahead of Cully, into the night. Into the river lit by the flashlight, but all I see is a wall of trees ahead.

We paddle a few more strokes before Cully says, "Okay, left. Definitely left."

I line us up for a left turn. It's my job to get us in the right vicinity and his job to draw us into a good spot so that we're in the current but can jump into the eddy if we get into trouble. I'm glad I don't have to worry about that part, because I'm too busy feeling sorry for myself.

My stomach's still not quite right, but nothing's right. My shoulder, the blisters on my hands, my lower back, my butt. My ant bites itch. It takes so much work just to hold my head up. And I know it's just a hallucination, but the wet splotch on the back of Cully's shirt has turned into my dad's face with that horror movie look it had right before I left for the race.

Nobody thinks I can do this.

Not even me.

"Sweeper," Cully says.

We're headed straight for a giant fallen log stretching halfway across the river, its trunk a foot above the surface and branches digging into the water every few feet.

"Draw left. Draw left!" I press the rudder pedal to steer left. We need to get in the slow water.

If we had both lights, if we could have seen what was on the left, we would have seen it in time.

Cully fumbles his paddle as he switches sides, but then he draws left. We both draw over and over, but the current grabs the stern. We're moving sideways with the current. My heart hammers. It's pushing us straight for the tree.

"Jump!" I yell. "Upstream!" If we're in the boat when it hits the log, our weight coupled with the force of the current will wreck it. Wreck us. "Don't go under!"

I bail upstream, away from the sweeper. The water is deep and swift. My head goes under. It's last year all over again. I brace for the impact. For the rock. It doesn't come. *Get*

your head above water. I pull and kick until I break the surface and the cool air gets my face. *Don't get caught in the
current.* It's too dark to see. I click on my headlamp. There's
the shore.

"Cully!" I yell. "Cully, get to shore."

I swim freestyle, head out of the water, and kick and pull
as hard as I can. The current tugs on me, but I'm moving.
I swim my way out of its grasp.

The current slows, and my feet touch the riverbed. I stand.
My chest heaves. Not enough air.

Where is he?

"Cully!"

Nothing.

I scan the river, but it's dark. I can't see him. Can't
hear him.

"Where are you?"

A sick feeling seizes my stomach. He could be underwater. He could be caught in a branch.

"Cully!"

His headlamp clicks on and glows dim in the shallows
downstream. "I'm here," he says.

The light sweeps the riverbank and falls on me. It grows
blurry. Hot tears on my cheeks."You okay?" I ask.

"Yeah, you?"

He's moving toward me. I want to crash through the water
and pull him into a hug.

I take deeper breaths. Everything slows down. My heart. My mind. The tears.

Back to the race.

The headlight on the boat is still, lighting up part of the log. My headlamp lights the rest. It's not just a log, it's a tree. It has eyes and teeth and a million spindly arms and it's holding my canoe sideways in its mouth. Any moment it's going to chew my boat to bits.

I don't know how to get the boat back.

God, I wish my dad were here. Wish I weren't the one in charge. The one who's supposed to figure this thing out. The responsibility is like a sandbag around my shoulders, pushing me into the ground.

Cully reaches out, fingers spread and arm shaking as if he's trying to lift the boat using the Force, then drops it, feigning exhaustion. He laughs a little to himself, like we weren't just in mortal peril. Like this is something to joke around about.

"This is serious."

"Just trying to lighten the mood," he says.

"Well, I'm sick of being the only one who cares."

"I care."

"Then act like it," I snap.

"Oh, exalted leader," he says in a solemn voice. "How shall we retrieve the boat?"

Asshole.

I'm not about to get back in that current, so I make my way onto the gravel bank where the trunk meets the ground. Cully splashes behind me. I climb onto the trunk. It's fat enough to walk across, but my legs are Jell-O. I crawl on my knees. The bark presses into my raw hands and scrapes at my tights. God, this hurts. My headlamp shines on the first branch sticking out vertically into the air. A few feet past that, the boat is stuck against a couple of branches that jut into the water. The water sounds faster running through the branches.

I lie flat on my stomach, wrap an arm around the far side of the trunk, and reach with the other. My fingers slip off the hull. I need to get closer to the middle of the boat, where it's widest. Where it'll be easier to get a grip on the gunnel. I scoot forward and reach again. Still too far. I scoot farther, to where another branch shoots into the air. I wrap my legs around the trunk, hook an arm around the branch, and reach. My hand clamps down on the gunnel and I pull, feeding the boat toward shore. It moves. I scoot my hand farther down the gunnel and scoot it again. And again.

"Got it," Cully calls.

I look back. He's on the tree with a hand on a gunnel, pulling up.

Cully straddles the log, scooting toward the shore with the boat. I follow behind.

We examine the canoe with our headlamps.

"Do we have something to fix that?" Cully asks, running his finger along a crack in the hull. The same crack I patched up last fall. The one Dad and I put in the boat last year. The pain in my side hits me again.

I can't do this. I'm not going to make it to the finish.

But I stuff that fear deep down inside.

"Of course we have something to fix it." I dig in the back of the canoe for our patch kit and start mending the crack. After fifteen minutes, after Leo has portaged the log past us, the wound in our boat is mended. I can't say the same for the one inside me.

37

"Sadie!"

"What?" I pull my eyes off Cully's back and see him, see the river, see everything with fresh eyes. I don't think that was the first time he'd called my name.

"Logjam," he says.

"Logjam," I repeat, and suddenly I see the huge tangle of debris blocking the narrow river before us.

It rained here earlier today. I can smell it.

"I think we could make it through that hole over there," Cully says, pointing ahead.

Right next to the black space Cully points to, I see a rabbit with an umbrella. It's got a stern look painted on its face, like I should know better than to try to squeeze through the hole. It says that I should be at home in bed, and why did I ever get back in a boat after last year?

"What do you think?" Cully asks.

I put down my paddle and press the heels of my hands into my eyes, and when I look again, the disapproving rabbit is still there, but when I squint, I can just make out the hole.

"Too narrow. If we can't find something better, I think we should portage." I see the light of another boat portaging river right, so someone else already came to this conclusion.

"Trust me. We can make that. I can see it better than you," Cully says, switching to a forward stroke. The boat starts moving and I'm too exhausted to fight it, so I press the rudder pedal and help Cully line us up for the hole. If we can avoid the portage, we'll save time and energy.

The nose goes through fine. Cully lies back in the boat to keep from getting beheaded by a branch. The boat shudders, and the sickening scrape of wood on the hull fills my ears before we come to a halt. Cully only made it through a little past his seat, which isn't the widest part of the boat. There's no way we're getting through here. We may have already cracked the hull, and I want to scream at him for being so stupidly stubborn. I told him it was no good.

I freaking told him.

Cully reaches up and tugs on a branch, trying to lurch the boat forward, but it doesn't move. He lifts his butt up to do it again.

"Stop!" I say, and his hand slips off the branch.

"Damnit!" someone calls from the bank. It's the other boat, the one portaging. "God-damn-stupid-fucking-mud!"

So we caught up to Mike Lewis.

He should be happy. At least he's not caught in the log jam.

"We're going to have to back up," I say.

"I still think we've got this," Cully says.

"You'll make it worse." I backpaddle a couple of times, trying to ease us out, but it's no good. At least there's no current pushing the boat.

Cully pushes off the log with his foot, but we're too stuck to move. He pushes again and again, but it's no use. The boat is good and stuck, and our weight isn't helping.

"We could climb over the logs. Maybe tilt the boat," he says.

"Not worth the effort. Let's climb out and swim it to shore," I say.

"Shit!" Mike yells from the other shore.

"Shit," Cully echoes.

"I'll get out first, and then when you get out, you push off the log jam."

"You-stupid-ass-useless-fucking-boat!" Mike shouts.

"Let's portage on the other side from him," Cully says.

I flip on my headlamp and check out the left bank. It's steep and covered in trees. I shine my light on the right side and see Mike struggling to get his boat up a steep bank with no trees, and apparently nothing to grab on to. "We'll portage left," I agree.

I slide out of the boat into the water. I kick and kick, away from the logjam, not moving anywhere, until the boat rocks and then lifts. Cully is out. I keep kicking, and suddenly there's a push, and we start moving upriver. I kick as hard as I can, pulling with my free hand, swimming the canoe toward the left bank.

There's a little bit of muddy bank before the trees begin and the earth takes a sharp turn up. My legs are like rubber when I try to stand. I wobble, slip, and fall, splashing to my knees and elbows. Dirty, fishy river water fills my mouth. I spit and spit before I stumble back to the boat and rinse my mouth out. Thank Gonzo and Erica for giving me some plain water. I could not handle any sort of mixed berry grapefruit shit right now.

I am so damn tired. Getting that boat up the bank already feels like an impossible task.

"Just one minute," Cully mumbles, crawling to the bank. He lies on his stomach in the water, folds his arms on the mud, and lays his head down.

My knees soften. Maybe one minute wouldn't hurt. Maybe one minute would make us faster.

"Damnit!"

Mike Lewis's shout from the opposite bank brings me back to my senses.

"Let's move," I say, nudging Cully with my foot.

"Two minutes."

Cully snuggles down into the mud, but a moment after I grab the stern handle, he's on his feet, taking the bow.

"How're we going to do this?" Cully asks, his voice laced with sleep.

I shine my headlamp up the bank, into the trees.

"We'll have to try to slide it up. I'll go first and pull. You push."

I flip up the rudder so it doesn't drag on the ground, and start up the hill, holding on to the stern handle. It's all a tangle of mud and tree roots, and every step is made worse by the weight of the boat and the effort not to fall and the fact that my legs are gummy worms.

We both slip in the muck more than once. My body's caked in it. A good ten minutes pass, and we've moved about ten feet. Maybe Mike had the right idea portaging the other side, except that he's still cursing over there.

Cully's end of the boat is probably only a few feet past the bank when we get stuck. There are just too many trees too close together, and the boat is just too damn long and unwieldy. I end up facing him as he tries to back through the space between trees.

"Try swinging your end to the left," I tell Cully, hoping we can thread the boat through a hole to the side.

Cully takes a few steps to the right, banging the hull against a tree.

"Your left, not mine," I shout.

"Why didn't you just tell me that?" Cully's voice is raised, too.

"Because it was obvious."

Cully steps to the left, until he runs into another tree.

We move forward a few steps, readjust the angle, move back a bit, readjust again, and I'm just so sick of it all, I want to scream.

"Push!" I yell at Cully.

"I did push. It's just stuck. See!" Cully lifts up his hands and steps away from the boat. It doesn't move. "I didn't sign up for this so you could spend sixty hours insulting me."

"No, you signed up for this because you needed your daddy to pay your tuition, when I'm going to spend the rest of my life paying back loans so I can go to school."

I hope it stings.

"I'm not here for my tuition," he grumbles.

I set down my end of the boat and move around a tree so I can see him better.

"What are you talking about? You already told me that's why you're here." I walk toward him. My body vibrates with anger.

He puts a hand up, shielding his eyes from my headlamp, and I click it off. Everything goes black.

I poke him in the muddy chest with my finger. "You told me you're here for your tuition," I repeat.

What a stupid-ass thing to try to lie about.

"He took it away," he yells. "Are you happy now?"

But I'm not happy. Cully was always an artist. From the time we were kids. He should go to art school.

"At the starting line," he says, "as soon as he found out I was getting in a boat with you, he called it off."

Johnny and Cully at the starting line. Cully red like a volcano. Cully saying *fuck him*.

But then I'm so confused. He didn't need to do this.

My eyes adjust to the darkness and Cully's face emerges in the moonlight filtering through the clouds. We're just a foot apart.

"Then why are you here?"

He turns his head away. Looks back. Rubs a hand over his forehead.

"Why would you get in the boat?" I'm raising my voice again, and I don't know if it's because I'm still angry or because I'm confused. "You don't care about this race. You never cared about it."

He opens his mouth, closes it, and then he takes a deep breath. He still won't look at me.

"Why aren't you answering me?" I shout.

His eyes turn back to me.

"Because I've missed you! Okay?" He's still half shouting. He steps back, tugs at his hair with both hands, and then takes a step closer. "I've missed you every day for the last six years. And I knew how much you wanted this. I knew you couldn't do it without a partner."

My heart is a freight train.

"You hate me!" I'm still yelling. Why are we both yelling? "You tore down the tree house."

"I took down the tree house because I was hurt and I was mad. People do stupid things when they're mad."

"I didn't do anything!" I shout, because every bad thing I did to Cully came after the tree house. "I didn't do anything to you!"

He huffs out a breath, and then he winds back up.

"You let go!" Cully shouts. He moves forward, his face a few inches from mine. His breath warm on my face. And then he's not yelling. "We didn't have to stop being friends. I held on, and you . . . you let go."

And there we are, at the finish all those years ago, when our dads were looking at each other with venom in their eyes. Cully's hand was warm wrapped around mine. He knew what was coming, too. He squeezed tighter.

I let go.

And I know it now, for the first time, that this is the root of everything that went wrong between Cully and me. I was the one person in his life who took him just as he was. Not his parents. Not his sister. And when it came down to it, when it was obvious that the Hinks and Scofields were over, he chose me, but I didn't choose him.

That day at the tree house, maybe he'd been waiting for me. That could have been our place, neutral territory. But instead, I pushed him away. I told him it was mine. I told him he had to leave. No wonder he ripped it apart.

I ruined things.

I ruined things, and I've spent the last day and a half being an asshole to him. And he kept going, just because he wanted to be friends with me again.

If he didn't hate me before, he should now.

Everything goes blurry. I start to wipe my eyes, but my hands are covered in mud. My chest heaves. So does his. I stare back at his moonlit face. I feel like I'm falling forward. Like that string that connects us is pulling me closer.

He takes a half step toward me and his eyes meet mine.

"I'm still holding on," he whispers.

I reach out and pull him to me.

My mouth is on his and his lips are dry and chapped. I press in harder, like all at once I'm telling him how sorry I am and trying to make up for six years of missing him. His hands find my waist, his fingers cool and damp from the mud. But the rest of him is so warm and the insides of his lips are so soft. I wrap a hand around his neck and—

"Could you two just get on with it?" Mike yells from across the river. "I'm gonna fucking vomit over here."

We both freeze. Cully steps away. His head turns toward the sound of Mike's voice. I turn away, too.

Oh my god. I kissed Cully.

It was never like that between us before. I don't even know if I want it to be like that now.

I kissed Cully, and—I didn't even ask. You're supposed to ask someone before you mash your face into theirs.

"I'm sorry," I say, without turning back to look. "I don't know why I did that." If he's completely disgusted, I don't want to see the look on his face. I take a breath. And another.

When I turn back, Cully is staring at the canoe. My stomach sinks a little. It's not like I was hoping he'd sweep me into his arms, but that was good. Like, really good. And it doesn't seem to have had any impact on him.

It's a relief that it's dark, because my cheeks burn with embarrassment and I don't know why. I don't like Cully like that. I could barely even tolerate him a day ago.

I guess it's good, at least, that he's not acting mad at me. And if we're not going to talk about it, I'm glad we have the boat and the race to focus on.

"Let's turn it upright," he says. "It'll be easier."

It's so freaking simple. I couldn't even see it.

We secure all the loose parts. He holds the bottom of the

canoe and I take one of the cross braces, and we turn the boat vertical. We're so close together, I'm grateful for the canoe between us. Grateful that he can't see my face. Grateful I don't have to look at his. The boat towers over us, unwieldy, and we take tiny steps, weaving through the trees. We twist it and turn it and adjust the angle. It wears on our already exhausted bodies, but eventually, the ground levels and the trees thin, and we've made it up the hill. We take turns dragging the boat across the soft ground, and somewhere in that time, the moon comes out from behind the clouds.

A cheer erupts from the opposite bank, and I guess that means Mike finally got his boat out of the mud. Slowly we weave our way back down to the shore, past the logjam, and see his bow light moving downriver as he paddles away.

By the water, there's a little sandy bit of shore that we set the canoe on. I stand in the shallows stretching, shining my headlamp downstream, where the river winds its way to Seadrift.

"Well, that was a mess." Cully's voice is soft.

I'm slow in turning to face him.

Mess is an understatement.

And it's not just the kissing.

We have so far to go, and I'm making a mess of the whole thing. Dad would have known what to do. That was one of the things I was supposed to be able to offer here. I'm supposed to know how to do this stuff. But I don't. And I've got Cully here, thinking I'm some sort of expert. And on top of the fact that I destroyed our friendship, I've made our partnership super weird, and I'm not even sure I can get us the rest of the way down the river. I'm not my dad.

I let my legs crumple beneath me.

Cully sits down, too, and I feel every inch of the foot he's left between us. "What's going on?" he asks.

"I'm making this up as I go, and I'm lousy at it." My voice cracks. "At this point last year, I'd already asked my dad if we could quit."

"You wanted to quit?" he asks, like he doesn't quite believe it. "I thought you didn't finish because you got hurt."

"Yeah, I got hurt. But I also wanted to quit. I was tired and scared, and I said it. I said it out loud, and Dad didn't even answer, and then we wrecked. And the thing is, I'm not sure if we wrecked because I made a mistake, or if we wrecked because some sick part of my subconscious knew it was the only way to get home."

And now the damn tears are rolling down my cheeks.

Cully inches closer, but not close enough.

I remember one night, hiding in my closet with our sides smashed together and warm, reading *A Wrinkle in Time*. He could read faster than me, so he would wait until I tapped his leg before he turned the page. Even now, I can still feel the soft flannel of his pajama pants under my finger. I remember thinking in that moment that my heart might just explode with love for my best friend, Cully Hink.

Everything in me wants to lean against him like I did that night in the closet. To rest my head on his shoulder. For everything to be good and comfortable and warm between us. And maybe I could do that right now, if I hadn't just kissed him.

"I don't think you did it on purpose," he says quietly, and it takes me a moment to realize that he's talking about the wreck, not the kiss, and I'm a little disappointed, because maybe we should talk about the kiss. "Even subconsciously," he continues.

"How can you say that?" I ask. "You don't even know me anymore."

He lets out a little half snort. "You haven't changed that much."

There's that tug in my chest again. The string that's connected us our whole lives.

"I didn't know whether to laugh or cry when I got that bag of Sadie Bears covered in eggshells," he says. "I really wanted those cookies."

I'm hit by a good bit of regret. "Sorry about that."

"Nah," he says. "I heard they called you Sadie Bear. We're even."

The way he smiles at me makes every moment of missing

him bubble up inside me. Now I'm the one who doesn't know whether to laugh or cry.

I stuff the feelings deep down in my belly. "We should get moving." We shouldn't be sitting here like this, wasting time. *Constant forward motion.* It's the only way I know how to race. It's how Scofields do it.

He falls back on the gravel. "Five minutes," he whispers.

My partner is hurting. And so am I.

This is how I become one of those people who lie down to rest on the side of the river.

12:44 A.M. MONDAY

I listen to the rhythmic rise and fall of Cully's breath beside me and fight the urge to shake him awake. It's good he can sleep. I hope it helps him. It's just hard to understand how he can be there, so peaceful, when I'm trying not to jump out of my skin.

My feet are in the water and my back is on the gravel. My ant bites itch like mad, even though I put more cream on, and I have to keep my eyes closed, because there's a freaky clown face in the trees eating one of those giant turkey legs. Eyes closed isn't much better, though. Horrible little movies play on the backs of my eyelids. A few of them are about the race. Boat after boat pulling up to the finish, each one with a Tanner in it who gets out and accepts a trophy and a bar of gold and a puppy that will never grow old. But mostly it's me, trying to kiss Cully, and a look of disgust spreading across his face, over and over like a bad GIF.

But if Cully is sleeping, then at least he isn't lying awake making that face. It's not like I'm blind to the fact that he turned out good-looking, but I've been so busy hating him that I don't understand where this part of me came from. Maybe race delirium. Because this is absolutely the last time on earth I should be kissing anyone, and he's the last person I should be kissing.

But in that moment, I didn't want to stop. I really, really didn't want to stop.

I press my palms into my eyes. It doesn't clear any of this up.

Time moves like a sloth, and then there are noises on the other side of the logjam. For a second, I think it might be an animal, and my insides tense. But I hear a grunt, and I know whoever's on the other side is dealing with the same crap that drove Cully and me to . . . to what?

The noises come closer, and then there's a light. I squeeze my eyes tighter.

"Everyone knows Scofields don't stop and rest." It's a man's voice. I can hear his boat dragging across the gravel.

"Get your light off me." I click my headlamp on so I can shine it right back and squeeze one eye open.

Robbie Scoggins drags his boat into the water

unnecessarily close to us. He's a friend of Johnny's and an all-around idiot. "Hey, that's bright," he says.

"Right back at you, jerk."

"I'll tell your dad I passed you during naptime."

"I'll tell him we had to wait here for four hours for you to catch us," I snap.

Cully puts a hand over his eyes. "Is it morning?" he mumbles.

"Just Scoggins being a butt."

When Scoggins paddles away, I can already hear someone else on the other side of the jam. Lots of someone elses. Lots of voices. At least one boat. Maybe more.

I want to say it, I want to tell Cully it's time to leave, but I bite my tongue. I owe him this rest, even if he wants to take it in a freaking train station.

"Might as well go," he says, rolling over on his hands and knees before slowly climbing to his feet.

I'm kneeling on the gravel when he holds his hand out to me and I take it. His hands are so much thicker now. So substantial.

He lets go as soon as I'm on my feet, and I want to slap the part of myself that feels disappointed.

Back to business.

We pull the boat into the water and take turns climbing in. Even with the pain in my butt and in my hands and in my shoulder, it's not quite as bad.

Whatever that was, whatever happened between us, I have to press it down. Keep it squashed deep inside me. I have to focus on the race and not let it enter my thoughts, because there's no place for it on the river.

1:18 A.M. MONDAY

TEXAS RIVER ODYSSEY

MILE 200

KEEP PADDLING!

At this point last year, my boat was cracked, my ribs were cracked, and my shirt was soaked in blood.

This year we paddle into the Victoria checkpoint, and I'm not bleeding. Nothing is broken. But my stomach is sick. I'm about to go farther than I did last year. I'm going to places I've never paddled in practice, let alone in the dark with a novice partner. I miss my dad more than ever.

I can't see the boat ramp in our headlights, but I know it's there. Another boat is pulled over. Its headlights shine downstream. Headlamps and flashlights dot the shore.

"Everything okay? Are you sick again?" Erica asks as soon as we pull in behind the other boat.

"We're fine. Why?" I answer, because she's not asking about all the fear and unsaid things churning inside me.

"You stopped for almost an hour. I was afraid one of you had broken a leg or something."

"Why would we break a leg?" I ask.

"One of the guys earlier did. A solo. He had to get rescued."

"That's awful," I say, and I should get some sort of gold star for not asking what place that puts us in.

"Why'd you stop, then?" she asks.

"We were resting."

She puts a hand on my forehead. "Are you sure you're not sick?"

"Positive."

"I'm . . ." Erica pauses. She's not a huge talker, but I've never seen her at a loss for words. "I thought you were going to destroy yourself." She holds something out to me. "Here. You've earned a cookie."

If that's not an *I'm proud of you*, I don't know what is.

The cookie is still soft, and it's orange and creamy. A Creamsicle cookie. One of Mom's.

Erica pulls my water jugs out of the canoe and replaces them with fresh ones.

"Thanks for the plain water," I tell her. "How did you know?"

"Cully told Gonzo he was sick of electrolytes. We figured if he was, you might be, too."

I hand her my old food bag, fasten the new one into place,

and wait while Cully and Gonzo finish talking. I wonder if they're talking about what happened. Maybe Gonzo's up there telling Cully he should just go ahead and get out of the boat before I try to make another move.

I feel so exposed.

Focus on the race.

"Ready?" I ask Cully.

"Yeah."

We take off, and a minute later the other boat from the boat ramp pulls up next to us and asks what's up with our lighting.

"Mark?" I ask, because I recognize his voice.

"Oh, hey, Sadie. Didn't realize that was you."

They pull up even with us on the left, giving us a better view of the river, and I explain about the end cap.

Up front, Cully laughs. "We've got an alligator gar swimming in our lights." Alligator gar are huge fish. Prehistoric-looking with long pointy snouts and pointier teeth. But they're not aggressive.

"How big?" Mark asks.

"Maybe three feet. There are two of them now," Kimmie answers.

"Just wait till you see them closer to the bay," Mark says. "They'll be longer than you are tall."

Cully and Kimmie both shudder.

"It's been a weird race this year," Mark says as

Cully and Kimmie fall into conversation up ahead.

"Yeah," I agree. I kissed Cully and I'm keeping pace with Mark Siegfried. It doesn't get any weirder.

"I mean, can you imagine having a tree fall on your boat?" Mark asks.

"Wait, what?" I ask.

"That happened to someone. What did you mean?" Mark asks.

"I just meant, I didn't think we'd see you again after Gonzales. You guys were flying. You should be coming up on Invista by now."

"Nah. It's not that kind of race this year," Mark tells me.

"What kind of race is it?"

"Kimmie's better when she rests. I mean, it makes her feel better. She's not in this to torture herself. So we stop and eat snacks on the shore, and a couple of times we've even slept."

"But . . ." I don't know what I'm going to say. *But you're so fast. But you could get first in class. You could maybe be one of the first five boats.* But I don't say any of it.

"I know how your dad runs the race. He's a machine," Mark says. "Don't get me wrong, I like running the race that way, too. But this is how Kimmie wants to do it, and I'm not going to push her to do it my way."

His words almost knock me out of the boat.

How did Mom and Dad do the race? Did they stop to rest? Did they pack blankets and camp out? I've never asked. Mom always says that the race just about tore them apart, and then it put them back together even stronger.

How often does it do that?

Then there's Ginny, saying she doesn't want to be responsible for anyone else. There's Dad and Johnny. One race undid all their years of friendship.

How often do people just stay torn apart?

2:21 A.M. MONDAY

The current is dead. Has been since Mark and Kimmie left us behind at Highway 59. We restocked there, and Erica gave me another cookie, and we set out for Invista, our next checkpoint.

If you look at the river on a map, this section looks like a piece of old string a cat vomited up. If you're actually on the water, it's worse.

A new blister rips open on my hand. You'd think I'd be finished forming blisters by now. I bite off the flap of skin and spit it in the river.

"I just want to pick it up and shake it out," Cully says.

"Shake what out?" Is this the beginning of him being delirious?

"The river. I want to shake all these kinks out and make it lie in a straight line. Put an end to all this back and forth."

"Do it," I tell him. "Please."

We're quiet for a while. My eyelids live at half-mast. I reach for an energy shot. God, I'm sick of these.

"There's nothing wrong with it, you know?" Cully says like we're coming back from a pause in a conversation.

"Nothing wrong with what?"

"With letting your parents pay for college," he says, and I wonder how long he's been ruminating on this. "Gonzo's parents are paying his tuition at UT next year. They've been saving for it since he was born. It's a gift. There's nothing wrong with accepting it."

I get it. I get what he's saying. The money my parents saved wasn't enough to pay for everything, but it would have helped. I would have taken it. But I also understood when it had to go into the house.

And I'd be lying if I said I'm not jealous. Of course I am.

"I understand that," I say. "But did they force him to paddle two hundred and sixty-five miles in a canoe to get it?"

Because there's something wrong with being out here because it's the only way you can get your tuition paid. And it's not that there's something wrong with Cully. There's something wrong with his dad.

3:07 A.M. MONDAY

Cully's head drops and lifts. Drops and lifts. He's nodding off.

My mouth opens, the words *get a snack* fully formed, when I force it shut.

A lot of people have a kind of hammock made for the person in the front. A wide piece of nylon that stretches across the boat from gunnel to gunnel right behind the bow seat. It snaps onto the sides with the same hardware we use for the spray skirt, which keeps the waves out during the bay crossing. The person in front rests their back on the hammock. From what I hear, it's a decent way to get some rest.

But Scofields don't buy boat hammocks.

I steer us to the bank river right and hang on to a low branch so we don't tip.

"What are we doing?" Cully slurs.

With my other hand I dig out the dry bag from behind me. It's a million times heavier than it was when I put it in the boat on Friday. That's what paddling two hundred miles will do to you.

"Put this behind you," I say, pushing the dry bag into the middle of the boat. "Lie down and get some rest."

"Are you joking?" he asks.

"Of course I'm not." Maybe it's a valid question, but it gives me a queasy feeling. Tears burn in my eyes. How could he think I'd joke about this when he's falling asleep sitting up? It would be cruel.

"Get some rest." Please don't let him hear the shake in my voice. "I've got you."

39

I've never actually paddled on my own while the bowperson rested.

It's hard.

Watching the river for logs and rocks from fifteen feet back is almost impossible. I didn't even manage to do it right in the bow last year. My depth perception is off in the dark. Everything is shades of blue and gray and flat. Most of the left side of the river is only lit by the moon. And pulling deadweight without a current is like paddling through molasses. The boat is unwieldy, and the river bends every hundred feet. Which kind of makes it good there's no current. The water's so still the canoe practically comes to a stop when I take a snack break or pee. And when the boat stops, it is so damn tippy.

I keep paddling. I keep us moving. And I resist the urge to wake Cully up and ask him to talk to me. To ask him how he feels about what happened between us. No matter how much I try to keep it out of my head, I keep going back to that kiss, wondering what would have happened if we hadn't been interrupted. Would he have stepped away, or would he have pulled me closer?

I grasp for other things to occupy my mind.

Water pours into the river at the Coletto Creek Confluence. It actually kicks up the current. They must have gotten even more rain down here than I realized. Also, that marks ten more miles to our checkpoint.

The trees are full of cartoon animals. Pigs and monkeys and snakes. A priest stands on the riverbank performing Mass for squirrels. I see elephants and giants. I even see Mr. Snuffleupagus. There's a dock on the side of the river with a hammock stretched between the piers. I could tie the boat to it and lie down while Cully sleeps. But when I get there it disappears, like a mirage.

Everything hurts. There's no other way to say it. My fingers. My feet. My butt. My arms. My back. All of my back. I try shifting left. Shifting right. Holding my elbow higher. Holding it lower. Sucking in my stomach and pooching out my stomach. Nothing helps.

And there's so far to go.

Invista. Portaging the two-mile logjam. The saltwater

barrier. Alligators. Crossing the bay. What if there are three-foot swells?

My eyes fill with tears. I can't keep going. It's too much. This is going to be another DNF. Another year where I have completely failed to do something I've planned for my whole life. Another year of my dad barely being able to look at me.

I put my paddle down, and I rest my elbows on my knees and my head in my gross, wrinkly hands, and I let loose. Huge heaving sobs. Snot drips out of my nose. I gasp for breath.

"Sadie."

It's Dad's voice, buried somewhere deep inside my brain.

I was eight, and I'd smashed my finger with a hammer. I was crying just like this. Whole-body crying, yelling *it hurts, it hurts.* The ice wasn't helping. How long would it last? Was it going to feel like this forever? Would this mess up my dodgeball game in PE the next day?

"Sadie, let me tell you something I learned on the river." Dad has an Odyssey story for every situation. "Every year there comes a point when I hurt so bad I think I can't go on. None of the tricks I use to make it hurt less help. I think of all the miles of river I have ahead of me, and I don't know how I can take one more stroke, let alone the thousands it'll take to get to Seadrift. And every time, I realize that the pain I'm feeling right now is bearable. What makes it unbearable is thinking about all that future pain. Worrying about it makes me hurt worse. Every year I learn this over again, to accept the pain I feel at that moment. I don't worry about the pain ahead. It's what gets me through."

"Yeah, but I don't want to get knocked out in dodgeball tomorrow," I said.

"Forget dodgeball. Think about how your finger feels right now," Dad said.

I did. And it turned out, it was bearable.

Which is not true here. I feel like shit.

But I wipe my nose on my sleeve and I pick up my paddle.

I can survive it, right now, in this moment.

And this one.

And this one.

40

"Cully. Cully, wake up."

The stars have faded. The horizon glows, and there's enough light now that I can see, even though the sun won't be up for another half hour. We've made it through the second night.

"Hmmmhmm . . ."

I pull my bug net and hat out from behind me.

Birds sing in the trees. But they're hard to hear over the steady buzz that fills my ears. The bugs are out. Mosquitoes. They prick at my neck and my hands. There's still not enough light to be sure, but I bet they're feasting on Cully's face.

Two mornings ago, I probably wouldn't have cared. I might have thought it served him right. It's strange how quickly things can change. For the last hour I've been wishing he were up so he could talk to me and make me laugh.

"Wake up!" I pull my bug net down over my hat.

Cully rubs at his face, but he doesn't wake up.

"Cully!" I yell.

Nothing.

I pick up some water with my paddle and fling it at him. A dark spot spreads on his shirt, but he stays fast asleep. Should I let him sleep? No. He can't wake up with a million bites on his face.

I take my paddle by the handle and scoot forward in my seat, reaching with the blade. But the boat's too long. I put a hand on the cross brace in front of me and take my butt off the seat. My paddle just brushes the ends of his hair. I lean farther.

A geyser of water explodes out of the river right next to me.

"Ahhhh!" I jerk away. Water pummels me.

The boat rocks. Cully's body rolls with it. I reach to the right, trying steady us, but it's too late. We roll to the side. I grip my paddle and plunge under the water. Cool water fills my clothes, my hair, my mosquito net. I kick to the surface and tread water. Streams of water pour off my head and down my face. When I open my mouth to take a breath, I inhale water from my mosquito net.

"What the hell just happened?" Cully yells as I pull my mosquito net up and take a breath.

He's a couple of feet away, his hand on the hull of the canoe. It's right side up but riding low. Full of water. He grabs his paddle, which is floating a few feet away.

Something huge slides against my leg. I kick away. A second later, silver scales surface and roll.

Cully kicks a few feet back. "What was that?"

"Alligator gar," I explain. "I was trying to wake you up, and—"

"You didn't have to dump me in the river!" A dragonfly lands on his head, and my entire chest goes squishy because it is unbearably cute.

"No," I say, but I can't help smiling and laughing.

"It's not funny."

"Let's just flip the canoe over and I'll explain," I say.

We swim the canoe toward the shore, until we can touch bottom. I fill Cully in while we dump out the water and climb back into our seats.

I wipe my face with my hand to get off any mosquitoes and pull down my bug net. "You should put on some bug spray," I say. "That's why I was trying to wake you. They were eating your face."

I start paddling, and he joins after he does sunscreen and bug spray and has something to eat.

"I thought maybe you got tired of me sleeping."

I laugh again. "No."

"Do you want a nap?" he asks.

"I'm awake now."

He laughs. "Me too."

And for the first time in six years, things feel right. It's like having Cully back. The old Cully. The one who owned half my heart as far back as I can remember. It makes me so ridiculously happy. But this Cully is almost six feet tall, and I can only name a handful of the things he's done in the last six years. There's something so sad and wrong about that.

Cully cracks a joke that makes me laugh, and some of that sadness disappears. We're still smiling, still making each other laugh, when we pull into the checkpoint at Invista twenty minutes later.

It was always a relief when Dad came through here at night, while I was at my grandparents' house. On the years he arrived during the day, we fought back black clouds of mosquitoes.

Erica and Gonzo wait at the bottom of a steep bank.

"How are you holding up?" Erica asks when we come to a stop.

"Hot. Sore. Tired," I answer. "But good."

Cully slides out of the boat, into the water. And really, I might as well join him. So I slide out, too, and the water is cool. It takes my weight, and I don't hurt so much. Maybe Cully is onto something with this. Maybe I should have been getting out of the boat with him yesterday. Maybe I would have felt better if I had.

"Your dad says to take the Haymaker cut," Erica says.

"What are you talking about?" It doesn't make sense, and not just because Dad has only bothered to come to one water stop. At orientation, they specifically told us to portage the logjam. That there wasn't enough water in the cut.

"I don't really know what it means. He just said, 'Tell Sadie to take Haymaker cut to Alligator Lake.'" Erica's face drips with skepticism. And sweat. "Sadie," she says, "what's up with these names? Neither of those sound like places you should be going."

"They're exaggerations," I say, because nobody has gotten seriously injured in either place. I think.

I stare downriver, like I might be able to see all the narrow channels that branch off river right—collectively called the cut. To see how much water is in them. To see if Alligator Lake is more than a mud patch.

If it's possible, if one of the channels really has enough water in it, we can save so much time. So much effort.

"When did you talk to him?" I ask, turning back to Erica.

"He showed up about an hour ago."

This little happy feeling blooms inside me. Not just happy. Hopeful. Maybe things are going to be okay between us.

Because Dad's been watching, and he wants to help.

41

The portage is two miles of ranch land, climbing over fences and getting eaten by mosquitoes and stepping in cow patties. And it's the last thing I want to do.

"I thought the water was too low for the cut," Cully says.

When the water is too low, the channels of the cut are mud and silt. And alligators.

"Must have been the rain," I say.

"That's fast."

"It's had a day to pour into the river. And I think they got more down here than we did. We passed some creeks that were really flowing last night."

"But why would your dad tell us? I thought he was mad that we were doing this together."

"I did, too."

"Do you think he's messing with us? That it's a trick?"

Sending us down Haymaker when it's not passable—it would be cruel. Even though Dad is upset I got in the boat with Cully, even if he is furious, he isn't heartless.

This is something else.

"No," I say. "I think it's a gift." A gift, and maybe an apology.

"Then I guess we should take it."

"Guess so," I agree.

We paddle on for over an hour, and I eat two breakfast tacos and some salty nuts. The right bank is all scrubby brush.

"We're on the lookout for a series of channels on the right," I tell Cully. It would be so easy to miss our turn, and we probably wouldn't even realize it until we hit the logjam.

"Have you ever done this before?" Cully asks.

"Once. With Dad." I don't tell him that we took the second channel that time, Early Bird cut, that it was two years ago, and that the river has changed since then. The river is always changing.

Haymaker is the third channel.

I think it's the third.

"Well, look who it is, defying the odds."

I glance over my left shoulder. The Sirens are coming up even with us. The sea-green shirts they started with are light brown.

"We weren't sure you two would make it this far without strangling each other," Lisa says.

They pull up even with us.

"Not me. I put my money on the two of you being hot and heavy by Cuero," Carrie says.

That kiss bursts into my mind and I swallow hard. My cheeks burn. I hope she thinks it's just the heat.

Cully stays silent, too. At least he doesn't laugh. At least he doesn't say that's the last thing he wants right now.

"Ready for the logjam?" Melissa asks. Thank god for Melissa.

"We're taking Haymaker," I blurt, so happy for a subject change.

"The cut's not supposed to be open," Melissa says. "That's what they told us at orientation."

"It's a fool's errand," says Carrie. "You'll end up turning around and portaging. Waste of energy."

"My dad said we could make it."

Melissa looks at me from the middle of the boat. "Will said you should take it?"

"Yeah," I say.

"It would be a hell of a lot better than portaging," she mutters.

The Sirens spend a good ten minutes debating, until we see the first opening in the scrubby bushes river right. And the second. And the third.

"This is it," Lisa says. "What's the verdict?"

"We trust Will," Cully says, and he draws us to the right as I adjust the rudder pedal.

"I'm in," Melissa says.

Carrie shakes her head. "No. Bad idea."

Lisa draws right, too. "Overruled."

Siren mutiny.

8:18 A.M. MONDAY

"I told you this was stupid," Carrie says as we all portage over another fallen tree blocking the waterway.

But I still think Dad must have known what he was talking about.

"We should turn back," she says when we portage the third fallen tree about a hundred feet later.

Cully holds my eyes for a moment as I feed the boat down the log to him. "We'll be okay either way," he whispers.

Which is kind. But I wish he didn't doubt Dad. Not when there's a snout and a pair of eyes just above the surface of the water ten feet away.

The first rule of paddling with gators is to give them plenty of space. And we do. The gator stays there. It doesn't move.

"It's still passable," Melissa says when we see the fourth log we need to climb over.

But it doesn't shut Carrie up.

"I knew this was a bad idea," she says. "Everyone knows Will is pissed at the girl."

Her words are like paddling right into a wall. Falling out of the boat onto a rock. As if I weren't worn down and beat up enough already.

Am I an idiot for thinking that he wants to help me?

"Shut up, Carrie," Melissa hisses. "He's her dad."

Cully slaps the water with his paddle. "Carrie's right," he says. "This was a bad idea."

My paddle stops. My mouth falls open. I can't believe he's backing Carrie up when we decided this together.

"You should turn around. Do the portage." Cully's voice is an ax.

He picks his paddle back up and digs into the water, still going forward, and I understand now. This was a bad idea for them. Not us.

I'm so grateful for him sticking up for me. For not letting me feel like the chump that Carrie thinks I am. If I could, I would leap across the boat right now and hug him and not let go.

We leave the sounds of the Sirens fighting behind and move even faster, and when we get to the other side of the fourth log, I don't get back in the boat.

That hollow spot in my chest hurts for all the years we lost together. It aches to be close to him. And I don't care if there's no room for these feelings in the race, because if

I'm being really honest, I want to kiss him again.

I pick my way through the shallow muck toward Cully and I hug him.

"Thank you for that," I mumble into his shoulder.

His arms fold around me. "He wouldn't do that to you."

I breathe him in. It's mud and river water and bug spray and body odor, and I take another breath.

"I missed you, too," I whisper. It was like I lost a piece of myself.

He presses his forehead into mine.

"Good," he whispers.

I close my eyes. We exhale at the same time.

There's this longing inside me, because even though we're so close, I want more.

He brushes his fingers across my cheek. They're wet and they're wrinkled, and my entire body goes electric because it's the kind of touch that means something. Something more than friendship.

I lean my cheek into his hand before I raise my chin. My nose brushes the side of his. My lips drift open and my eyes close.

A splash comes from up ahead. Alligator.

We break apart and look downstream. But we don't see an alligator. It's a boat. A four-person coming toward us from the direction we're heading.

"Couldn't make it through Alligator Lake," the bowman

tells us as he climbs out to portage the log. "It turns to muck up there."

Cully looks at me for a long moment. I study his face, hoping to see some disappointment there, but I can't read him.

"What do you think?" he finally asks.

We watch them lift their boat over the log and climb over. They couldn't make it through. But we're only two people. Less weight. More agile. I have to believe Dad told me this because he knew we could do it.

"I want to keep going," I say.

So we do.

We paddle the rest of the channel until we reach the wide expanse of Alligator Lake. When there's not enough water, it's a muddy field. But when there's enough water in it, it's a lake. A lake of shallow, slow water. Full of alligators. More than one pair of eyes follows us from just above the surface. My paddle scrapes mud on the bottom, and I stop digging as deep.

"Are you catching mud, too?" I ask.

"Sometimes," he says.

We're halfway across when I feel the scrape vibrate through the boat. We slow to a stop. Must be a log under the surface. I really don't want to get back out.

"Pull hard."

"Gotcha."

I match his stroke and pull with my whole body.

The head surfaces a few feet ahead of me. The boat tilts left.

Shit. Shitshitshitshitshitshitshitshitshit. We can't go over. Alligators don't bother you if you don't bother them. But paddling on top of them is beyond intrusive. My heart thuds in my ears and it's beating a million miles an hour and the fear is taking over my body.

Don't panic. Fix it.

I take a big, deep breath.

"Stabilize on the left!" I say. Cully puts his paddle flat on the water to keep us from going over, and I pull as hard as I can. The alligator rises higher. The boat tilts farther.

I jab my paddle down on the right and push against the mud as I pull us forward.

"Now paddle!" Cully takes a stroke.

We budge.

"Harder!"

My arms, my legs, my back, my hands all scream in protest, but I pull. And I pull again. We scrape forward. The boat levels. We move forward as the alligator swims away.

My heart is still a jackrabbit when we reach the channel that dumps us back into the river. Every inch of my skin tingles. That is the most insane thing I've ever done, but we made it.

Dad must have known that in a tandem, we'd be just light enough to get through.

And I feel a little bit taller, because he didn't just know we could get through. He trusted that whatever we ran into, we'd be able to handle it.

Is it wrong that I'm glad that Cully's not going to RISD next year? Wrong that I'm hoping he'll stay here and go to Texas State? Wrong that I don't want this thing between us to just live on the river? That I want it to follow us back home?

Is it wrong that I keep wondering what he looks like with his shirt off? Am I objectifying him?

Would he mind?

These questions roll through my head on the way to the Salt Water Barrier. Mile 249. But they all wash away when Allie is onshore, her arms folded across her chest, her boobs resting on them like they're a shelf. She's wearing a minidress. An actual minidress. And it's covered in cherries.

CHERRIES.

Something boils up inside me. What the hell kind of person does this?

She was lucky to be with Cully. She's an idiot for throwing that away. Especially for Tanner.

"Nobody wants you here!" I yell.

I put my hands on the gunnels and lift myself up, but my arms fail. Allie's eyes turn into ping-pong balls. "Nobody likes seeing you play dress-up on the side of the river!" I lift myself up again and swing my legs into the water. I stand up, stumble, and catch myself.

"If you want to be here, be like that lady!" I point to the costume woman, who's in a white wig, a crown, and a powder-blue skirt suit, with a handbag crooked in an elbow. "That lifts people's spirits."

Her Royal Majesty forces a smile and waves the little British flag in her hand.

"Hold up, Sadie," Erica says, putting her body between Allie and me. "She was just here to see your brother and her car got stuck in the mud. She's waiting for someone to push it out."

"Someone could have helped her ages ago," I say, because Tanner should be long gone. Hours gone. "She's trying to mess with us!"

I look at Cully for confirmation, but he's not looking at Allie. He's looking at me with this half smile like I just burped the alphabet or something.

"Your dad warned Allie off when he found out what she

and Tanner were doing," Erica says. "And your brother left about five minutes ago."

"Wait, what?" I snap my eyes away from Cully.

"Coop Bynum got whacked in the head with a branch," says Gonzo. "Probably has a concussion. It was kind of a mess. Slowed them down. He's out of the race. And then you passed a million boats when you took the cut. You're in seventh place." Gonzo turns to Cully. "Your dad's not too far ahead, either."

"What?" we both ask this time.

I turn back to Cully, and the goofy grin has slid right off his face. I did my best to give up the hard-charging, get-to-the-finish attitude when Cully threatened to quit. I thought I was giving up making the top five. But we're so close. Sixteen miles left. Ten more river miles and then six more across the bay. We could beat them both and make top five. It would be the sweetest victory.

"There's a whole mess of boats behind you, so if you want this, you better move," Erica says.

My eyes meet Cully's and I cock an eyebrow at him.

All I can see are his brown eyes across the canoe when he says, "Let's do it."

We paddle hard. Fast. Like when the gun went off. We pull at the brackish water below the Salt Water Barrier.

Sweat drips down the sides of my face and rolls down my back.

The river is mostly straight, with big, gradual turns, and we are flying. Past all the low, scrubby bushes. Past people's houses.

Once, we catch sight of Tanner and Hank in their bright shirts up ahead, but they disappear around a bend.

"I don't—need you—to do that—for me—anymore." Cully's words come in a rhythm punctuated with his strokes.

"Do what?" I ask.

"Step in. Defend me," he answers.

"What?"

"What you did—with Allie," he says. He must have been ruminating on this the whole time. "I don't need it." He takes a few strokes without speaking. "I had—to figure it out. Without you."

"Okay." My stomach sinks. "I'm sorry." My words come between quick breaths.

"No. It's okay. It was funny," he says. "I just don't need it."

I guess it's his call, ignoring Allie. Maybe it's better.

We keep going. We keep up our pace. We put miles behind us.

I hated it all those years, watching Johnny put Cully down. It ate at me.

I was eleven and he was twelve. It was late May, already boiling hot outside, and we'd spent the morning working on the tree house. Cully's mom had a new half gallon of vanilla ice cream in the freezer. We each ate two scoops for lunch before getting back to work. Around dinnertime we stopped by Cully's. Johnny was just home from a training run with Dad. He stood in their kitchen with flames coming out of his ears. The ice cream carton sat in a creamy white puddle.

It had spent half a day on the counter.

Johnny acted like I wasn't there. He backed Cully into the corner by the sink, red faced and shaking. And the yelling—he yelled at Cully like he was a grown man instead of a boy.

I was hot, sweaty, thirsty. But mostly I was done. I was so done with all of it.

I slapped at Johnny's arm. "Leave him alone!" I yelled. "It was an accident!"

Johnny's eyes didn't leave Cully, but his hand reached out, rough on my arm, and pushed me away.

"Everything you eat for the next week is going to be covered in melted ice cream," Johnny shouted.

I don't know if he really would have done it. I just knew it had to end.

I grabbed the carton and climbed onto the counter behind Johnny, shoes and all. Ice cream soup sloshed around the container. Condensation dripped down my hands as I lifted it high and tipped it over Johnny's head. Cully's eyes went wide as saucers. Ice cream poured over Johnny's hair and splashed on the counter and his shoulders and Cully. A still-frozen blob paused on his head before it slid down the side of his face.

Cully's jaw hung open and a stream of ice cream ran down his nose and into his mouth.

My feet hit the floor with a thud. "Ruuuuun!"

Cully slipped in the puddle, but his dad didn't try to stop him. Didn't move. We bolted out the door and didn't stop until we got to my house, panting and hot. We fell on the living room floor and just lay there until Mom came home. We didn't tell. But Cully didn't go home that night.

He was a near-permanent fixture at my house until our dads raced together a week later.

"Did he hit you when we were kids?" I ask now, because I never asked back then.

"He spanked me. When I was little," Cully says. "But not like you're thinking of. Not with a fist. He drew a line there. His dad hit him."

"I'm sorry," I say.

"For what?" Cully asks. "For my dad?"

His pace doesn't lag. His words come short and hard between strokes.

"I should have held on," I say. "I should have never left you alone with them. You could have lived at my house."

God, what would have happened if I'd never let go?

Would we still be best friends? Would he be my boyfriend? Would I have felt so desperate to finish the race if I'd still had Cully? Or would our dads have poisoned our relationship in little ways?

"I've missed you. I told you, I missed you every day." He's quiet for a couple of quick strokes. "But it got easier at home, after you were gone. He's—he's never going to be the dad I wanted. He'll never be like your dad. Or Gonzo's. I ate dinner at Gonzo's just about every night of seventh grade. But when I got to private school, I figured out I was good at soccer. Sports helped. I learned how to tuck my chin and take it. I realized it wasn't actually about me. Maybe I wouldn't have gotten there with you around to pour ice cream on his head when he got mad at me."

"I would have done that a million times for you," I say.

"I know. I loved you, too."

43

We're pulling so hard. So fast.

I hurt. Every stroke hurts. And with every stroke I hear the words *I loved you, too.*

Loved.

Not love.

It's almost eleven fifteen when we pass beneath the Wooden Bridge. It's the last public access. Last place we'll see our bank crew. Last chance to put on our spray skirt before we hit the bay.

Erica and Gonzo are waiting at the boat ramp just downriver. A longboat is pulled out on the grass.

I hop out of the canoe and bob underwater. The water's not much cooler than the air, but it still feels good on my face and my scalp. I pull my hat back on when I surface. "We have to dump all the extra weight for the bay crossing."

Erica hands me an empanada, and I shove half in my mouth with wet fingers and start chewing. She takes my trash and water bottle. My mosquito net, bug spray, Desitin, and sunscreen go next.

"Take the lights and the batteries," Cully tells Gonzo.

I unscrew the end cap on the stern. My fingers wrap around nylon, and I pull out the bright blue spray skirt like a magician pulling scarves out of her sleeve. I find the stern end and lay it across my seat and spread the rest up toward the bow. It's like a waterproof tent that lies flat over the top of the boat to keep the waves out of our canoe in the bay. There are openings where Cully and I sit.

Gonzo leans in next to Cully. "Dude, that's your dad over there." His voice is low.

My head whips from the boat to the shore. Sure enough, Johnny Hink kneels next to his three-man boat, making repairs.

"No way," I say, my mouth still half-full.

"A tree fell on their boat." Erica hands me a new water jug. "They've had to keep making repairs. It's cost them hours."

What are the chances we'll get out of here without him noticing us? I would pay money to see Johnny Hink's face at the finish if we beat him.

"Be fast," I whisper to Cully.

He nods.

New water goes in the foam holders. Erica gives me a bag with a few snacks, just to be safe. I duck underwater and come up on the river side of the boat, then slide on my life vest and zip it up. On the spray skirt I find the snap with the black arrow drawn above it, and pop it into the marked snap on the boat. And I keep snapping. So many damn snaps on this thing. Cully does the fastening on the shore side of the boat.

"Just fasten the middle. Leave the bow and the stern open for us to get in," I remind him.

Erica and Gonzo watch in the water. They're not allowed to help.

By the time I'm finished, my fingertips bleed. I jump into my seat, but Cully is still snapping behind the bow seat.

"John Cullen."

Cully keeps a hand on the boat as he turns. Johnny Hink stands ankle-deep in the river, mud splattered across his white racing tights and his orange shirt.

"I'm proud of you, son," Johnny says.

Cully's head jerks back an inch. My head jerks back an inch. Erica's and Gonzo's heads jerk back an inch. This has to be the first time those words have crossed his lips. Ever.

"You've done well. Better than I expected." Johnny's voice projects, like he knows everyone onshore is listening. "I think you've earned that tuition. I think you've earned Rhode Island."

Did he take a blow to the head?

Cully's forehead wrinkles. "You mean that?"

"I do." Johnny lifts his chin. "Come talk to me for a minute."

Cully's eyes meet mine before he lets go of the boat, and I bite my tongue to keep from saying that my brother is putting miles between us. Cully stumbles the first step up the boat ramp, but he recovers. He walks to his father. They both stand with hips slung forward, shoulders rounded. It's the Odyssey posture—what fifty hours in a canoe do to you.

Johnny brings a hand to Cully's shoulder.

"You've run a good race," Johnny says. He tips his head toward the shore. "Your mom's over there. Why don't you take a load off? Let her drive you to the finish. I'll see you there."

Oh.

Oh no.

"Wait," Cully says. "You want me to stop?"

A hush falls over the shore.

I press my lips together and squeeze the gunnels with my hands.

"Look," Johnny says. "You've already set out to do what you wanted to do. You've proved yourself. You've been on the water for, I don't know, fifty hours. You've come two hundred and fifty miles. It's quite a feat. More than most boys can do. There's a rough bay up ahead. Let's just go ahead and call it."

Johnny's hand moves to Cully's arm, like he's ready to pull his son the rest of the way up the boat ramp.

Cully's head turns. His eyes meet mine. I can't fight it. I don't want to. How could I begrudge him this? Without him, I wouldn't even have started the race this year. And anyway, he deserves to go to that school. If quitting now will make amends for throwing away a friendship so good, so pure, I'll do it.

I'd do it a million times for Cully.

"Go." I slide out of the boat so there's no confusion. "Take it."

His eyes squeeze tight. His chest expands and contracts. When he opens his eyes again, I know he's going to take it. It's the whole reason he started this.

He turns back to his dad. They're the exact same height.

Cully straightens an inch.

"No." His answer comes down like a hammer.

What?

Johnny's fingers tighten on Cully's arm. "Think hard about this, John Cullen."

Cully jerks out of Johnny's grip.

No one moves onshore. Everyone is watching. The rest of Johnny's boat. Race officials. Other bank crews. My dad.

My dad.

My dad is here.

"You set me an impossible task." Cully's words are loud. Forceful. "And when it turns out I can do it, that I might even beat you, you can't handle it. You try to make me quit. Is that what you call being a man?"

Cully walks to the river. Through the water. I scramble into the boat.

"If you get back in that boat, it's off," Johnny calls. "Rhode Island. Texas State. I'm not paying for any of it."

"I don't want it," Cully yells. "Not on your terms."

The boat rocks when Cully climbs in. It makes waves big enough to reach the opposite shore.

To reach Seadrift.

To reach home.

The breeze ruffles the spray skirt in the front and back where we didn't finish snapping it. We've rounded a bend and the boat ramp is well out of sight when Cully puts his paddle down. His head bows. He cradles his face in his hands. I can just see the tips of his thumbs below his ears. His shoulders shake.

"Cully!" God, this stupid boat, this stupid river between us when all I want to do is be up there with him.

"Cully." I tuck my paddle under my seat and put my hands on the gunnels. I'm about to slide into the water and swim to him when something crashes through the woods onshore.

Right. We're in alligator country.

The noise comes closer, and I realize it's not an alligator.

"You're strong!" someone shouts from shore.

Cully's head lifts.

"Stronger than you think!"

I catch a glimpse of him through the bushes. That gray plaid shirt. That orange hat.

There's a catch in my chest.

He's here. He followed us.

"You're almost there!" Dad yells. "Just take the next stroke."

Cully wipes his nose across his sleeve. He picks up his paddle. I take mine, buoyed up by Dad's words.

"Just take the next stroke."

Cully digs his paddle into the water. As I do the same, the first tear spills onto my cheek because I am so ridiculously grateful that he followed us. That we're not alone.

"And the next one," Dad calls. "You're almost there. Just take the next stroke."

We're moving now. He runs along the shore, dodging trees.

I sniff up a runny nose. Cully does, too.

"Paddle through the pain.

"You're almost there.

"Just take the next stroke."

Cully laughs. "Only your dad would do this."

I laugh a little, too, and say, "Isn't it great?"

This is the dad I've been missing for the last year. The one who jumps a chain-link fence and runs through someone's backyard to show us he believes in us.

"You're almost there," Dad calls.

"You're so strong."

He runs with us, down the river, toward the bay, until he reaches a concrete wall around someone's yard.

"You're almost there."

His words carry us the last two miles to the bay.

12:01 P.M. MONDAY

Dad told me once that the six miles you paddle across the bay are just as hard as the two hundred sixty you paddle to get there. I wouldn't know. I've never crossed the bay. Not until now.

But I know how it works.

The trees end. It's all marshland and tall grass. We're almost to the end of the river. The wind lifts my hat and I tuck it inside the spray skirt. Whitecaps cover the bay.

"Time to suit up," I say.

"What?"

"You need to finish the snaps on the spray skirt and put on your life jacket."

"Right," he says, like he's just realized where we are.

I keep paddling while he finishes his bay prep and cinches the spray skirt around his chest, then I cinch mine.

As soon as we pull into the bay, water crashes into the side of the boat.

"We're going to pull as hard as we can till we get to Seadrift, okay?" I tell Cully.

We'll enter the bay and paddle out about fifty yards, then hook a right. We'll follow the shore to Foster Point. Distance-wise, it's longer than paddling straight for Seadrift, but staying close to shore provides shelter and makes our bay time shorter. Paddling straight out into the bay could mean hours of extra paddling.

From Foster Point we'll turn left and cross into the rough waters of the bay, where the wind will toss us around like a leaf. We'll paddle to the other side, to the spoil island that borders the barge channel. Once we reach the spoil island, we'll turn right, cross the narrow barge channel, and follow the shoreline to Seadrift.

While we do this, we'll do our best not to get hit by any fishing boats or barges.

There's a boat in the distance. Highlighter-yellow shirts. Tanner and Hank.

Voices come from behind us. I check over my shoulder.

"It's your dad. He's catching up to us," I tell Cully. He doesn't have to say how much he wants to beat his dad. It radiates off him. And I want it as much as he does.

If we can just pass Tanner and Hank, we'll be in the top five. We'll have beat them both. It's better than I could dream of.

"Does he have his spray skirt on?" Cully asks.

I glance again and see the bright blue. Damn, they're fast. "Yeah," I answer.

We have the advantage here. It's harder for the longer boats on the bay. They don't navigate the swells as well. They tip more easily. More likely to swamp. But they also have more arms. More paddles pulling in the water.

The wind whips at the hair that's fallen out of my braids and flattens the tall grasses on the shore to our right. It pushes against us, like it doesn't want us here. My arms, my shoulders, everything in me wants to lie down and rest. Everything in me is spent, and the water is getting rougher. I dig in and I pull. Over and over again. Sometimes I only catch air, but I keep pulling.

Stay ahead of Johnny.

Catch Tanner and Hank.

"I don't think we're moving!" Cully yells over the wind.

He's right. Foster Point isn't any closer.

But everything onshore looks smaller. "The wind is blowing us off course!" I shout. It's blowing us into the middle of the channel. Into the rough water.

But it's too late to try to correct. Forget the shelter of Foster Point. We're doing this the hard way, heading diagonal, straight for the tip of the spoil island.

12:46 P.M. MONDAY

The constant up and down, back and forth, nauseates me. Plowing perpendicular into a wave doesn't work. The water breaks over the canoe, pooling in the spray skirt and possibly seeping into the bottom of the boat. Taking them parallel doesn't work, either. It's a good way to tip over. The waves roll in from the same direction, and I adjust the rudder, aiming to send us over them at an angle. Cully powers us forward, and I spend half my strokes with my paddle flat on the water, bracing us. We push forward. The waves rock us back and forth, and time drags by like molasses.

Then a big one comes. The world goes sideways and I slap the water with my paddle, but it's too late. We crash into the bay.

I have to get out of the spray skirt quick. I pull and kick my way out. My feet only find water. It's too deep to stand. The boat floats upside down, on top of the water. I throw my arms onto the canoe before it can blow away and scramble up the hull to lay my chest across the top.

The boat and I bob up over a big wave.

Cully's head breaks the surface.

"You okay?" I ask.

"Okay," he answers.

"We can't flip the boat here. We need feet on the sand."

Cully looks to the opposite side of the bay. The side we

were headed for. It's a dot on the horizon. No question we need to backtrack.

I push my way to the front of the boat and grab one side of the bow. Cully grabs the other. Waves slap me in the face and the taste of salt water fills my mouth. Water shoots up my nose and burns my sinuses and every broken blister on my hands stings as we kick our way to shore.

We're twenty feet out when the water gets lighter. My feet touch sand. I stumble, but I find my balance. I stand a foot away from Cully, who sways with the water.

His eyes are already scanning the bay. I follow his gaze and find what I knew I'd see. Johnny Hink is out there. Ahead of us.

Cully's eyes meet mine. They're dripping in defeat. I want to go to him. For us to collapse into each other. To curl into a ball together onshore and sleep until tomorrow.

"Ready?" he asks.

Maybe he's not defeated. Maybe he still wants to catch his dad. I'd love to see Johnny outraced by the son he never loved properly and the girl who dumped ice cream on his head. It's not going to happen. We can't beat him in the race, but I think I'm okay with it, because really, we beat him at something more important.

"Come on," Cully says, and I shuffle through the water to the stern and wrap my fingers around the gunnels.

We lift, and I grunt because I swear the boat weighs

eighteen tons. Water pours out of the holes in the spray skirt, and I grab the other gunnel with one hand and we flip the canoe.

I peer inside the spray skirt and find my water bottles rolling loose inside. I reach in and grab one, find the mouthpiece and pop it in my mouth. I bite down and take a pull.

Salt water.

I spit it into the pale brown water around me.

I take a pull of water from the other and swallow.

"Check your bottles," I say. "One of mine has been compromised."

1:25 P.M. MONDAY

I can't see Johnny when we set out again.

We push forward and it feels like a hundred hours of being slapped around by the waves.

But the spoil island grows bigger on the horizon.

Slowly.

Slowly.

Slowly.

We're even with the end of it, angling toward the shore.

We keep pulling.

We're to the tip.

We're ready to make the turn.

That's when I see them. Two guys stand in the shallow water next to the island, their boat on its side. They wear highlighter-yellow shirts.

They don't see us.

There's a freaking hummingbird in my chest.

I can see my brother's face all those years ago. *Face it, Sadie, you just can't keep up.* I see him in the kitchen, avoiding my eyes. I see him at Spring Lake, trying to get me to go home.

Then I remember the whistle on my life jacket. I raise it to my lips and blow.

For a moment, the shrill sound drowns out the waves and the wind and everything else.

"You okay back there?" Cully asks.

My brother's face lifts away from his canoe. His jaw falls. If I could, I'd take a picture and frame it.

We're going to beat him. We're going to reach the finish before my brother and Hank.

We paddle for another ten minutes, drawing closer to the finish line.

Something huge and black zips across the water. It hits the side of our boat with a thud. The wind pins it to us.

Cully's paddle bangs against it. "What the—?"

My stomach sinks.

It's a canoe. A three-person shell with a spiderweb of duct

tape and fresh patches across the hull. The partially snapped spray skirt whips in the wind.

It's empty.

I brace on my left with my paddle in one hand and grab a loose bit of the bright blue spray skirt. White vinyl stickers on the side spell out the words NEVER SAY DIE.

That's right. Erica and Gonzo said his boat got damaged. No.

I hit the water with my paddle.

"Damnit!" I yell.

"What?" Cully's voice barely carries over the wind.

"It's your dad's boat!"

"What?"

"Your dad!" I repeat. "He's out there!"

"He'll swim to shore," Cully says, taking the next stroke toward the finish. Toward beating both his dad and Tanner.

I see them now. Three dots in the water. Cully's right. They could swim to shore. They might even walk to shore. Huge parts of the bay are shallow enough to walk.

If the race officials don't think it's life-threatening, we could be disqualified just for taking them their boat. I could still not get my finish.

But it's been over fifty hours. They're in the middle of the bay with no water, no phone, no spot tracker, no flares. And even with binoculars, nobody's going to spot them from shore.

Damnit.

"We have to," I yell to Cully. Because even if it means we're DQ'd, even if it means I don't get my patch, I'm not gambling with anyone's life. Even Johnny's. "It might be an hour before we can tell anyone. They'll drift."

I can still see Johnny back at the last stop dangling everything Cully wants in front of him to make him quit. To keep his son from beating him.

I get why Cully wants to keep going. He's probably right. They'll probably be fine. But what if they're not?

"Cully," I say, "you're the better man."

He uses his paddle to swing at the next wave like a baseball bat. "No!" he yells.

But he draws the boat to the right.

I adjust the rudder pedal, and as he paddles, I use the stern rope to tie Johnny's boat to ours.

Waves crash over the bow and I cinch the spray skirt tighter around my chest. Without it, we'd swamp in about thirty seconds. As it is, the pump is working overtime to empty the boat. We're rocked back and forth, side to side. Johnny's canoe gets tossed by the waves and blown in the wind. It slows us down like we're dragging a parachute. We pull as hard as we can and we move slowly. So slow it doesn't feel like we're moving.

Everything hurts. My stomach has gone sour again. I pull a small sip from my water tube, but I can't stand the sweet grapefruit flavor anymore. My stomach clenches and rolls, and everything comes back up. I vomit onto the spray skirt and the side of the boat, but I don't bother to wipe my mouth. Just spit until the taste of the salt water spraying on my face takes over.

3:05 P.M. MONDAY

A whistle cuts through the air and someone raises a paddle. They see us. Two of them swim our way, pulling a third, floating on his back.

"John Cullen?" Johnny says when we get close. Ted Stern nods at me.

"What's wrong with Walt?" Cully asks.

"Muscle cramps," Ted says.

Walt grunts.

"What do you need?" I ask.

The boat rocks and Johnny puts a hand toward our gunnel.

"Don't touch this boat!" I yell, ready to beat his hand away with my paddle. We might still be in the race. I'm not getting disqualified for anything unnecessary.

"Just give us our boat back," Johnny says. "We'll get to the finish on our own."

I untie the boat and make sure it gets in Johnny's and Ted's hands. "Don't let go this time," I say before we paddle away.

I don't know why I thought they might say thank you.

We turn the boat toward shore and pull. An hour passes. Or maybe fifteen minutes. I'm too scared to look away from the waves long enough to check the time. We fight the wind and waves and we paddle until we see the pavilion onshore, the stairs, and the wooden awning where we'll take pictures. My watch reads 3:51 p.m. when we pass the buoy in the water that marks the actual finish line. Tears spring into my eyes.

Erica and Gonzo are there. Mazer. Mrs. Gonzales.

And Dad.

We made it.

"Tip right?" I ask Cully.

"Yeah."

Deep breath. We both lean to the right, knocking our canoe over on purpose for once. I slide out of my spray skirt and go under, letting the water hold me for a moment. There's no paddle in my hands, no sharp pain in my shoulder, no next stroke to take. I made it all 265 miles, and I am so completely satisfied.

When I surface, Cully is already there. A warm happiness spreads through my chest. I pull him to me, close my eyes, and shut out everything but Cully. His arms go around me. My temple presses into the rough stubble on his cheek.

"You smell terrible," I whisper.

"So do you."

I pull him tighter. "I couldn't have done this without you."

"Me neither," he says.

46

There's a hand on my back. A third hand.

I break away from Cully. Dad stands waist-deep in the bay. His blue eyes meet mine.

There are so many things to say. But I'm so damn tired.

He puts a hand on the boat and nods toward the stairs. A silent *go on up.*

Two tall blue poles rise out of the grass onshore. The white board that spans the tops has the words TEXAS RIVER ODYSSEY in red letters.

I've dreamed of walking under that finish line my entire life.

Walking away from my boat, I feel like I've forgotten something. But I grip my paddle tight in one hand. Waves slap me around, but as I climb the stairs, the rail in my other hand is so steady it's unreal.

My feet find dry ground. My body still sways. I survey the finish. A couple dozen spectators and volunteers in lawn chairs under the pavilion and on the grass. A handful of racers napping or eating. A line of five boats on the lawn. A longer line of port-a-pots up by the road.

Dad and Ginny pull our boat out of the water and lay it across the grass in front of the finish line.

"Fifty-four hours, fifty-one minutes," a race official tells us. "That puts you in sixth place. Second in class."

One boat away from our goal.

But it turns out, I don't care what our time is or who we beat. I just care that I'm here, with my arm pressed against Cully's.

Erica unclips Mazer from his leash and he runs at me. I bend down and give him a good scratch before he moves on to Cully, who gives Gonzo one of those back-pat hugs.

"I'm gross," I warn Erica, but she hugs me anyway.

"Thank you so much," I whisper.

"I did it because it's hard," she says.

"You're fucking invincible," I tell her.

"So are you."

Gonzo hugs me next. He's put his pompadour back together, but he's still in athletic shorts and a river-stained shirt. I understand for the first time that I've had the privilege of seeing Gonzo with his guard down, not the polished-up version he presents to everyone else, and for some reason, it gets me all choked up.

"I'll never be able to thank you enough," I tell him.

"Just promise you'll never take a boat out during a lightning storm again," he tells me.

I laugh. "Promise."

We let go of each other, but he keeps a hand on my arm.

"Maybe you had a point about *Cool Runnings*," I say.

"I know." He lets his hand fall. "But so did you."

Mrs. Gonzales hugs Cully, then cups his face in her hands and tilts his chin down so their eyes meet. "I am so proud of you."

Leslie Hink stands beside the pavilion, watching another woman be mother to her son.

Cully and Mrs. Gonzales stay like that a moment, before she turns to me. "Sadie. You are so strong." She pulls me into a quick hug.

Dad is only a few feet away, hands in his pockets. Someone's missing.

I look more closely at the people in the chairs. Coop, Randy, and Hank are eating burgers. Coop's eyes and nose are bruised purple and scabby. But my brother isn't with them.

I turn to Dad. "Where are Mom and Tanner?"

"At the hospital. Your mom thought Tanner needed stitches," Dad says. "He stepped on a stingray."

"Did you tell them to put a butterfly bandage on it?" I ask.

It takes Dad a second to remember before his chin wrinkles, holding back his laugh.

"I told them I had to be here for your finish." He holds out a hand to Erica, who puts his phone in it. He must have handed it to her before he got in the bay. "Someone has to take the pictures," he says.

His words hit me in the chest. My dad chose to be here. For me.

"Go ahead," he says, pulling his phone up to picture height.

We pose with our bank crew first. And Mazer. He's not leaving my side.

"One of just Cully and me," I say, and Erica and Gonzo stand off to the side, leaving Mazer with us.

I slide my arm around Cully's waist and squeeze him tight. His arm goes around my shoulders. We smile at the camera, and then I turn my head. I've spent so much time looking at his back. Now I take in Cully's brown eyes, his copper hair, his golden skin. His freckles are out of control, and I can feel the goofiness of my smile. I don't know what the future holds for us. I just know that right now I want to stay in this moment, happy that we made it here together.

Dad and I carry the canoe across the grass and line it up in order of finish with the other boats. We're next to Mark and Kimmie's boat. Tanner's canoe is one ahead of them. Conner

Howell took fourth and the Wranglers took third. But the best thing is seeing that it isn't a six in the spot for first place. A four-person canoe is resting in the top spot, the words NO SLEEP TILL SEADRIFT in white letters on the side. Molly, Mia, Erin, and Juliette took the whole damn race! It's the first time an all-female boat has ever won, and it makes me so ridiculously happy. I spy them across the pavilion talking to Kimmie. Maybe they're trying to recruit her. I wonder if they'd take me on next year, too.

A few people walk around, checking out the boats. Someone catches Dad by the arm. An old racer whose name I can't remember.

"Find me later," Dad tells him, and we finish our walk to the pavilion.

Cully and I settle into two beautiful reclining lawn chairs, and I melt into mine. Just resting my back against some-thing is a ridiculous luxury.

Dad comes back and sits next to Gonzo and Erica and Mrs. Gonzales like they're old friends and takes a sip from a drink that was already in the cup holder.

I ease off my shoes and examine my feet.

"That's not right," Erica says, because they're ghostly white and covered in wrinkles, but every racer in this tent arrived with feet just the same.

Cully takes his shoes off, too. "I'm not sure I'll ever be fully dry again."

I hold out both hands to show Erica how every section of every finger has a blister, and the line of blisters across the tops of my palms.

My cold burger and fries are the best thing I've ever eaten. I sip on a half-melted chocolate milkshake in between bites.

Gonzo sucks the last of his shake through a red straw, making a loud gurgling noise. "Sorry the food's been sitting out so long."

"The tracking app said you'd get in about an hour and a half sooner than you did," Erica says.

"Yeah." Gonzo leans forward. "The app made it look like you and your dad were paddling on top of each other for a while."

I'd just as soon never tell anyone what we did for Johnny Hink, but the story tumbles out of Cully's mouth.

Everyone turns to look at the bay, like they might spot Johnny's boat out there. Everyone except Dad, who's looking at me with a serious expression. Evaluating me.

"What else happened out there?" Erica asks.

So we tell them about Cully losing his paddle and getting the boat pinned against a tree and the ants in my pants and everything else we didn't have time for at the checkpoints. And they're telling us about the water moccasin that dropped out of a tree two feet in front of Erica, and the property owner who tried to charge them fifty bucks for trespassing, and staying up all night to watch our dot move across the app on their phones.

Then Mom's back with Tanner and she hugs me and tells me how proud she is of me.

"You ran a good race," Tanner says, which is as much of an apology as I could ever expect from him.

They join us, Mom and Tanner. The Bynums, too. Tanner soaks his foot in hot water. Allie's here, too, and I don't yell at her to go away because Cully doesn't care. They tell us about losing their headlight, and Coop getting whacked in the face by a branch because of it, and all the bad blood there was between us has washed away. After Coop left, they made the hard choice to sit out for two hours until there was enough light for them to see. And they have another story about getting stopped by an entire herd of cows while they were portaging the logjam.

"So much cow shit," Tanner says.

I'm able to laugh and cringe in all the right places, because it's so much like the finish I always dreamed of. Like it was when we were kids.

But for the first time, I see that finishing doesn't actually matter. I got everything that I wanted out of this race before I ever crossed the finish line.

≈

We all lie back to nap for a bit. I wake to the sound of Dad's voice. He's talking to Mom, but when he sees me awake, he crouches next to my chair.

"Come sit with me, kid," he says.

He pulls me out of my seat with a calloused hand. I follow him again, past the pavilion this time, far away from Tanner and Mom and Cully. We sit on the seawall, dangling our legs. Dad's feet just brush the surface of the water, and little waves roll over them. He studies his hands in his lap.

On the bay, a boat appears on the horizon. We watch in silence for a few minutes as it slowly moves closer. Three people in the boat. Only two of them paddling. It must be Johnny. People yell and clap a bit, but it dies down. That level of enthusiasm is hard to keep up the whole time a boat inches toward the finish.

I glance back at the pavilion. Cully's still sleeping. When I first agreed to paddle with him, I thought I could just leave him behind at the finish again. That everything could go back to how it was before last year's race. That I would be Dad's tough, strong daughter. It's all I cared about.

But thinking I could use Cully like that, thinking that he was just some sort of tool to get down the river . . . I was such an idiot.

"Those were the brightest lights I've ever seen on the river that first night," Dad says, just as the words "I'm not giving him up again" come out of my mouth.

"What was that?" Dad asks.

"Wait, you saw our lights?" I say.

He waits for me to repeat myself, but I don't. I want him to explain.

"Everyone saw your lights. That first night when you came blazing down the river with them, it made me wish I'd done something like that the year we raced. What happened to them the second night?"

"But you weren't at our water stops."

"I went back and forth between you and your brother. But I saw you on the water a fair bit. Called your mom with updates all the way down the river. Erica and Gonzo were a good crew."

"You were hanging out with Erica and Gonzo?"

"I like those two."

"Why didn't I see you?"

"Didn't think you'd want to see me." He studies his hands. "I knew it had to cost you a lot to team up with a Hink. You had to be pretty angry with me to do that. I tried to make up for it with the cookies and the tip about the Haymaker and Alligator Lake."

"How'd you know we could make it through?"

"Second place was a tandem who zipped through there. I was watching on the app," Dad says.

"I thought you didn't like all the technology the race uses now."

"Yeah, well, when your kids are on the water, it's reassuring."

"But why?" I ask. "You barely talk to me." My eyes burn. Dad lets out a heavy breath.

"I owe you an apology, Sadie. A big one. I sulked over not finishing that race, and when I came out of it, when I realized what an ass I'd been, you could barely look at me. I've been mad at myself for the last year, but I've never blamed you."

"What?" I ask. Because this doesn't fit with anything that's happened in the last year. "You've always blamed me. That's why you said you didn't want me in a boat with Tanner."

Dad pulls back to look me in the face. Wrinkles crisscross his forehead. "When did I say that?"

"I was eavesdropping on you and Mom in the kitchen. You thought that I would ruin his chances of finishing, too."

Dad turns back to the water and stays quiet for a minute. "That's not what that conversation was about," he finally says, and I wait until he decides to finish. "You know, your brother gets that competitive edge from me. He's willing to sacrifice a lot for a win. Too much. I didn't want him in a boat with you because he'd be like me. He wouldn't listen to you. He'd put the finish above his partner. I just didn't realize it would push you into a boat with John Cullen."

"Call him Cully," I say automatically as the shame of

calling him John Cullen hits me again. Then I let Dad's words seep into my brain. "I was that way with him at first. I was a jerk. Wouldn't let him rest. Gave him hell every time he messed up. But he called me on it. He threatened to walk away, and I had to take a good look at myself. I didn't like what I'd done very much."

Dad gives a little half laugh. "Not the first time a Hink and Scofield were at each other's throats during the race."

"That year with you and Johnny—what happened?" I ask.

"Everything," Dad says. "Nothing. We couldn't agree on anything that race. If he wanted to portage, I thought we should stay on the river. And . . . he needed a break. He didn't have the grit that year to paddle nonstop, and I wouldn't let him. I let my ego come before our partnership. And . . . and I made a bad call. I got turned around and took us the wrong way on the bay. It could have been a lot worse than it was. We got in this big fight, waist-deep in the water. It turned into a shouting match, and he hit me in the jaw."

"That sounds really familiar," I say.

Dad's head snaps around. He looks me in the eye. "Did Cully hit you?" His voice is steel.

"No!" I almost shout. I stare into his eyes. "Hear me when I say this. He's *nothing* like Johnny. He's *not* volatile."

Dad's face softens. His shoulders relax. "Yeah, I've kind of realized I'd figured that kid wrong." He turns back to the bay. "Gonzo told me what happened with Tanner and

Allie. Your brother's a real piece of work sometimes. I hate to think he gets that from me, too."

He's quiet for a moment. "During the race that year, Johnny told me this crazy story about how you stood on his counter and dumped melted ice cream over his head. Told me your mom and I were too soft on you. That you were out of control. I couldn't believe he'd lie to me like that about my own kid."

Oh. I always thought since my parents never mentioned it, maybe Johnny didn't tell. But I guess it was stupid to think that the ripples from that incident didn't turn into waves. Huge waves.

"Dad."

"Yeah?"

"I stood on Johnny Hink's counter and poured ice cream on his head."

Dad's eyebrows shoot up. He rubs his stubble. "Well, then."

My stomach sinks. But then Dad laughs. Deep laughter. Body curled, knee up, hand pressed against his mouth laughter. "I think I might owe that man an apology," he finally says.

"I swear, Dad, I had to. You should have seen the way he was yelling at Cully. I didn't know it would make you hate each other."

"Don't hold yourself responsible for something that happened between two grown men."

I need to tell him.

"I'm not giving Cully up again." I make my voice as hard as I can. "So don't ask me to."

"I didn't ask you to give him up the first time." Dad's quiet for a minute. "But I see why you thought you had to. These are our mistakes you've been living with. I should have stepped in. Should have made things right with Johnny for your sake if nothing else. Or just adopted the kid so we could keep him around."

The memory of kissing Cully explodes into my mind.

"You shouldn't have adopted him."

Dad twists around to where Cully is in the lawn chair.

"So it's like that?" he asks.

I think back to the way his fingers touched my face when we were in the cut.

"I think so," I say. "I hope so."

He stares at me for a long moment, then shoots his eyes to Cully. "I guess I owe your mom twenty bucks."

We both laugh.

He puts an arm around me and pulls me close. His chin rests on the top of my head.

"My point in all this, in bringing you over here," Dad says, "is to say that I'm sorry and that I love you. You are so damn strong and so brave, and I couldn't be more proud of you right now if you'd paddled that boat to the moon. And it's not about finishing. It's not that you came in sixth place, which is really something. It's that you went out there and you put your whole self into it."

I know him too well to believe that. "Come on, Dad. You can't pretend you aren't proud that I came in sixth. I know how much that means to you."

"Of course I'm proud of how well you did. But I'm proud of how you did it. You put your partner above the finish. You realized that to get there, you two had to take care of each other. And when a jackass like Johnny Hink got in trouble, you went out there and helped him. It's better than he would have done for you."

He looks out at the water, where Johnny's boat approaches the finish.

"That's why I decided not to race this year," he continues. "I took a good look at how I'd treated you, and I didn't much like it. Didn't like myself very much, either." He turns his head away from me, wipes his eyes, and sniffles. "I really hope you can forgive me." His voice breaks as he says it.

I wipe my eyes with my wrinkled hands and lean into my dad. "Of course I can."

He pulls me into a hug. We stay there, with his arm around my shoulder, and watch as Johnny's boat reaches shore. As Johnny skips the photos, leaving his wounded partner behind, and walks straight for Cully. He wakes his son.

Dad starts to stand, but I put a hand on his arm. Everything in me says to go over there. To grab what's left of my milkshake and pour it on Johnny's head. But I can still hear Cully's words in my ears.

I don't need you to do that for me anymore.

Instead, I watch as Cully stands, rubs his eyes, and leads his dad away from the pavilion.

I watch heated words fly between them.

And then I watch Cully walk away.

"We're not done here, John Cullen," Johnny calls after him.

"Yeah. We are," Cully says. "We're really done."

He walks to me and Dad, holds out a hand, and says, "Let's go clean up."

Erica drives us the four blocks to the motel that leaves rooms unlocked for racers to shower.

"Want me to wait?" she asks.

Cully shakes his head. "We'll call you if we need you."

We leave our shoes outside the door of the room—an Odyssey tradition to show someone is showering in there—and walk inside.

It's an old place, built at least fifty years ago, and probably not updated much since then.

I let my bag fall on the carpet with a *whup*.

"Do you want the first shower?" Cully asks.

I shake my head. "Take it."

He goes into the bathroom and the door clicks shut. I can hear the water running inside, and a minute later the door cracks. "Can you bring my bag in here and give me my dopp kit?"

He's already in the shower when I carry in his backpack and dig around until I find a toiletry bag I can only assume is a dopp kit. Steam rises above the closed curtain and billows out when I slide the bag in to him.

Then I lie down on the cold floor of the bathroom, not caring about germs or dirt or other people's hair, and I close my eyes.

"What was your dad saying?" I ask.

"Doesn't matter," he says.

He's in there. Showering. Naked. A flimsy shower curtain away. But it feels like a million miles.

"It matters to me," I say.

A quiet minute passes.

"He's mad that we brought him his boat. Mad that I walked away at the Wooden Bridge. Embarrassed. Says I disrespected him in front of a crowd of people," Cully says. "Like he didn't do the same thing to me."

"What are you going to do now? Texas State?" I can't deny that part of me wants Cully to go to school fifteen minutes down the road. We could see each other every day.

"I'll stay at Gonzo's until he cools off. Defer my admission. Get a job. Apply for loans and grants. It's not like I'll be the first kid to figure out how to pay for school on my own. Maybe I can go to RISD in the spring. Or in a year."

I don't know which part of this makes me love him the most, only that I love him all 265 miles down the river and all the way back. All the way to Rhode Island or anywhere else he lands, whether I get to love him as a friend or I have the chance to love him as something more.

I run my tongue over the inside of my teeth. I also know that after two and a half days on the river, my mouth is foul.

Suddenly, I'm up and I'm flossing and brushing my teeth, and my legs and my arms and my entire body are made of rubber, and I don't know if it's from extreme exhaustion or from Cully. I'm waiting in the room while he finishes up, because it's too hard waiting in there with him on the other side of the shower curtain. He comes out fresh and clean, and then I'm in the bathroom peeing on an actual toilet. I sit in the shower because I'm too wobbly to stand, but I'm using soap and shampoo and watching the dirt run off my body and down the drain in a brown stream. Then I'm clean, in a black cotton dress, walking out of the bathroom.

Cully is on one side of the bed with his eyes closed. Asleep, he looks so peaceful it's impossible to tell he spent the last two and a half days paddling. I see so clearly how he is still the boy I've known my whole life, just older. It seems so ridiculous now that I ever could have hated him.

And even if I'm wrong, even if he doesn't feel the same way about me that I do about him, I have to ask. I lie down on my side, face-to-face with him, and press my foot into his. His brown eyes drift open. I touch his face and his cheek is smooth.

"Can I kiss you?" he whispers.

Everything inside me glows.

I cock an eyebrow at him. "Goulash."

His soft laugh is everything.

His chest is warm underneath my hand. His fingers are in my hair and his lips are soft against mine. We stay like that, kissing, our feet tangled together, until someone knocks on the door and asks what's taking so long.

We climb off the bed onto wobbly legs. I catch his hand as we walk out the door into the bright June sun. All the blistered and raw parts of my hand press into his.

And I don't let go.

Author's Note

Anyone familiar with the Texas Water Safari will recognize it as the inspiration for the Texas River Odyssey. My dad paddled the Safari as a teenager, back in 1964, after reading the 1963 *Life* magazine article about it. I grew up thinking of it as *that crazy canoe race my dad did.* In 2012, the race came back into my life when my husband paddled it with three friends. I followed along, spectating at water stops and checkpoints. Long before his team ever made it to the finish line, the beginnings of Sadie's story were already forming in my head.

The Water Safari community is made up of a generous group of people who have the absolute best stories. Nothing I could dream up could compare with what they have experienced. I encourage anyone interested in learning more about the Safari to visit texaswatersafari.org.

Although the Odyssey has its origins in the Safari, all the characters and events in the story are completely fictional.

Acknowledgments

The people who made this book happen could fill a whole fleet of canoes.

Thank you to my agent, Michael Bourret, for your keen insight, for loving this story, and for finding a home for it. Thank you to my editor, Maya Marlette, for all your brilliant edits, for your support, and for writing the best emails. I couldn't have landed in a better boat. You are both first in class, every time.

Thank you to the whole team at Scholastic including Melissa Schirmer, Keirsten Geise, David Levithan, Mallory Kass, Jessica White, Elizabeth Tiffany, Aimee Friedman, Shannon Pender, Josh Berlowitz, Janell Harris, Taylan Salvati, and our sensitivity reader Joseph Chavez.

Big thanks to Bethany Hegedus, my first mentor, who changed my writing completely. To early readers Salima Alikahn, Shelli Cornelison, Vanessa Lee, Laurie Morrison, and Laura Sibson. Thank you to beta readers Kate Branden, Elizabeth Hayt, Brynn Speer, Sarah Pitre, Heather Curry, and Melanie Jacobson. Special thanks to Salima and to Stephanie Kotara, who have cheered me on for over a decade now. And to Emma Kress for navigating these new waters with me.

Thank you to my advisors at the Vermont College of Fine

Arts. To Tom Birdseye, who helped me get Sadie and Cully to the finish line that first semester. To Margaret Bechard, who helped me see my new beginning. To Jane Kurtz, who helped me write from inside my character's skin. To Tim Wynne-Jones, for loving this story from the start. And to David Gill, for helping me get Sadie and Cully to the finish line the second time and for so often seeing my story more clearly than I could see it myself.

Thank you to my Tropebusters and to the Writers of the Lost Arc. I couldn't have found better families at VCFA.

I owe a huge thanks to the people who shared their canoeing knowledge and their racing stories with me. To Holly Orr of Paddle with Style, who is a skilled canoeing teacher and was so patient when I made every mistake you can make in a boat. Thank you to Chris Kelter, for being my racing partner and an all-around great friend. Thank you to Tom and Paula Goynes for sharing Safari stories over pie. And thanks to John Dunn, for always being willing to tell me about your racing days and for inventing the Cussing Lamp.

Mom, Dad, Kelly, thank you for raising me to love books and for always keeping me well supplied.

To my kids, I am so lucky to be your mother. Thank you for always being excited about me becoming a "book writer," and for the happy dance when I got the good news. You are more incredible than I could have dreamed, just as you are.

To Woody, who does hard things, thank you for everything, always.

About the Author

Holly Green has never paddled in a 265-mile canoe race, but she has paddled a sixteen-mile race, and that feels like a reasonable length. She is a former potter turned tech trainer turned writer who loves traveling, hiking, and swimming. She holds an MFA from the Vermont College of Fine Arts and lives in central Texas with her family.